# Dying Wish

By

Hope Everly

DYING WISH

# Dying Wish Playlist

Lexi:

Breath me – Sia
Love Hurts – Nazareth
Fix You – Coldplay
Too Good At Goodbyes – Sam Smith
Elastic Heart – Sia

Lucas

Say Something – A Great Big World / Christina Aguilera
The Scientist – Coldplay
Tears Don't Fall (Acoustic) - Bullet For My Valentine
Say You Won't Let Go – James Arthur
Always Remember Us This Way – Lady Gaga

Maddison

Fight Song – Rachel Platten
Unstoppable – Sia
Superwomen – Alicia Keys
Try – Pink
Happy – Pharrell Williams

Nelly

Tourniquet Remastered 2023 – Evanescence
Bring Me To Life – Evanescence
My immortal – Evanescence
Creep (Acoustic) – Radiohead
I'm No Okay – Citizen Solider

# Dedication

This book is for anyone who has ever felt the weight of loneliness pressing down like an anchor. For those who've carried sadness heavy in their chest, who've felt overlooked, unwanted, or invisible.

I wrote these words because I've been there too. Many of us have. And if you're reading this, I want you to know: you are not walking through it alone.

There are people who care. People who love you. People who want to hear your story, even when you feel too quiet or too broken to tell it. Sometimes the hardest thing is finding the courage to speak, to reach out, to ask for help, to believe you deserve it.

This is your reminder, from one soul to another: you are seen, you are valued, and you are not alone.

Hope

# Trigger Warning

Dear Day Dreamer,

Let's cut the crap. This isn't a sweet bedtime story.

What you're about to step into is dark, jagged, and laced with things most people would rather bury. **Depression. Self-harm. Suicide. Bullying. Harassment. Swearing.** All the lovely little ghosts that don't stay in the closet no matter how tightly you shut the door.

If you're not ready to carry that weight, it's okay to put this book down. Protect yourself first. The shadows will wait; they're patient like that.

But if you keep reading, understand this, it won't be pretty. It won't be easy. It will be real. And sometimes, real feels like bleeding ink across a page.

Consider this both your warning and your invitation.

Step carefully. The dark has teeth.

Yours in shadows,

Nellyfish

# Chapter 1

## Lucas

The cafeteria buzzed with noise, trays slamming, cutlery scraping, voices bleeding into one low hum. Sunlight slanted through the tall windows, sharp and golden, cutting across the worn linoleum like it was trying to brighten a place that didn't deserve it. The air reeked of burnt coffee and yesterday's leftovers.

I leaned back in my chair, arms stretched, hands resting on my thighs like I owned the damn room. It was a front, I knew that, but it was a good one. I always had to look like I had it together.

Beside me, Lexi slumped low in her chair, dark circles carved under her eyes, the weight of the whole world pressing her down. Across from us, Maddie tried to beam sunshine into the room, her smile too bright, too forced, as if it could smother the storm brewing.

And then there was Nelly, arms folded, eyeliner thick, dagger eyes sharp, practically vibrating with anger, like she was one word away from tearing us apart.

"Well, don't look at me!" Nelly snapped, her tone sharp enough to cut glass. Her eyes flicked across the table, daring someone to blame her.

Maddie faltered, gaze darting between Nelly and the rest of us, torn and unsure where her loyalty belonged.

Then Lexi's voice cut through, flat, edged with steel. "He needs to grow up."

It stung, though I'd never show it. I shrugged, plastered on a smirk, and let my voice drip with arrogance, the armor I knew best.

"It's not my fault her boss wanted a piece of all this." I gestured to myself, grin cocky. "Are you jealous?" I leaned toward her, wiggling my eyebrows.

Her arms snapped tighter across her chest. She turned toward me like I was dirt under her shoe. "Why would I want to touch you?" Venom laced every word. "I think everyone has had a turn of you."

That one hit deeper than I wanted to admit. I leaned in anyway, kept my grin sharp. "That's because I am so damn good!"

She didn't even blink. Just rolled her eyes.

"You're the one missing out, cupcake." I winked, relentlessly.

Her glare sliced into me. "She thinks you're my friend, and you refuse to call her back. She's taking it out on me now!"

That jab landed hard. Still, I forced my smirk to stay, even while it twisted something inside.

"We're all friends," Maddie tried, her voice too soft, too desperate.

Nelly scoffed, eyes cutting to Maddie with cold amusement. "You need to realize what this really is."

Lexi rubbed her neck, gaze lowered. When she finally spoke, her voice was low, resigned. "Yeah… I think it's time we call it."

And just like that, the bottom dropped out of the room.

I leaned forward, the smirk carved onto my face, because if I stopped smiling, they'd see just how broken I was. "Yeah, I mean, it's not like I've got any chance of scoring with any of you."

The table froze. For a heartbeat, even the cafeteria seemed to fall silent.

So, I tilted my head, grin curling darker. "Mind you, I've always had a fantasy of screwing a pregnant lady."

Lexi's recoiled, disgust twisting her features. "Just when I thought you couldn't get any more disgusting."

Perfect. I leaned back, pretending her words bounced right off. Easier to be the asshole than the broken piece of shit inside.

Maddie's sunshine dimmed. Even she folded her arms, defeated. "Do you not remember why we meet here every week?"

Nelly sighed, flat, cruel. "He's been dead two years, Maddie."

Maddie crumpled. I hated myself for watching instead of reaching.

"I'm sure he didn't mean forever." Nelly added, shrugging.

Lexi shifted like her chair was made of nails. She wouldn't meet Maddie's eyes. "Yeah, Madz. We tried, but we're not the same people we were back in high school."

And me? I leaned back; arrogance plastered over panic. If I stopped playing the clown, Joshua wouldn't just be gone, he'd be erased.

"No, I definitely grew up into a fine specimen. You girls are lucky I still hang out with you."

I dragged my eyes over to Lexi, grin curling. "Except you, Lexi. I am lucky to hang out with you. When are you going to give in to my charms?"

"You need to give up, Lucas." Her arms folded tighter. I didn't want you two years ago. I don't want you now."

"I'll have you one day."

And that's when Maddie snapped. Her voice shook with fury and grief. "Why can't you all just get along for a couple of hours a week? Why can't you do it for Joshie?

Her eyes cut to me first, "You do nothing but brag about your conquests."

Her words sliced deep. She was right. But I couldn't let it show.

Then her gaze swung to Lexi. "And you do nothing but argue with Lucas and obsess over your ex."

Lexi's voice cracked as she spat, "Well, he did knock me up and then disappear back to his wife."

Then Maddie turned to Nelly. "And you, you just sit here and hate on us, and the world, and everything in it."

Her voice broke. "For Joshie, you could put it aside. Just for two hours a week. To do what he wished in his last dying breaths. He was so good to all of us. God, we used to be best friends."

Her chair scraped back hard. She stormed off.

The silence left behind was suffocating.

Nelly smirked, voice low and mocking. "Well, look what you two did. You broke little Miss Sunshine."

I laughed it off, though my stomach knotted.

Lexi turned on me, eyes blazing, then looked back at Nelly. "Us?" It was you who brought up Joshie being dead. You know how that upsets her."

I raised my brows, tone dripping with mock innocence. "And they call me the insensitive one."

Nelly laughed, short and sharp, then pushed from the table. "If Madz is back in her perfect little life, I'm done here."

Her chair scrapped back, final. She didn't even look back.

The silence pressed in thick. Lexi stared at the empty space like she might break if she blinked.

I leaned forward, grin slipping back on. "Well, looks like it's just the two of us."

She rolled her eyes, exhaustion carved into her face.

I pushed further. "Fancy a little rendezvous in the bathroom stalls?"

"Oh my god, Lucas. Have you not realized how pregnant I am?"

Pregnant. The word still punched me in the gut. Of course I knew. I always knew.

I shrugged, smirk intact. "You'd help me cross 'pregnant hot chick' off my bucket list."

"Well, since you say it like that..." Her voice dropped husky, lips caught between her teeth.

My heart jumped. "Really?"

"No! Dickhead." The venom in her glare burned deep.

I laughed it off, though it stung. "Fine. Nothing here for me either. I'm out.

I stood, smoothed my shirt like I was on a runway, and sauntered off, smirk fixed in place. I didn't dare look back.

Because if I did, she might see right through me.

# Chapter 2

## Lexi

I pressed my hand against the swell of my stomach, trying to steady myself as the cafeteria's noise slipped into a dull, watery blur. The laughter, the chatter, the scrape of trays, everything melted away, like I was sinking beneath the surface while the world kept moving above me.

And then I realized.

They'd left. All of them. One by one, chairs scraping back, voices clipped, eyes turned away. And here I was, alone. Like somehow, I was the one who ruined it. Like I was the problem.

Maybe I was.

Maybe it was me, sitting here with a baby growing inside me, the proof of every bad decision pressing out against my skin. Maybe they're sick of hearing the edge in my voice, the bitterness I can't always swallow. Maybe they look at me and only see failure.

A girl dumb enough to fall for a married man. Dumb enough to believe she mattered to him. Dumb enough to cling to his lies that he'd leave his wife. Dumb enough to end up like this.

Heat burned behind my eyes, but I bit it back, hard. No way was I going to cry here, not where anyone could see. I'd pretend everything was fine until I couldn't anymore. But it wasn't fine. It hadn't been fine in a long time.

And maybe the truth was, they didn't leave because I offended them. Maybe they left because I don't fit anymore. Because deep down, I've never really belonged.

I pressed harder against my stomach, as if I could hold myself together with the weight of my own hand. But the truth clawed its way through anyway, ugly, merciless.

Argh, why? Why the hell do I put myself through this every week?

My throat tightened. His name whispered through my head before I could stop it.

*Joshie.*

That's why. Always him.

It wasn't about me. Not about Maddie and her bright smiles that hid her cracks. Not about Nelly and her razor-sharp edges. And definitely not about Lucas with his damn smirk he wore like an expensive accessory.

It was about Joshua Edward.

The four of us, dragging our fractured selves back to this shitty café, to this same table every week, bleeding out in different ways, bound by the same reason. Him.

And I can still see us, back then, like ghosts haunting the edges of memory.

Maddie perched on the bench, sunlight spilling over her like it belonged to her. Her black curls shimmered as she tossed her head back, laughter spilling too easily, too brightly, as if she could bend the world toward joy. She was always like that, sunshine on command. Sometimes it was real, sometimes it was a mask, but either way, she made people believe in it.

Nelly lingered on the edge, pale skin catching the light against the black curtain of her straight hair. Her gray eyes stayed fixed on the ground, fingers twitching against her sleeve, restless, like she might vanish into the cracks. She carried heaviness everywhere, a shadow draped across her shoulders, making you wonder if she'd ever felt at home in her own skin.

Lucas sprawled across the bench like he owned it, six-foot-four of cocky arrogance stretched over wood. His tan skin glowed, his light brown hair catching the sun just right, those sharp blue eyes already too aware of their effect. Back then, his grin was boyish, wide, unguarded, the kind that pulled people in. That was before it sharpened into the smirk he wears now, that dimple sinking into his right cheek like a reminder of everything infuriating about him.

And me? I stood off to the side, sharp-tongued, arms crossed, pretending I didn't care if I was left out. But my chest ached with the lie. The thought of being forgotten terrified me more than I'd ever admit.

But Joshie…

Joshie was different. He sat in the center, not because he demanded it, but because it was natural. Six feet of calm strength, wiry muscle beneath his shirt, short black curls catching the light. His dark skin glowed warm in the sun, and when he smiled, the whole damn place lit up.

He didn't have to be loud. He didn't need banter or sharp edges to hold attention. His presence was gravity. He anchored us, stitched our jagged pieces into something whole. And when everything else felt like it might splinter, he made us believe, just by being there, that somehow, everything would be okay.

God, we really were friends once. Real friends.

It wasn't high school that tied us together, not classrooms or lockers or shared years. It was him. Joshua Edward, the glue that took five broken pieces and made us whole.

Joshie would've given you anything: his jacket, his last bite of food, his shoulder when you couldn't hold yourself together. He carried us when we couldn't carry ourselves. He loved us like family.

Nelly was the girl smudged in charcoal, hiding out in the art studio where no one noticed her, quiet, forgettable, a shadow. If it hadn't been for Joshie, I might never have even known she existed.

He went into that studio, pulled her out, and told us… told me, "This is Nelly. She belongs here too."

And because it was him who said it, we believed him. We believed in her.

The memory sharpened like glass, cutting through the present. I could see it so clearly, the school courtyard alive with chaos. Boys shouting across the football field, sneakers squeaking on the pavement, the sharp tang of cafeteria fries drifting from the doors. It had been loud, messy, constant. And yet, when I looked at the faces around that bench, the noise blurred to nothing. They were my world then. The only ones who mattered.

And then there was Lucas.

Argh, Lucas…

Even now, sitting alone in this cafeteria, the thought of him made my chest clench. I leaned back into the memory, watching the boy he had been sprawled lazily across the bench, pretending he didn't care about anything. Back then, he was different, softer somehow. Before the smirk, before the endless bravado, before he turned himself into the kind of man I couldn't stand.

Why couldn't he have stayed that way? Why couldn't he still be *that* Lucas?

He hadn't been smooth or clever with girls. He hadn't needed to be. He was just a regular guy, awkward sometimes, fumbling his words, but real. You could talk to him, have a conversation without it twisting into innuendo or some crude joke about his latest conquest. Back then, he was just… Lucas. And God help me; I almost missed him.

My thoughts shifted to Maddie and how she used to be, her laughter cutting through the heaviness like

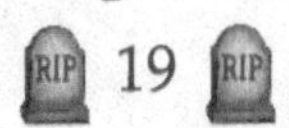

sunlight breaking through storm clouds. She hadn't really changed. Maddie was still Maddie, bright, hopeful, determined to find the silver lining even if it killed her.

Back then, she believed in the best in people, even when they gave her every reason not to. Maybe it was strength. Maybe naïveté. Or maybe life just handed her that brightness and never asked her to pay for it.

But me?

Sitting here now, pressing a hand to the curve of my stomach as the real world buzzed around me, I wasn't sure I believed in anything anymore, not in Maddie's sunshine, not in Lucas's charm, not in Nelly's sharp edge. And definitely not in myself.

# Chapter 3
## Joshua

*7 years earlier*

I adored Maddie. Honestly, who didn't? She was light bottled into a girl, joy wrapped in golden-brown skin and black curls, laughter spilling out of her like she had a direct line to happiness itself. But standing beside her could feel like staring at the sun too long: you needed shades, maybe even SPF 50, just to handle the sheer brightness.

Sometimes it burned. Sometimes I needed a breather from all that glitter.

Still, people couldn't resist it. Everyone gravitated towards her, orbiting like she was their own personal star.

And me? I wasn't the star. I was the anchor. The gravity. The glue. The one who made sure we didn't spin off into space and never come back. And honestly? I was okay with that. Someone had to hold us together.

I leaned forward on the bench, clapping my hands with a grin.

"Alright, my little misfits, listen up. I was thinking: tonight, my place. Movies, popcorn and, yes, brace yourselves… a little truth or dare."

Boom. Just like that, I had their attention. I always did. Not because I was the loudest, okay, sometimes I was, but because I was the one who made plans, the one who refused to let us drift. Keeping us together was my job, my pride, my whole heart.

Maddie squealed, clapping like I'd just promised her front-row tickets to a Hemsworth shirtless convention. "Yes! Perfect!"

Nelly rolled her eyes, all gothic gloom and sarcasm, but I saw the tiny shift: she leaned a fraction closer. That was Nelly. Acted like she didn't care but wanted to belong. That's why I'd pulled her into our orbit in the first place. My Nellyfish.

And then there was Lucas. Lord have mercy. Long limbs, sun-kissed skin, that cheeky grin ready to launch some ridiculous dare, probably involving stripping or kissing or something equally stupid.

Classic Lucas: hiding everything behind a grin, always watching Lexi when he thought no one noticed.

I noticed. I always noticed.

Lexi. Sweet, complicated, forever-trying-to-please Lexi. I saw the guilt flicker across her face before she opened her mouth, the way her shoulders curled like she was bracing for a hit. I swear I felt the weight pressing down on her chest as if it were my own.

"I'm sorry, Joshie. I can't."

Ouch. Right in the heart.

I tried to hold my smile steady, Joshie, the anchor, the glue, but it slipped, just for a second. Just enough for her to see.

Of course, Lexi couldn't stand the silence, so she rushed to fill it. "I got invited to the bonfire party. By Jamie."

And boom, there it was.

Beside me, Lucas's brow shot up like a flag on game day. His voice dripped with something that was supposed to sound casual but didn't fool me for one second. "What, the footballer?"

Mm-hmm. Lucas thinks he's subtle. Spoiler: he's not. The way his tone sharpens every time another guy's name passes Lexi's lips: child, please. He's got it bad.

And I don't know how Lexi, queen of overthinking, hasn't picked up on it yet. Honestly, I don't know why he won't just grow a pair and tell her how he feels.

But then again… maybe I do.

Because Lexi doesn't look at boys like Lucas. Oh no. She's got her eyes glued on the shiny ones, the captains, the golden boys, the ones who can throw a football fifty yards and still manage to wink at the cheerleaders.

She chases the glitter; half the time it's just tinfoil.

Don't get me wrong: Lucas is not hard to look at. Six-foot-four, sun-kissed skin, eyes so blue they make you think of summer pools and poor decisions. Please. If he ever came out in a crop top, Maddie and I would need resuscitation.

But he's not the "popular jock," and in Lexi's world, that seems to matter. Too much.

Lexi's cheeks flushed, pink creeping up her neck, but she forced herself to meet Lucas's stare. "Yes. That's the one. I think he likes me."

My chest squeezed, because I could see it: those words sliced straight into Lucas. He didn't even have to say anything; jealousy is a thing he wears like cologne.

Maddie leaned into Lexi, sunshine in human form. "He's so friggin' cute."

Lexi's guilt softened into a smile. That was Maddie's magic: crack open storm clouds with one grin and make you believe the sun had always been shining.

I sat there watching, feeling that old ache. We were growing up, drifting, our paths tugging us in different directions, and still I kept trying to be the glue, the anchor who refused to let us split apart completely.

I straightened on the bench, slipping into that calm, grounding tone I always used when things felt like they might crack. "Well, the rest of us can catch up. Make a night of it."

That was my role, wasn't it? Not the loudest, not the brightest, but the one who wove us back together with a single thread. The reminder that we belonged, here, with each other.

Maddie's giggle rang out, grin spreading like sunlight. "As long as there's ice cream and hot men, I'm in."

I leaned toward her, mischief sparking in my eyes. "Oh honey, if I'm picking the movies, you *know* there'll be hot men." I wiggled my eyebrows dramatically, earning her laugh. "Chris Hemsworth will have his shirt off within the first twenty minutes. Mark my words. And let's be real, if we ever stumble across that man, we already agreed we'd share. Equal rights when it comes to a little slice of Australian hot ass."

She burst into bright, easy laughter and for a second, I let myself believe the world could really be that simple.

Nelly shifted, arms crossed like armor, expression flat as usual, but angled closer. "I'll come if you don't complain about me drawing on my iPad."

I smiled. I'd take that. That was Nelly's version of saying she needed us.

Maddie shot Nelly a sunshine-gone-sassy look. "You miss half the movie with your head buried in that thing."

Nelly shrugged. "I've got my art exhibition next weekend. I need to finish some pieces."

"That's fine, Nellyfish," I said, softening. "At least you'll be out of that crypt you call a bedroom. You know sunlight won't actually kill you, right?"

Her lips twitched. Almost a smile. I count it as a win.

My gaze slid to Lucas. He was sprawled across the bench, legs everywhere. Normally, he'd trade stupid flirty comments to make Lexi roll her eyes, but today his shoulders slumped, jaw tight. Those blue eyes looked far away, like he wasn't even sitting with us.

No banter. No grin. Just silence. And it killed me.

Lucas had been drifting lately, pulling back like I'd done something wrong. Maybe I had. Maybe I'd pushed too hard urging him to tell Lexi how he felt. But it kills me watching him orbit her like a lost planet while she chases the shiny jocks.

I can see where this ends if he keeps holding it in. Lexi's going to hurt him, not because she's cruel, but because she's blind to what's right in front of her.

If she breaks him, he might bury that soft part of himself for good. That thought makes my chest ache.

I wanted to shake him, to yell, to MAKE him tell her. But instead, I sat back, crossing one leg over the other, pretending I wasn't watching him unravel.

I leaned forward, snapping my fingers dramatically. "Hellooo? Earth to Lucas! LUCAS!"

Maddie giggled, covering her mouth, eyes sparkling like sunlit glass. Lucas blinked, like he'd been dragged out of a dream, and gave me a half-baked smile that didn't fool me. "Oh yeah, sure man. I'll be there."

"Mm-hmm," I thought, narrowing my eyes at him. He still had that storm-cloud look.

Maddie squealed, pulling the room back. "Ahhhhh! Make sure you have chocolate chip ice cream. And both of those Hemsworths present."

I flung myself back on the bench, mock-serious. "Girl, I'll make sure they're both present. Thor and Hunger Games, abs for *days*. Consider it done."

Laughter bubble over, loud and wild. For a second the world beyond our bench blurred away. It was just us, whole.

Beside her, Nelly huffed, folding her arms tighter around herself like a shield. "You know there's more to life than boys."

I shook my head with a dramatic sigh, wagging my finger like I was her sassy life coach. "That attitude? Uh-uh. That'll get you thirty minutes with no electronics forced to watch men with no shirts on. You gotta *learn* to live, girl."

Then Lucas, always the one to test the cracks, opened his mouth. "We all know you like girls, Nelly."

The words dropped like a bomb.

Maddie's giggle cut off mid-breath. My hands froze. Lexi stiffened. The air turned brittle and sharp.

Nelly's eyes went wide. Her breath snagged. She looked gutted, like he'd reached inside her chest and yanked out her secret for everyone to see. Then she ran. Sneakers slapping the pavement, black hair flying, gone before any of us could move.

My stomach dropped. Each step she took felt like a punch to my chest. Every footfall tore another thread from the fragile tapestry I'd been trying to stitch together.

Maddie's arms crossed, fury flashing across her face. Lexi shot up, fire in her eyes.

"What has gotten into you?" she snapped. Then Maddie said to Lexi: "Let's go see if she's okay."

They stormed after Nelly.

And suddenly it was only Lucas and me. Silence settled, thick and suffocating. I could feel Lexi and Maddie's absence like an open wound. Nelly's ghost lingered in the empty space.

I crossed my arms, trying to hold everything in: disappointment, frustration, the ache of seeing us splinter.

Lucas stood, face twisting into that faux-confused mask he used when he didn't want to own his actions. "What?"

My voice was calm but razor-sharp. "Don't play dumb, Lucas. That wasn't about Nellyfish. That was about Lexi, about her going to that damn party with Jamie. You know it. That was not on, man."

He bristled, brushed off his jeans like he could brush away his guilt. "I don't know what you're on about."

Please. I knew better. I *always* knew better.

I saw through masks, armor, walls. Lucas wore his like a neon sign.

Then, as if none of it mattered, he turned his back and walked away, sauntering into the crowd with that lazy swagger like he hadn't just snapped the last fragile thread holding us together. The sea of students swallowed him.

I sighed, rubbing my chin.

Why can't he tell her how he feels? Lucas wastes so much energy hiding, pretending every things a

joke. But I see it: the way he looks at Lexi when he thinks no one notices, how his whole body goes rigid when her name is tied to another boy.

He could deny it all he wanted, but not to me.

"Sometimes I wonder why I even like guys," I muttered under my breath, tired and sharp, honestly. "They're so damn confusing. So closed off."

The courtyard gave no answers. Football-field shouts, sneakers squeaking, laughter spilling down the steps, life went on  like nothing had happened.

But something had. Something big.

I felt it in my bones: our group was cracking, breaking apart piece by piece. And for the first time, I wasn't sure if even I, Joshie the glue, could keep us whole.

# Chapter 4
## Joshua

***7 years earlier***

My room always smelled like a strange mashup of things: popcorn, my mom's lemony laundry detergent, and probably a little too much of my body spray (don't judge, I like to smell fabulous).

The curtains were pulled tight, but of course the moon had to sneak its nosy little self in, slicing the floor with silver light.

The four of us crammed into my room like sardines, limbs tangled on beanbags, spare cushions, and the edge of my bed. The TV glow flickered over our faces, turning us into ghosts one second and shadows the next.

I was sprawled half off the bed, claiming my space like the diva I was, keeping one eye on the movie and the other on my friends, because that's what I did. Always watching. Always making sure no one unraveled.

Nellyfish leaned forward on her beanbag, wide-eyed like she'd just discovered fire. "I didn't think this movie would be so interesting," she whispered, as if admitting it to loudly would ruin her image.

I smirked, proud of myself for picking the film, but before I could take credit, Maddie beat me to it. Of course she did.

She curled her legs beneath her, her grin so smug it could've lit up the whole room. "I told you, Nellyfish. It's not what you think it is. And you haven't even seen the best part yet."

Warmth pooled in my chest as I watched them: Maddie, radiant as ever; Nelly, slowly being pulled out of her shell. Moments like these, simple, small, crammed together in my room, were the glue. The reason I fought so hard to hold us together. Despite the cracks. Despite the chaos of who we were becoming.

For nights like this, we still felt whole.

I flapped my hand dramatically at Maddie, slipping into my best mock-stern impression. "Shush, don't give it away, Madz. This is the first thing I've seen in forever that's managed to get Nellyfish's nose out of that damn iPad."

Nelly's cheeks flushed pink under the TV's glow. She ducked her head, as if shrinking small enough would make us forget we were talking about her. She didn't argue, though, which was progress. With Nelly, no protest was as good as a compliment.

Lucas sprawled on the floor, legs stretched out, his shirt riding up just enough to show off the tan he loved to brag about. He frowned at the screen, voice dripping with judgment. "I just don't understand why she doesn't see Peeta for who he really is. She's always using him and going back to Gale."

Maddie predictably let out a dreamy sigh, eyes glued to the TV like she'd already married the man on screen. "But Gale is so handsome," she swooned. "He's the one I would choose."

I rolled my eyes so hard I was pretty sure I saw the back of my skull. Typical Madz, always swooning, always convinced some brooding boy with nice cheekbones was the answer to life's problems.

From the corner, Nelly tilted her head, her tone dry, as if she honestly couldn't care less. "Which one is Peeta again?"

I chuckled, the sound low and warm, but I sharpened it with a pointy edge. "He's the pining one. Much like Lucas."

The wicked grin that followed was deliberate. Lucas's head whipped toward me, his face twisting in mock offense, but I just smirked and popped a piece of popcorn into my mouth.

Somebody had to say it. And if it wasn't me? None of them ever would.

Lucas snapped upright like I'd just slapped him with a truth he wasn't ready to face. "Dude, that's not me at all."

Please. The boy couldn't even lie without his ears turning red.

Maddie dissolved into giggles beside him, her laughter bubbling bright and sweet, like she'd been waiting for this moment. She stretched out her leg and nudged him playfully with her foot. "When are you going to tell her?"

Lucas blinked, all fake confusion, his voice dipped in innocence so thick I almost rolled my eyes right out of my head. "Tell who?"

Maddie leaned back, arms folded, that sly smirk curling across her face. She was enjoying this way too much. "Oh, so you're fine calling out everyone else today, but not yourself?"

I swear I could see his jaw lock, the muscle twitching like he was holding everything back with his teeth. Instead of answering, he flung his hand toward the TV like it was some kind of life raft.

"Shush., this is the best part."

I couldn't help the laugh that slipped out of me, soft but loaded. My eyes glittered, because I saw it. I always did, the things he thought he kept hidden, the way he carried himself whenever she was around.

"Yes, Lukie…" I drawled, letting my voice drip with meaning. "Sure… the best part is coming up."

And for a heartbeat, just one stolen moment between the flickers of the screen, I caught it.

The way his eyes shifted. Softened. Warmed. His cheeks went pale pink, the way they always went when he was thinking about Lexi.

He didn't even realize he did it. But he did.

And oh, did it make my chest ache, watching my best friend burn up in feelings he'd never admit. Not even to himself.

# Chapter 5

## Lexi

***7 years earlier***

The bonfire cracked and hissed a few feet away, flames clawing toward the night sky as smoke drifted into the salt-heavy air. Music thumped from a speaker half-buried in the sand, a steady bassline that made the ground hum beneath my bare feet.

Laughter rose from the cluster of football players and cheerleaders scattered around us, red plastic cups in their hands, their bodies silhouetted by firelight and the silver glow of the moon over the water.

Jamie leaned against his cup like it was an accessory, his smirk lazy, practiced. I stood close enough to smell the faint tang of beer on his breath, nerves prickling through me as I tried not to shift under his gaze.

"So yeah, I never really noticed you before," he said, shrugging like it was nothing.

Heat rushed to my cheeks. My laugh came out awkward, thin. "I've been in your English class all year. And last year we had math's together."

His eyebrows lifted in mock surprise. "Wow, funny."

I shifted my weight, scratching my arm to give my hands something to do. "I guess."

He tipped his cup back, swallowing slowly before lowering it again, his eyes dragging down the length of me. "So, what… did you just get hotter or something? 'Cause no way I would've missed a girl who had a body like yours."

The words landed heavy, shame prickling across my skin. I forced a small, hesitant smile, trying to laugh it off even as my stomach twisted.

I swallowed hard, searching for steady ground. "I was thinking that maybe… maybe we could go out and grab a shake after school sometime."

For a heartbeat, I thought I'd said the right thing. That maybe he'd smile and nod, and this could feel normal. But instead, his grin curled into something sharper.

"Is that like code for…" he winked, lowering his voice as he leaned closer, "because we don't have to wait for another day. There are dunes back there, and I've got condoms in my car."

My heart lurched. Panic fluttered in my chest. "Well, I… we only… this is the first…"

He cut me off with a scoff, his words coated in disappointment that felt like a slap. "Oh, so you're a prude. I thought when I invited you here, you were a sure thing. You were so excited when I asked you."

The fire cracked behind us, cheerleaders' laughter spilling like glass shattering, and I felt suddenly, painfully small.

"It's not that… I guess I could go…"

The words tasted like ash in my mouth, but I said them anyway, because the silence that followed his judgment felt worse than agreeing to something I didn't want.

The firelight blurred as Jamie's eyes slid past me, scanning the crowd. His smirk shifted into something hungrier, already chasing another target.

"I gotta go…" his eyes narrowed like he was trying to recall, "…Vicky?" He barely looked at me, his tone was dismissive, careless. "I just remembered I have to speak to my mate about something very important."

And then he was gone.

He jogged across the sand, calling after another girl, his voice dripping with flirtation. "Hey Kristy. Wait up. Slow that cute ass down, I want to talk to you."

Laughter swelled. Music pounded. But all I heard was the hollow crack inside my chest.

I crossed my arms tight against myself, forcing the words out through clenched teeth. "My name is Lexi. And 'mate'... my ass."

Tears stung before I could stop them. My throat closed up, heat rising to my face as I blinked furiously, desperate to hold it together. But the truth slammed through me anyway.

*Why do they always do this to me?*

I sat down in the sand, hugging my knees to my chest. The noise of the world faded to nothing, but my chest still ached from the sting of being used, of being treated like nothing more than a body.

There is no "special one" out there. Not really.

The idea of someone who cares enough to actually see me, to learn my name like it means something, to want to know who I am before taking what he wants… that's just a fantasy. A stupid dream made for movies and fairy tales. Not for girls like me.

The truth hit sharp and cold: boys don't care. Not about the late-night talks, not about what makes me laugh, not about the little things that matter. They care about one thing, and once they've had it, they're gone. You're forgotten. Replaced.

So maybe it's time I stop waiting for someone different. Stop hoping. Because hope is what keeps breaking me.

I pressed my chin harder into my knees, swallowing down the lump in my throat. From now on, I'd know better. I'd remember what they are and what they want. And I'd stop pretending there was more.

Better to accept it now than keep getting crushed by the same lie.

My hands shook as I pulled out my phone, the glow of the screen blurring with tears. I pressed it to my ear, swallowing the sob clawing its way up.

"It's me." My voice cracked, low and broken. "Can you come get me?"

DYING WISH

The night spun around me, waves crashing against the shore, smoke from the bonfire stinging my nose, laughter ringing sharp like glass.

And all I wanted was to vanish.

# Chapter 6
## Joshua

***7 years earlier***

Maddie was curled on my bed, giggling at the screen like she didn't have a care in the world. Nelly leaned forward, her pale face lit up by the movie, like she'd forgotten for five seconds that life annoyed her. Lucas was half-slouched in his usual *I'm too cool for this* pose, long legs stretched out, pretending he wasn't secretly invested.

And then: *buzz… buzz… buzz.*

The shrill ringtone cut through the hum of the movie.

I groaned, tossing a pillow at him and throwing my head back with the kind of dramatic flair I was born with. "Don't get it, man. Let it go to voicemail. We're mid–Katniss Everdeen, and this is sacred."

But Lucas's eyes flicked toward the phone, that softness creeping into his voice. "It's her."

Of course it was. It was always *her*. I didn't even bother looking up. I knew. We all knew.

"We all know who it is," I muttered, reaching for a handful of popcorn I suddenly didn't want.

The buzzing stopped. Silence stretched. And then: *buzz... buzz... buzz.* Louder this time. More desperate. Like even the damn phone was begging.

Lucas's jaw tightened. His whole body went rigid, like he was already halfway out the door. "But she might need me. She might be in trouble."

That was it. I snapped my head toward him, fixing him with a look sharp enough to cut glass. My voice came out calm, but heavy, the kind of calm you only get from holding frustration too long.

"You're never gonna get her that way, Lucas. Always being there to pick up her pieces. You're not her boyfriend; you're her safety net. And you're gonna break yourself if you don't put your damn foot down. Let her realize what she's doing to you."

The words landed like lead. He didn't argue, didn't even flinch, just sat there, swallowing it down, trying not to choke.

The movie kept playing, but none of us were watching anymore. The room felt colder despite the flicker of the TV. And somewhere out there, Lexi's voice was calling into the dark.

And this time, no one was picking up.

Or so I thought.

Lucas' hand shook when he grabbed the phone, like it weighed a hundred pounds. He always acted cool, lazy smiles, cheeky grins, that easy drawl, but right then, the phone might as well have been a live grenade. His knuckles were white, his shoulders stiff.

The ringtone buzzed again, drilling into us. Maddie shot me a look, brows creased, but I stayed quiet. Watching. Because Lucas wasn't just *answering a call,* he was bracing for impact.

And then he pressed it to his ear. His whole body shifted, like he'd stepped into another world.

"Hey. Are you okay?"

God, his voice. Low, steady, velvet-soft in a way he only got when he was worried. It cracked something in my chest I didn't want anyone to see. He didn't even sound like the Lucas we all teased. This was the Lucas who cared too much, the one he tried to hide.

Silence. Then his reply came fast, sure, no hesitation. "I'll be there in twenty."

Just like that. No questions. No excuses. Because that's who Lucas was, always orbiting the people he loved, ready to throw himself into their mess just to keep them afloat.

The call ended. The glow of the TV snapped back across his face. He stood there a second, staring at the phone like it had burned him. His jaw was tight, his eyes stormy.

I couldn't say anything. My chest ached just looking at him.

Because I knew, no matter what time she called, no matter why, he would be there. Always. And part of me hated how much I admired him for it. Part of me hated how much I wanted that kind of devotion aimed at me.

Lucas shoved the phone into his pocket, face unreadable. But I'd known him too long, the stiff shoulders, the clenched jaw. Yeah, he was rattled.

I crossed my arms, tilting my head, sigh slipping out dramatic. "You never learn, Lucas."

His head snapped up, blue eyes flashing with that defensive edge he got when anyone scraped too close to the truth. "I would do it for any of you."

I arched a brow, smiling sharp enough to sting without being cruel. "Uh-huh. Keep telling yourself that. But running every time Lexi snaps her fingers doesn't make you her knight in shining armor, it makes you her errand boy. And errand boys don't get the girl."

The muscle in his jaw ticked. His hand dragged over the back of his neck, like he could rub the frustration out.

"You need to stop looking too much into things. I'll see you guys tomorrow."

He grabbed his bag and hoodie and stalked to the door. A moment later, the click of it shutting behind him left the room heavier.

I leaned back on the bed, shaking my head, though I couldn't help the small smile tugging at my lips. "That boy has it bad."

Maddie twirled a black curl, her eyes softer than her words. "I think they'd make a cute couple. But you know Lexi… she only has eyes for the footballers."

I chuckled, fanning myself like I'd just spotted a shirtless Hemsworth. "To be fair… have you *seen* their abs? That's top-shelf eye candy. I wouldn't say no to a quarterback with dimples and a six-pack."

Maddie's smile faltered. She hugged her knees close, her voice fragile. "Yeah, but that's all it is. They're only interested in one thing. Lexi's already given it up a couple of times, only to end up broken. Lucas would be shattered if he knew what she's really been up to."

I sighed, humor slipping, weight pressing on my chest. Because Maddie was right. And Lucas? He wasn't built for heartbreak, not the way he felt about her.

My grin softened, fading into something quieter. "Well, best he doesn't find out then. Because Lexi still thinks sex is some magic spell to snag a guy or keep one. And baby, it's not. It never is."

The words lingered heavily in the air. Lucas was already gone, out chasing after the one girl who would never sees him the way he wanted. The irony cut deep. Maddie knew it, I knew it. Hell, even Nelly knew it. Everyone but Lexi and Lucas.

Nelly shifted, arms crossing like a shield. Her voice sliced sharp. "Will you guys be quiet? I'm trying to watch the movie. Lexi and Lucas' pathetic love lives are exhausting. Same story, every time. He's been trailing after her like a lovesick puppy for years. Someone needs to tell him it's not going to happen."

Her words burned, cruel and true. I kept my eyes on the screen, but every word carved deeper. I cared about Lucas too much to see what made him special get stripped away.

My flamboyant mask slipped, truth bleeding through. My voice came low, steady. "Someone's going to get really hurt. And I don't think it's going to be Lexi."

The air tightened, suffocating. Even the movie couldn't distract from the cracks forming between us.

Maddie let out a dramatic sigh, curling up like a princess waiting for her crown. "God, it's like watching *Titanic* again. You know it's too long. You know that selfish bitch had enough room on that damn door to let him on. He didn't have to die."

I narrowed my eyes, warning soft but pointed. "Madz…"

But she flicked her hair like she was auditioning for a shampoo commercial.

"What? We all know it's true. I would've shared my board with Leo. Geez. That girl had real issues."

She tried to laugh it off, her giggle bouncing, but it landed hollow. Not even her sunshine could chase away the cracks running through the room tonight.

I shifted, arms wrapped tight around my knees, eyes fixed on the flicker of the TV without really watching. Nelly's words echoed sharp as broken glass.

*Lovesick puppy. Broken record. Not going to happen.*

I wanted to shake her. Shake Lucas. Shake Lexi. Hell, maybe even myself. Because the truth of it sat like a stone in my chest, heavier than I wanted to admit.

And somewhere deep down, right in the place I usually smothered with sass and jokes, I was terrified she was right.

And this wouldn't end with a happily ever after.

# Chapter 7
## Lucas

***7 years earlier***

The beach was colder than I expected, one of those chills that sank straight through my hoodie and into my bones. The fire roared behind me, voices carrying over the crash of waves, cheerleaders, footballers, the whole golden crowd.

Their laughter blended into one sharp, grating sound, and I hated it. Whether they were laughing at her or just laughing at life, it didn't matter. I knew what it felt like to be on the edge of it, and I could see the way Lexi's shoulders shook as she sat there alone, like she was bracing for the world to swallow her whole.

My chest tightened. Screw the crowd. Screw the stares. I pushed past them, jaw clenched, eyes locked on her. Every step felt like her pain was lodged somewhere inside me too.

"Hey, Lex," I said, keeping my voice steady even though my insides weren't. "You ready to go?"

Her head snapped up. Tears streaked her cheeks, her eyes wide and broken. Just like that, the rest of it, the fire, the noise, the mocking voices, faded out. All I saw was her.

She nodded too fast, a sob breaking loose as she stumbled toward me. Then she was in my arms, clinging to me like I was the only thing holding her up. My heart cracked wide open, but my arms wrapped around her without hesitation, tight, certain.

"Thank you, thank you, thank you…" The words spilled against my chest, her voice trembling, her whole body shaking like she might fall apart if I let go.

I lowered my chin on her hair, keeping my voice calm and low, as if saying it enough could stitch her back together. "It's okay. I've got you."

And then I heard it, muffled against me, the one thing that nearly undid me completely. "Thank you, Lukey."

*Fuck,* hearing her call me that did things to me. Every nerve in my body lit up for her, something primal woke inside me every time she used it, something no one else had ever reached.

I pulled back just enough to see her face, catching her eyes in the dim glow of the fire, green, always too bright, even when full of tears. It gutted me. My chest twisted as I asked, soft but sharp with worry, "Are you alright? Did he hurt you?"

She shook her head, too quickly again, like if she moved fast enough the ache wouldn't show. But I saw it. With her, I always did.

"I don't want to talk about it," she whispered. "Can you take me home?"

My answer was out before she'd even finished. "Sure. Come on."

I wasn't about to press her, not now, not when she was cracked down the middle. So, I slipped my hoodie over her head and steered her away, slow and steady, keeping myself between her and the glow of the bonfire, between her and the voices that still carried over the waves.

Every step away felt like peeling her free from all of it, the smoke, the fake smiles, the careless words. And if I could've carried the weight for her, I would've. No hesitation.

She walked close beside me, and I held myself taller, broader, like maybe I could be the shield she needed. She didn't have to know I was shaking too.

As long as she felt safe with me, that was enough.

The car was quiet. Too quiet. Just the low hum of the engine and the rhythm of tires on the road. Streetlights flickered past, slicing shadows across her face, and every time the light hit her eyes, I caught that ache there. It made my stomach twist.

My hands gripped the steering wheel tighter than I meant to, knuckles pale. Like if I held on hard enough, I could keep everything from falling apart.

She finally spoke, her voice cracking, thin, desperate to break the silence. "Your dad has a really nice car."

I glanced at her quickly, then back at the road. Her hands were knotted in her lap, twisting like she was holding something in. I tried to keep my tone steady. "Yeah… I've gotta look after it though. If I scratch it, I'm the one who has to pay for it."

The words came easy, but a pause followed. I let out a breath, lowering my voice, teasing, though heavier than I meant. "Pretty sure you're not that interested in my dad's car though, Lex."

The words hung there, thick as smoke. She didn't look at me, just stared at her lap, and it killed me not to know what was running through her head.

I finally asked, quiet but edged, "Are you going to tell me what happened tonight?"

She shook her head, nails digging into her palm like she could claw the truth out of herself. Her voice barely a whisper. "It's stupid."

*Stupid.* That's what she always said. But the tears in her eyes, the way her shoulders curled, none of it was stupid. Then it spilled out. "Well, turns out he just wanted to have sex with me. When I hesitated, he just moved on and chased another girl right in front of me."

The air left my lungs like I'd been sucker punched. My jaw locked, hands clamping harder on the wheel. The image of Jamie face, smug and careless, flashed in my mind, and I wanted to put my fist straight through it.

But what came out was sharper than I meant. "You were going to sleep with him?"

I hated my own voice, the mix of hurt, jealousy, fear. It sounded like accusation when all I felt was a sick, sinking ache.

She faltered, guilt in her tone. "I…"

Something in me snapped. The thought of her letting some idiot footballer touch her, like she wasn't worth more, made my chest burn.

"You barely know him, Lex! That's all those guys want… sex. You're better than that."

Her arms folded tight, shutting me out. Her reply was quick, biting. "I asked you to pick me up, not a lecture. You're not my father. It's not every day someone like that shows an interest in me."

Her anger stung, but worse was the truth underneath… she didn't believe she deserved more.

I risked a glance at her, my voice rough. "You can't just give that up because some football player notices you. He doesn't know you, Lex. He doesn't know your favorite color is green. Or that you're terrified of spiders. Or that you cry every single time you finish the last scoop of your favorite ice cream."

I swallowed hard, forcing the lump in my throat down. My chest was tight, heart pounding, but I couldn't tell her the rest, that Jamie didn't deserve her, that none of them did. That I'd been here all along, knowing every piece of her, wishing she could see me the way I saw her.

The words slipped before I could stop them. "Because you wonder if it's going to be discontinued and that might be the last mouthful you'll ever have."

It was silly. But it was her.

Her head snapped toward me, cheeks flushed, her voice sharp. "God, Lucas, it's just sex. You're talking like I'm still a virgin. It's not like I'm expecting him to marry me."

The words cut through me. *She's not a virgin.*

I couldn't breathe. My grip faltered, the car swayed before I corrected it. My chest cracked open, raw and aching. With who? How many times? Poisonous thoughts spiraled.

Joshie's voice echoed in my head: *You really need to get your feelings for Lexi under control.*

I stared straight ahead, jaw tight. But inside, it was chaos.

Her voice sliced through, bitter. "What, you have nothing to say? All you boys think the same. All you boys want the same. If we don't give you what you want, you just move on to the next."

I forced myself to look at her, my voice softer, wounded. "Is that what sex means to you?"

She shrugged. "It's what it means to everyone. A bit of fun, and hopefully the boy likes you enough to call afterward so you can keep doing it."

Her words hollowed me out. My brows furrowed. "And that is what girls expect?"

She smiled, but it didn't reach her eyes. "Yes."

The answer gutted me. I gripped the wheel tighter, silent, wishing I could prove her wrong. That she was worth more. That I wanted to be the one to show it.

But all I could do was drive, my chest aching with everything I couldn't say.

Streetlights blurred across the windshield, gold and white streaks cutting the dark. My eyes stung, my throat tight.

The silence pressed in, heavier than any argument.

*I always thought girls wanted someone who cared enough to know them first.*

Not just their body. Their favorite color. The way they laughed. What scared them at night. I thought that's what it was supposed to mean.

But sitting there beside her, hearing her voice… maybe I'd been wrong all along.

Maybe I was the fool.

And maybe I'd built it into something it wasn't.

The ache of everything I couldn't say filled the space between us. So, I just stared at the streaks of light outside, wondering if either of us truly believed the lies we were telling ourselves.

# Chapter 8
## Lexi

***7 years earlier***

The sun beat down over the beach, the salty air clinging warm against my skin. Waves rolled in, slow and lazy, catching the light in glittering arcs while gulls circled overhead, scavenging like they were planning to take over.

Maddie twirled in her swimsuit, hands on her hips like the sand bowed down for her. Nelly hung back with her camera, capturing it all, her laugh soft and fleeting as Joshie cracked another joke.

And Joshie, God, Joshie, he was the sun in our orbit, pulling us all in with that easy smile and fearless energy.

Then there was Lucas. Laid out on the towel, grin sharp enough to gut me, cocky enough to act like he owned the entire beach.

And me? I laughed until my stomach hurt. Until the ache of the real world dissolved into salt air and sunshine. For a while, we were untouchable, five kids on the sand, stitched together from mismatched pieces that somehow fit.

### *Present Time*

I can still hear that laughter on the wind. Still feel the way we patched each other up after heartbreaks, fights, secrets. We weren't perfect. We were misfits. But we were true.

At least, back then.

Time cuts deep no matter how hard you hold on. Life drags you in different directions whether you want it to or not.

Nelly chased her art, off to college, her fingers smudged with charcoal and her head full of bigger dreams. Maddie fell in love, settled down, frosted cakes at her bakery, and smiled like she'd solved the riddle of happiness. Joshie went to law school, steady as ever, becoming exactly who we all knew he'd be.

Lucas slipped into nights that blurred together, bartending through neon and smoke, charming the world with that grin.

And me? I drifted. Job to job, city to city. Nothing permanent. Nothing solid. Just enough to survive another week.

It was five years after school when we found our way back to each other, a night out, a celebration for Joshie.

But that memory doesn't glow like the beach. It doesn't shimmer with summer warmth. It cuts like glass, sharp and irreversible. That was the night, the night that cost us Joshie.

*2 years earlier*

The karaoke bar pulsed with chaos. Neon lights buzzed overhead, threatening to burn out, while drunken voices butchered ballads into the mic. The floor was sticky, the tables stained with beer, the air thick with sweat and noise.

And there we were, the five of us again. Shoulder to shoulder, like nothing had changed.

Maddie glittered under the lights, cheeks flushed, curves poured into a dress too bright to ignore. Nelly dressed like she'd wandered in from a funeral, sharp edges wrapped in black, pretending she didn't want to disappear. Joshie still had that grounding presence, steady and magnetic, holding the pieces together without even trying.

And Lucas… damn, Lucas. Leaning against the wall with that cocky grin, the whole room tilted toward him without him lifting a finger. He didn't chase anymore, he didn't have to.

And me? I held my glass tight, pretending the burn of alcohol was enough to numb the ache inside. Pretending the smile I wore wasn't another mask.

Here's the truth: men always want the same thing. Doesn't matter the promises, the charm, the attention. In the end, sex is the bargain, the currency. I'd learned to play that game. Learned to survive by it. And somewhere along the way, I got good at being cold.

But with them, my people, it used to feel different. Real. More.

So, I raised my glass, forcing brightness into my voice. "Let's let loose tonight. Forget everything. We deserve this. No stress, no bullshit. Just fun."

They cheered with me, but even as I grinned, I was calculating. How many more shots until the cracks showed? How many drinks until I picked someone, anyone, who wasn't Lucas to take the edge off?

Because I swore, I wasn't going home with Lucas. Not him. Not tonight.

What I didn't know then was how much that night would cost. How much my words would matter. How much *Joshie* would matter.

It started with me, with the suggestion. A little extra kick to make the night better.

Lucas produced the little bag like a magician, his grin too easy. "Well, I asked around and managed to get five. Guy swore it's the good stuff. Said we'd have a night to remember."

Maddie lit up instantly, her joy loud and blinding. "This is going to be amazing! It's been ages since we've all been together."

Joshie shifted, hesitation written in every line of his body. "I don't know about this, guys. If I get caught, my career's over. I can't risk it."

For a second, his voice nearly cracked through my haze. *Nearly*.

But Maddie's sunshine smothered it. "It's one tablet, Joshie. People do it all the time. Lighten up. Nothing bad's going to happen." Her smile carried us, reckless and convincing.

And then Joshie exhaled, long and heavy, before finally nodding.

That was it. The moment. The cut in time that split everything open.

Later, I would wonder why.

Why him? Why not me? Why not any of us?

We all took the same pill. We all drank the same drinks. We all danced in the same blur of neon and bass. But only Joshie didn't come back.

I can still see him, that smile, the way he wove through the crowd like he was still watching over us. And then gone. Swallowed by the lights, the chaos, and our carelessness.

By the time we noticed, it was too late.

And that's the part that claws at me in the dark. The part that will never let me go.

Because I should've seen it. I should've saved him.

And Joshie would still be here.

# Chapter 9
## Lucas

***2 years earlier***

The fluorescent lights in the bathroom buzzed overhead, sickly and cold, bouncing off tiles cracked with age. The place reeked of disinfectant and stale smoke, the kind of stench that clung to bar bathrooms, where secrets went to rot.

I caught my reflection in the smeared mirror, straightening my shirt, jaw tight. My pulse was racing, but not from nerves. From want. From the promise of what I thought was finally mine.

"Tonight's the night… she's giving me all the signs. Finally, you're in, Lucas."

I braced myself, sucking in a breath, that stupid grin tugging at my mouth

*Go get her.*

But when I turned, the world split clean in two.

"Josh?" My voice cracked on his name, sharp and wrong. "Josh? Is that you?"

He was there. Crumpled in the back of one of the stalls. Face down on the cold tiles, body limp like a discarded coat.

My chest seized. The room spun. Then my legs moved before my brain caught up. I was on the ground, knees burning against the tile as my hands shook violently, grabbing at his shoulders, flipping him onto his back.

"Josh. Joshie, wake up. Joshua, come on, you need to wake up!"

My words tore out of me, frantic, broken, louder than I'd ever been in my life. I shook him harder, desperate, the sound ricocheting off the walls like punishment. Each echo came back at me like a reminder:

*You weren't here. You weren't here. You weren't here.*

But he didn't move. Not even a twitch. And that was it. That was the moment.

Too late. Too much damage already done. His heart, his kidneys, whatever poison we'd all swallowed that night, it had chosen him. And I wasn't there to stop it.

Because while my brother, because that's what Joshie was to me, a brother, was dying on a bathroom floor, I wasn't looking for him.

I was chasing my fantasy. I was chasing *her.* And I will never, ever forgive myself for that.

My fingers laced over his chest, pressing down, again and again, begging him to come back to me as I shouted for help.

"Somebody call an ambulance"

The hospital was worse.

Too bright. Too sterile. Too fucking cruel. Fluorescent lights buzzed overhead, white walls stripped of anything resembling hope. Machines hummed and beeped, mocking us with every sound. The air stank of antiseptic, as if bleach could wash away what was happening.

Joshie lay there, too still. His chest rose and fell like each breath cost him more than he had to give. Tubes tangled around him, wires trailing across his skin, the machines doing the work his body couldn't.

And I stood there with them, Lexi, Maddie, Nelly, watching, waiting, breaking.

But inside? I was rotting.

Because while they saw helplessness, grief, the horror of what we were losing, I saw the truth.

I wasn't there for him. I wasn't the friend he deserved. I was the guy too busy chasing a piece of ass while my best mate, the one who held us all together, lay dying alone on that dirty bathroom floor.

And that's the night I learned who I really was.

A player.

A coward.

A fuck-up.

A disappointment.

Not the guy Joshie needed. Not the guy Lexi believed in when we were kids. Not even close.

Just Lucas, the guy who gives girls what they want for a night because that's all he's good for.

And the sickest part? That night made me everything Lexi ever wanted in the first place. And it cost me my brother.

# Chapter 10

## Nelly

***2 years earlier***

Nothing brings you down from a buzz… a high… faster than your friend being rushed to hospital in a life-threatening condition.

The hospital was too bright. Too white. Too clean. It stung my eyes, burned my skin. Like standing in a world stripped of everything warm, everything real.

I hated it. I hated the hum of the machines, the sterile sting of antiseptic, the way the fluorescent lights droned above us like flies circling something already dead.

Joshie lay in the bed, pale against the sheets, his chest rising in shallow, broken movements. Tubes tangled across him like chains, but they weren't keeping him here. Not really. Not for long.

The others stood close, Maddie with her tears staining her pretty face, Lucas with his jaw locked like clenching hard enough might hold him together, and

Lexi… pretending she wasn't crumbling even though I could see it in her eyes. But me? I just stood there hollow.

Joshie was my only real friend. The only one who ever saw me. *Really* saw me. He gave me the name *Nellyfish* the first week he pulled me into the group, said I floated around like I was lost at sea until he found me. Like a jellyfish.

He made me laugh at it, turned something ugly into something mine. And now he was slipping away. And with him… so was that part of me.

His eyes fluttered open, heavy, but when they landed on us, on me, that warmth was still there. That stupid, impossible warmth that made you believe everything was okay, even when the world was on fire.

"You guys have been so good to me," he rasped, voice weak but steady. "You've pushed so hard to try and get me the help I need. But I can feel it. The doctors have said there's nothing more they can do."

The words gutted me. They tore through me like glass. I wanted to scream, to rip the machines from the walls, to tear this whole place apart until they fixed him, until they saved him.

But I just stood there. Silent. Because that's what I always did.

Lucas whispered, "I'm so sorry, Joshie," his voice cracking like glass splintering. Maddie sobbed softly, clinging to Lexi like she'd fall apart without her.

And me? I couldn't move. Couldn't speak. Couldn't breathe. Because when Joshie died, I knew I'd die too. Not in body, not right away, but in every other way that mattered.

He was the only one who made this world bearable, the only one who pulled me out of the dark and said I belonged. And now, watching him fade, I felt the color bleed out of everything.

The day Joshie left, Nellyfish would go with him. And all that remained was Nelly, cold, hollow, waiting for the tide to finally take me under.

Joshie looked small in that bed. *My Joshie.* His chest rose in uneven little gasps that sounded like they cost too much. And yet somehow, even like this, his eyes still held warmth. Still found each of us. Still made it feel like we mattered.

Maddie's voice cracked beside me, full of regret that cut like glass. "I shouldn't have…"

Joshie shook his head weakly, the faintest smile tugging at his lips. "I don't want any of you to blame yourselves. I did what I did knowing the risks, as we all did. I don't want this changing anything."

But it already had. It already broke us.

Lucas leaned forward, his jaw tight, eyes wet. He looked more boy than man in that moment. His voice wavered as he whispered, "But man… this will. You're going to leave us."

Joshie coughed, his breath rattling, then forced his gaze across us. His eyes were glassy, but that warmth was still there. He never let it go, even now.

"And for that, I want you to make me a promise. We've started to drift apart, barely seeing each other these days. I'm sure this will leave you feeling a lot of things. And I know you'll need each other more than ever now. So, promise me, meet up every week. Keep an eye on each other. Look out for each other. Be there for each other. And hey…"

A faint smile pulled at his lips, shaky but still him. "Maybe talk about me occasionally."

Maddie was the first to answer, she always was. Her voice shook as she clutched his hand like she could anchor him here. "I promise, Joshie. We will never forget you. We love you."

The room went quiet, the kind of silence that screams. The machines hummed, the lights buzzed, but all I could hear was my own heart breaking in my chest.

Because this wasn't just goodbye to Joshie. It was goodbye to the only person who ever truly saw me. Joshie was leaving, and when he did, the last piece of me that still believed in anything good was going with him.

I couldn't breathe. Couldn't move. My body locked, throat raw, eyes stinging with tears that wouldn't stop no matter how hard I tried to swallow them back. My sleeve was soaked, but I kept wiping at my face like it would matter. Like anything could matter without him.

Joshie's head shifted slightly on the pillow, the effort alone costing him everything he had left. His voice cracked, rough and broken, but it was his voice… his voice calling for me. "Nellyfish?"

I froze. *Shit.* I froze. My heart felt like it would crack open right there. Nobody else ever called me that. Nobody else ever would.

I pressed my hands hard against my mouth, holding myself together long enough to answer. My voice shook, trembling out of me like shards of glass. "Yes… yes, I will."

His lips twitched into the faintest smile, a shadow of who he used to be, but still him. Still Joshie.

"Thank you. I promise to look down over you, if I can… guide you. You four are hopeless."

He tried to laugh, *God*, he tried, but it broke into wet, jagged cough that ripped through his chest. The sound carved me open. He shouldn't have been joking. He should have been living.

"I don't…" A coughing fit wracked him. "I don't know…" He stopped, gasping, then tried again. "…I don't know what you'll do without me…"

The words fell apart with him. His head sank back into the pillow, eyelids fluttering, I swear I felt the floor drop out from under me.

And then my tears stopped. Like someone turned off the tap. Like all my emotions ceased to exist.

Not like Maddie, who howled, collapsing forward, her whole body breaking under the weight of it. Not like Lexi, who reached for him, sobbing so loud it tore through the sterile air. And not like Lucas, who tried to hold them both up while his own face was streaked with tears.

No, I just stood there, frozen. My hands covered my mouth, my eyes wide, my heart shrieking inside me while the world tilted into silence.

And then the machines screamed. The shrill alarms pierced the room, stabbing into my ears, a cruel, mechanical confirmation of what I already knew.

Joshie was gone.

The color drained out of everything in that moment, the room, the air, my life. Joshie had been the only one who made me feel like I wasn't a mistake. The only one who made me believe I belonged. And now he was gone.

A part of me died right there with him. The part that could laugh. The part that could hope. The part that could live.

And all we had left were his words. His last wish. A chain to bind us together when the only thing I wanted was to follow him into the darkness.

# Chapter 11

## Maddison

The slam of the door rattled through the house louder than I intended, shaking the frame and making me flinch at my own anger. My steps were sharp against the floorboards as I stormed into the living room, the noise almost necessary, proof that I was still here, still holding myself together.

Ray followed behind me, slower. Steady. Always steady. His eyes tracked me the way they always did when he knew the storm wasn't aimed at him.

"Woo, baby girl," his voice light, teasing, trying to catch me before I unraveled. "What's got you worked up, slamming doors like someone stole your last dollar?"

I spun too fast, arms folding across my chest before I realized how defensive I looked. My voice cracked, sharp and trembling, fury barely disguising the ache beneath.

"I can't with them anymore." The words shattered out of me like glass on the floor.

Ray tilted his head, rubbing his chin, patient like always. But I couldn't stop. The anger was already spilling out, tangled with the grief I usually locked behind smiles and affirmations.

"Two friggin' hours. That's all. But noooooooo… that's too much to ask out of their miserable lives. Two hours a week to sit there, put on a happy face, and be nice."

I hugged myself tighter, pressing my arms against every soft place I hated; every curve that reminded me I wasn't who I wanted to be. Every failed test. Every month of hope that turned to nothing. Every reminder that my body betrayed me.

And underneath it all, Joshie's absence. The empty chair. The missing voice.

I was supposed to be the glue. The sunshine. The one who beams "it's all good, it's all fine" until people believe it. Positive affirmations. Gratitude lists. Fake-it-till-you-make-it smiles. That's who I was to everyone else.

But not to him. Not to Ray.

His face softened, his voice dropping into that place only he used with me, the place that reached past the mask. "Baby, some people just can't do it. They're too wrapped up in their own mess to see the bigger picture."

I wanted to scream at that. Tell him I couldn't hold this together anymore. Tell him the smile I painted on every week was cracking. Tell him my body didn't feel like mine anymore, that I hated myself more than I let anyone know.

Instead, I just stood there, arms crossed, trying to stop my hands from shaking. Because if I let it all out, if I said the truth out loud, I was afraid I'd never be able to put the mask back on again.

My face crumpled before I could stop it, anger slipping into something worse… grief. My arms, so tight across my chest moments ago, loosened and fell uselessly at my sides. My voice barely held steady as the words scraped out.

"I just need those two hours. Those two hours to forget. To remember Joshie. To escape and remember the days we were all best friends."

Ray stepped closer, slower this time. His movements were careful, gentle, like I was already shattered, and he was afraid one wrong touch would splinter me completely.

His voice was low, aching, echoing the truth I couldn't bring myself to say. "To remember when things were a little easier."

Tears stung my eyes until they blurred everything. "To the days when we were all there for each other. When we actually listened instead of tearing each other apart. When we knew what was going on in each other's lives instead of pretending."

The weight of it crushed me, the reminder that Joshie was gone, and we were only shadows of who we'd been.

Ray brushed my arm, grounding me. His voice was steady, warm even while I crumbled. "You know I'm always here for you, baby girl."

I sagged against him, my body folding like it couldn't hold itself up anymore. My voice cracked, betraying the smallness I tried to hide. "I know."

Sniffles broke out of me, ugly and loud. Ray pulled me close, his embrace steady while I fell apart. "Oh, baby."

I buried my face in his chest, hating how much of me depended on him seeing the real me, the messy, broken me no one else ever saw. To everyone else, I was Maddie the sunshine. Maddie the glue. Maddie who always smiled and said everything was fine.

But not here. Not with him.

I pulled back slightly, swiping at my damp cheeks with the back of my hand. My words stumbled, fractured. "It's just…"

Ray tilted his head, his thumb brushing across my arm. His voice was the anchor I clung to. "You need someone else to hear you. I understand. We'll get there. We have the appointment on Saturday. We get another try."

*Another try.*

The words lodged sharp in my chest, caught between hope and shame. *Another try* meant another reminder my body couldn't do the one thing it was supposed to. Another reminder that even with all my smiles, all my pretending, I was still failing.

But I nodded anyway, because that's what I did.

I force a breath out, "I don't get it, Ray. How can you still… want me?"

The words spilled bitter and trembling. "I've put on so much weight. My body doesn't even work properly. Every time the doctor tells me it's another negative, I feel like less of a woman. Like I'm failing you. Failing us."

The silence pressed hard, suffocating, until I dared to lift my eyes.

Ray's gaze didn't waver. He cupped my face in his hands, rough palms, warm against my skin. "Baby girl," he murmured, his voice thick with conviction. "You are not failing me. You are not broken. You are not less."

He brushed away my tears, eyes burning with truth. "Your body is not the only thing I love about you. It's not even close. I fell in love with you, your laugh, your fire, the way you light up everyone's life even when you're breaking inside. And yes… " his grin flickered, playful even here, "…that sweet ass too. But Maddie, you're everything to me. *Everything*."

The words burrowed into the hollow parts of me I usually kept locked away. I wanted to believe him. God, I wanted to. But the war in my head wouldn't stop.

I wrapped my arms around myself. "When I look in the mirror, I don't see what you see. I see the weight I've put on, the dark circles, the woman who can't give her husband a child. I see someone who's pretending to be happy so the people she loves don't fall apart. And I'm so tired, Ray. I'm so tired of pretending."

Ray didn't flinch. He pulled me against his chest until I could hear the steady drum of his heart.

"Then don't pretend with me. Ever. You don't need to. Let the world have the sunshine Maddie. Give me the real you. Tears, scars, weight, pain, all of it. That's who I want. That's who I love. That's who I married. You're a strong woman, Madz. It's what drew me to you… along with that fine ass."

I let out a small chuckle, swatting his chest. "Stop it, I'm crying, and you're complimenting my ass."

Ray grinned, eyes glinting. "I'm your husband, baby girl. I can do whatever I please."

His playfulness softened into something steadier. "I said in good times and bad, in sickness and in health. And I meant it. Every word. I intend to keep that promise, Madz. Through all of it. And yeah…" he winked, "…your ass will always be my weakness."

A laugh slipped through my tears. Fragile, but real.

Heat crept up my cheeks. "Stop," I muttered, though I didn't mean it.

He leaned in, mischief sparking. "I say we don't wait till Saturday's appointment. We start the baby-making now."

I shook my head, a shy smile tugging at my lips. "Well… you know I can't say no to you."

He kissed my forehead, lingering there. "That's my girl."

But then, his expression shifted, serious again.

"How about I make curry chicken tonight? Chocolate pudding for dessert. We curl up with your favorite movie. Just us."

The smile slipped away. My arms folded tight over my middle. "You know I can't, babe. Saturday's weigh-in… the nurse will…" My throat closed. "…they'll say I haven't been trying hard enough."

Ray's jaw tightened, arms crossing. "I don't give a shit what they say. I like you the way you are. You're barely eating these days as it is."

The silence stretched, heavy with what I couldn't say, that I hated myself for this. That I wanted to believe him but couldn't, not when the scales always told me otherwise.

Finally, I whispered, broken, "If I don't lose the weight, they'll drop us from the program. And then we don't even get the chance."

His eyes darkened. "Well, the way they're going, they'll give you an eating disorder before they give us a baby."

Then his voice softened again, fierce with love. "I don't care about weigh-ins. Tonight, you're eating with me. No IVF, no baby talk, no stress. Just us."

He brushed my jaw until I looked at him. "I love you the way you are. I didn't marry a dress size, Madz. I married you. All of you."

Something cracked inside me. The tears still came, but this time they carried a faint smile with them.

I dropped my gaze, cheeks warm. "Your body, your mind… your personality. I like the whole package."

His grin returned, cheeky again. He patted my backside. "Now get that ass of yours in the kitchen and keep me company while I cook."

Ray winked over his shoulder as he swaggered toward the kitchen. Always steady. Always certain. Always carrying me when I couldn't carry myself.

And that's why I loved him. He was my number one supporter. I didn't know how I got so lucky. Built like he belonged on billboards, sexy as hell, and yet he looked at me like I was the prize.

I'd told him a hundred times he needed his eyes tested. He'd just laugh and say his vision was perfect. One day, I half expected to wake up and find out this was all a dream.

From the kitchen came his voice, warm and teasing. "You know I only do my best work with my girl by my side."

A small smile tugged at my lips as my feet carried me toward him. For tonight, at least, we could be Madz and Ray again, not the couple weighed down by clinics and appointments.

Just us.

But life has a cruel way of reminding you that warmth never lasts.

# Chapter 12
## Nelly

The house was a corpse. Skin flaking from the walls, eyes cracked and filthy, breath stale enough to choke a saint. It smelled exactly like what it was: unwanted. Abandoned. A perfect reflection of yours truly.

The door groaned when I shoved it open, long and low, like even it was tired of putting up with me. Figures. My own house had joined the *Sick of Nelly* fan club. Membership: everyone.

I slouched through the hallway, dragging my boots across the boards. Every step felt like gravity had it out for me, pressing harder, daring me to collapse. The air clung thick and heavy, pressing in like the house wanted to see how long I'd last before I cracked.

I didn't bother with the lights. Shadows suited me better.

By the time I got to my room, my hands were trembling. Blinds half-hanging, sunlight sneaking through in jagged stripes, like knives across the mess. Papers, drawings, empty bottles everywhere. One still full, waiting for its turn.

The whisky, my one loyal companion. Beside it, the orange pill bottle rattled when I picked it up, like it was laughing.

And on the wall? Joshie. Taped-up photos, yellowed and curling. Scars I couldn't stop scratching at. Some ghosts you don't banish. Some you hang up like wallpaper.

I dropped into the chair, body jerking like the strings had been cut and someone sloppy tied them back together. Pressing my palms into my eyes until sparks danced, tiny fireworks in a cave.

"Arghhh." It tore out of me, sharp and jagged, like glass splitting.

Back down at the desk: options, futures, endings. What a buffet. Whisky. Pills. Razor blades.

"Inny, meany, minny, moe," I muttered in a flat, sing-song voice, bitter as bile. "What poison wins tonight?"

My hand hovered. Whisky. Pills. Blades. Blades. Pills. Whisky. The finest menu for the terminally hopeless. Five-star dining for the damned.

Would anyone even notice if I didn't clock in tomorrow? Probably not. Maybe Madz. She'd cry pretty at the funeral, her sunshine cracked but still trying to hold the sky together with duct tape and optimism. Pathetic, really, that the only person who might actually weep for me is the one always insisting everything is fine.

I rolled the pill bottle in my fingers. It felt feather-light. Too easy.

"The pills," I whispered, soft, almost tender. "Clean. Quiet. No mess for anyone else."

A laugh bubbled up, humorless, hollow. "I'll even wash it down with whisky. Classy exit. Five stars on Yelp for sure."

My thumb pressed against the lid. Just one push and…

The shrill scream of my phone sliced through the silence like a banshee with perfect timing. I jumped, muttered a curse, and glared at the glowing screen. Figures. Even my death scene couldn't get stage time without an interruption.

I swiped my sleeve across my face, more annoyed than ashamed, and answered. "What?" My voice sounded brittle, hollow, corpse-like. Fitting.

My boss's voice shrieked down the line, sharp and grating, like nails dragging across a coffin lid, already dripping with disdain.

"What was that shit you sent me for the Baxter account?"

I shut my eyes, pinched the bridge of my nose. *Lucifer, give me strength not to hurl this phone at the wall and watch it shatter like my will to live.* My grip tightened instead.

"You wanted edgy and new. That's what I gave you."

Silence. Then the scoff, smug, dismissive. The sound of someone who decorates their soul with beige wallpaper.

"No. What you gave me was depressing and dark."

A jagged laugh tore from my throat, humorless and cracked. "Congratulations. You've just described me. And also, trendsetting."

Because let's be honest, the world *is* dark. Shadows, rot, broken glass. Kids grow up fast; may as well learn what they're stepping into. But no, my boss wanted rainbows and bubblegum, clowns with dead eyes and bunnies with plastic smiles.

"It's for a kid's play center," he snapped. "We can't show this crap to the client. Get back on your laptop and redo it. Tonight. Clients are back in tomorrow."

My palm pressed against my forehead, fingers digging in, the pill bottle whispering temptations beside me.

"Fine. Guess you're not ready for edgy and new."

His voice sharpened, cutting clean as a scalpel. "Happy and fun, Nelly. Clowns. Bunnies. Dinosaurs. This is your last chance. Unless you want to go back to writing obituaries, oh wait, sorry, newspaper ads, you'll get it right. And you'll get it to me tonight."

I pulled the phone away, stared at it like it had just spat on my grave. My lips curled into a bitter smirk, dry as ash.

"Clowns and bunnies," I muttered to the empty room. "Guess I'll save the funeral theme park idea for later."

Of course. Typical. Here I was, ready to make my grand exit, and life wouldn't even let me slip quietly into the grave. No, apparently I was destined to draw cartoon bunnies for sticky-fingered brats whose greatest tragedy was dropping their ice cream on the pavement. What a legacy.

I tossed the phone onto the desk, the crack of plastic against wood sharp enough to echo in the corpse of the room. My eyes dragged back to the pill bottle. My chest felt heavy and hollow, like a coffin waiting to be filled.

"Clowns, bunnies, dinosaurs," I muttered, voice flat as dirt. "That's me. Real happy-fun-time Nelly."

The sarcasm seared my tongue, but underneath it, the weight pressed harder, heavier, like something crawling inside my ribs.

Silence followed. The kind that makes your skull buzz. My chest rose too fast; jaw locked until my teeth ached. The only sound was the faint hum of the whisky bottle, vibrating against the desk like it was alive, singing its siren song.

"Well," I spat into the emptiness, sharp and venomous, "looks like you'll just have to wait. Can't traumatize the kiddies. Lucifer forbid they find out too early what the world really is, a meat grinder dressed up in glitter."

The chair screeched against the floorboards as I shoved back. The sound was jagged, angry, perfect.

My legs felt weak, like I was slogging through a swamp of bones and tar, every step pulling me down deeper.

Behind me, the glow of my phone dimmed to black. The pill bottle stayed exactly where it was, patient, smug, like it knew it would win eventually.

And maybe it would. Coffins don't chase. They just wait.

# Chapter 13
## Lucas

The bar hummed with the usual Friday-night noise, but it was background music to me. Always was. Didn't matter where I went, the story stayed the same, I was the hottest guy in the room, and everyone knew it.

That wasn't arrogance anymore. That was survival.

Shannon, the bartender, leaned across the bar, arms folded, giving me that look she always did, the one that said she was onto me.

"Why are you here on your night off?"

I smirked, lifting my glass like it explained everything. "Needed a drink."

She raised a brow, nodding toward the neon glow spilling in from the street. "There are a lot of bars around, Lukey."

My grin widened as I slid back into the role I knew too well, the one that never let anyone too close.

"Yeah, but none where I get a staff discount and such a charming bartender."

I threw in a wink for good measure. Armor. Always armor.

She rolled her eyes so hard it made me chuckle. "Yeah, I know your game, Lukey. Go use it on someone else."

I tipped my drink to her, chuckling low in my throat. "Worth a try."

Her laugh was sharp, unimpressed. "Not with me it ain't. I've seen your moves, and I've seen where, and how many women, you've put that thing into."

I leaned back on my stool, hand pressed to my chest in mock offense, my grin never faltering. "Hey, don't be jealous that the ladies can't get enough."

She shook her head, amused but not buying it. "Jealous isn't the word I'd use, Lukey."

Before I could fire back, her eyes flicked toward the door. That sly smile tugged at her lips.

"Don't look now. Little Miss stage 5 clinger at nine o'clock."

I stiffened, just for a second. She saw it. She always saw too much.

Sure enough, Cindy breezed in like she'd been rehearsing the entrance, eyes locked on me like a dog on a bone.

"Lukey… it's you!"

Her voice was syrupy, too sweet, and my jaw tightened. I rolled my eyes, masking the irritation with a lazy sip from my glass.

Behind the bar, Shannon stifled a laugh. She lived for this.

Cindy closed the distance, her wide-eyed eagerness faltering when I didn't melt into her arms. Her voice wavered. "Lukey?"

I didn't move. Didn't blink. Just let the silence stretch, the only sound the ice clinking in my glass.

Her smile faltered. "Lukey, are you ignoring me?"

I dragged out another sip, long and deliberate, before setting the glass down.

On the outside, I was every bit the untouchable player she thought she wanted. On the inside, my stomach twisted. Because the only name I wanted on my lips wasn't hers.

It was Lexi's. It had always been Lexi's. And she still didn't see me, not really. Not the way I'd built this whole damn act just to survive without her choosing me.

I finally set my glass down, slow and deliberate, meeting Cindy's eyes with the kind of faux confusion I'd mastered years ago.

"I'm sorry, are you talking to me?"

She blinked, tilting her head like she thought it was some kind of joke. "Lucas?"

I sighed, smooth and easy, like I hadn't rehearsed this a hundred times before. "I'm sorry, love, I think you have the wrong person. My name's John."

Behind the counter, Shannon groaned loud enough to draw a couple of stares. Cindy laughed nervously, the sound cracking. "Stop being silly, Lucas."

I held her gaze, letting the mask slip just enough for my tone to turn firm. "I'm sorry, sweetheart. I really don't know who you are. You must be mistaken."

Her smile froze, then cracked, twisting into something bitter. She crossed her arms, her words sharp, meant to cut.

"You're an ass, Lucas. I'm not blind or an idiot."

The whole bar seemed to hear her, her voice slicing through the haze of laughter, clinking glasses, and bad jukebox music.

But me? I didn't move. Didn't flinch. Just leaned against the bar, wearing the same mask I'd worn for years, the one that kept people out.

The one that made sure no one saw the boy underneath. The one still stuck on a girl who never wanted him the way he wanted her. The boy who'd learned not to get feelings.

Cindy slapped me across the face and then spun on her heels, her footsteps sharp against the sticky floor. The door banged shut behind her, anger trailing after her like smoke.

I rubbed my face, turned back toward the bar, and reclaimed my stool.

Shannon shook her head, arms folded tight across her chest. "You're a real ass, Lucas."

I let out a laugh, low, careless, the kind of sound I'd trained myself to make when I was anything but.

"I told her what it was. Just a bit of fun. No strings."

She rolled her eyes so hard I thought they might roll away and not come back.

I smirked anyway, leaning back against the stool. My voice came easy, dripping with charm I didn't even feel.

"But once they get a taste of this…" I winked, shameless.

On the outside, I was every bit the player. Untouchable. Desired. Always in control.

But inside? *Fuck,* inside I was still that boy at seventeen, watching Lexi walk away with someone else, realizing in one brutal heartbeat that all she believed men wanted was sex.

So, what did I do? I became that man. The man she said we all were. The man I thought she'd finally want.

And I've been stuck playing him ever since.

Her arms stayed crossed, her tone cold enough to freeze whiskey mid-pour. "You need to learn not to shit in your own backyard. They all know you work here, Lucas. You can't pretend to be someone else when they all come here expecting to see you behind the bar. And to be honest? I'm sick of dealing with your fangirls."

I bit my lip, the practiced move, the mock-sexy grin I'd perfected over years of late nights and easy lays. The one that usually worked. The one that usually made the sting of words like hers slide right off.

She didn't even blink.

The smirk faltered, just for half a second, but I straightened up, folding my arms across my chest like armor. My voice came out smooth, sure, the way I needed it to.

"I ain't going to change. I love this lifestyle. No strings, no commitment, no responsibilities. Different women, different likes, never boring. It's what girls really want. They like it when guys want them."

Shannon's face hardened like stone. "Guys like you are disgusting. You give girls such low self-esteem. They end up sleeping with any guy that looks their way, anyone who gives them attention, hoping he'll stick around."

Her words should've hit harder. Maybe they did, somewhere deep down, in that bruised place I didn't dare go. But my mask was already in place. I didn't even flinch.

My smirk stayed steady, almost taunting. "They love it as much as we do. They always come back for more. They wouldn't do that if they hated it."

She narrowed her eyes, her voice cutting flat and final. "There's no helping you."

I grinned wider, though inside the smile felt more like a scar. "I'm perfectly happy, thank you. I don't need help."

Her laugh was sharp, bitter, the sound of someone who'd seen too much to believe the act anymore. "Yep. Your sort always are."

And then, the moment cracked.

A woman slid onto the next stool, perfume hitting me sharp and sweet, cutting through the stale beer and smoke. She didn't even look at me when she spoke, her voice calm and practiced.

"Vodka and orange, please."

Shannon turned away, busying herself with bottles and ice.

I leaned back, getting a better view, still smirking, still playing my part, but the truth gnawed at me like it always did. Because I was wrong about one thing.

I wasn't perfectly happy. Not even close.

But hell would freeze over before I was ever going to let anyone see that.

"Sure thing, coming right up," Shannon said, grabbing a glass.

And just like that, I switched gears. Cindy? Gone. The argument? Forgotten. My charm clicked on like a light switch. This was my game, my mask, my armor.

I let my lopsided grin slide into place as I turned to the woman beside me. "Well, hello there, gorgeous."

She tilted her head, smiling back, a little shy but already hooked. "Hello."

Shannon slid the drink across the bar with that tired smile of hers, but I caught the look in her eyes, exhaustion, frustration, the silent reminder that she'd seen me play this same hand a thousand times before.

She knew how it ended, how it always ended.

I didn't miss a beat. "Shannon… that one's on me."

If Shannon kept rolling her eyes like that, she is going to strain something.

"Great. Remember the talk we were just having? Shit… backyard."

I chuckled, waving her off like her words couldn't touch me. "Yeah, yeah, yeah."

Then I leaned toward the woman, lowering my voice into that smooth, practiced tone that never failed me. "So, why's a pretty thing like you buying your own drinks?"

Her giggle came soft, cheeks warming as she tucked a strand of hair behind her ear. I could practically feel Shannon's eyes burning through me from behind the bar.

But I didn't stop. I couldn't.

I'd perfected this mask. It was my comfort. My distraction.

I leaned in closer, grin sharp and calculated. "Your boyfriend should not leave you unattended."

Her laugh was light, easy. "I don't have a boyfriend."

And there it was. The answer I'd been waiting for.

My smirk widened, victory sliding into place like it always did. "Well, it would appear it's my lucky night."

Her eyes darted away, shy, before coming back to mine. That bashful smile tugged at her lips, and I knew I'd won.

But under the buzz of neon and the hum of chatter, the truth hit the back of my throat like whiskey that burned too long.

This wasn't luck. It was the same tired game I'd been playing for years. And no matter how many times I won, it never felt like enough.

It never felt like I'd really won.

Because no one ever compared. Not to her. Not to Lexi, the woman whose magic I could never break free from.

The room was dim, shadows spilling across the sheets as we tangled together. Her lips were hot and insistent, her body pressed to mine like she was starving for something I couldn't give her. For a while, I let myself sink into it, the heat, the hunger, the illusion.

Sammy pulled back with a breathless laugh, her cheeks flushed. "Oh, Lucas, you know how to get a girl's attention… and to keep it."

I smirked, giving her the same line I'd given a hundred others. "I aim to please, sweetheart."

Her giggle bubbled out, nervous but eager. She brushed her hair from her face, trying to look casual. "I'm not normally like this… just going home with the first guy I meet at a bar."

My grin didn't falter, though her words barely touched me. "But it was good, right?"

I flashed her a winning smile. She smiled in return, softer this time, as if she wanted to believe we'd shared something real.

"Yes… it was a pleasant surprise."

Her eyes lingered on me like she was hoping I'd be different, like she saw something worth holding onto. "Meeting you might have been just what I needed," she whispered. "I've been going through a rough time. I was actually at the pub to meet a girlfriend; she was going to cheer me up. But meeting you… maybe this was the cheering up I needed."

Her words kept spilling, desperate for an ear, for someone to hold her pain. But all I could think about was how heavy the room suddenly felt.

I sat up, eyes flicking to the clock on the nightstand. "Is that the time? Sorry, I've got an early morning. Work tomorrow."

Her face froze, confusion and disappointment flickering across it. "You're… kicking me out?"

I didn't answer at first. Just smirked like it was nothing. The mask. Always the mask.

But inside, my chest ached. Because this wasn't cheering her up. This wasn't connection. This was me filling the silence, chasing skin while my best friend was six feet under and the girl I wanted was pregnant by another man, a man who didn't want her.

And no matter how many women I touched, no matter how many smiles I faked, it was never Lexi's face I woke up next to. And my best friend was never coming back.

I held up my hands, playing it off like it was harmless. "Don't see it as being kicked out, as in…" I dragged it out, stroking my chin like I was actually putting thought into the words. Then I slipped the mask back on, smooth and practiced. "A wonderful, fun night had. And now it's over."

Her smile crumbled, tightening into something bitter. Arms crossed, voice sharp. "So, no exchange of numbers? No catching up again? That's it? I was just some itch you had to scratch?"

I shrugged, letting the casual roll of my shoulders do the talking. Detached. Unbothered. "I don't see it as that."

But of course she did. I could see it in her eyes, she wanted a connection, someone to offload to. I was not that person. I don't do offloading. My bottles are already filled, and if I take on anyone else's mess, mine will implode.

If anyone actually knew just how messed up, I truly was...

The sheets were still a mess around us when I leaned back against the headboard, plastering on that lazy grin I'd perfected years ago.

"You're a beautiful woman, Sammy," I said smoothly, voice dripping with charm I didn't feel. "And I got to experience you. And you got to experience all this."

I gestured at myself like I was the prize, like this was some kind of mutual win.

Her lips parted, the warmth draining from her eyes as the realization hit her like a slap. "Oh my God," she whispered, disgust etched in every syllable. "I did it again."

Her arms folded across her chest like a shield. Her voice rose, brittle, furious, the same words I'd heard a hundred times before. "You're a pig just like the rest of them. Are there even any decent men left in this world?"

Her hand came down across my face with a sharp crack. My head snapped to the side, skin stinging. Two for today. Not my worst record, but close.

When I turned back to her, I was smiling. Yes, you bet I was smiling. That's what I did. That's who I was now.

Inside, though? The sting of her slap was nothing compared to the one I'd been carrying for years; the night I'd been chasing ass while Joshie lay dying in that bathroom stall. The night I lost my brother.

No matter how many women I touched, no matter how many smiles I faked, every single one of them only reminded me of the one I couldn't have, Lexi. And how badly I messed up that night.

This… being slapped, being called a pig, being despised, it felt right. It felt like penance. It felt like what I deserved.

Sammy yanked on her clothes like every thread had betrayed her, storming for the door with all the fury I'd expected.

I leaned back, voice dripping arrogance I didn't feel. "Well, if I knew you liked it rough… maybe we can catch up for one more go?"

And yes. I said it, because I had to make sure, she wasn't just mad at me. I had to make sure she hated me.

She spun, eyes blazing like she could burn me alive. "You're a dick."

I laughed, low and careless, the sound bouncing sharp off the walls like broken glass. "Wouldn't be the first time I've heard that, sweetheart."

Her face twisted, red with fury. "I wouldn't come near you again if someone paid me."

I stood then, naked, hands on my hips, grin plastered in place like the carefully placed shield I'd developed over years, one I couldn't take off. "Okay, sweetheart. But thanks for tonight… I really enjoyed it."

Her scream split the air. "ARGHHHHHH!!!"

Then the door slammed so hard the walls rattled.

Just like that, silence. Only the faint echo of her anger lingering like smoke.

I sank back onto the bed, chuckling like none of it mattered. Like the sting in my cheek wasn't still burning. Like her words hadn't landed right where I already knew I was weakest.

The truth was, every time a woman stormed out, the silence afterward was the same, heavy, suffocating.

And no amount of charm, no amount of skin-on-skin distractions, could drown it.

Still, I grabbed my phone. My thumbs moved fast, scrolling through numbers, old texts, familiar names.

There was always another option. Always another body to fill the space.

Because if I stopped, if I sat still in that silence, I'd have to face the one thought I never outran:

Lexi.

Always Lexi.

# Chapter 14

## Lexi

The phone buzzed, Lucas's name glowing on the screen like a curse I couldn't shake.

**Lucas:** *"Did your night turn out as fun as mine?"*

And then the photo came.

*Jesus Christ.*

Lucas sprawled across some black silk sheets, a single sheet barely covering the one part of him I least wanted to see. That smug grin plastered on his face, like he'd won some prize. Like this was worth bragging about.

I stared at it, bile rising in my throat.

Did he actually think this was attractive? That I cared? God knows what diseases he's carrying, sticking that thing into half the city.

I gagged, tossing the phone down onto the rug like it had burned me.

The nursery wasn't really a nursery yet, just four bare walls that echoed when I breathed too loud. A flat-pack cot sat in the middle, box ripped open, bolts and screws scattered across the floor like confetti from a party I hadn't been invited to.

I sat cross-legged on the rug or at least tried to. Hard to do when your belly's this big and your legs ache this much. The instructions stared back at me like they were written in another language.

*Bolt A into leg B with washer C before tightening nut A.* Over and over.

I pressed my fingers against my temples, muttering into the silence. "Why can't they sell these things already built? Who actually enjoys this shit?"

The phone buzzed again. Another photo from Lucas.

At least he had gray track pants on this time, though they hung so low I could still see the sharp V of his hips. My stomach churned. My fingers flew across the screen.

**Me:** *"You're disgusting, Lucas. I hate to think about what diseases you have. I hope you don't kiss your mother with that mouth."*

I hurled the phone onto the carpet and dragged the cot box closer. The diagrams mocked me, neat lines, bold arrows, daring me to admit I wasn't strong enough for even this.

My chest tightened, heat rising to my face. "I can't do this." The words cracked out of me, sharp and broken, swallowed by the empty room.

And for the first time in a long time, I didn't know if I meant the cot… or all of it.

Tears stung hot, blurring my vision. I clutched my swollen belly. The skin stretched taut beneath my palm, alive with every flutter that reminded me there was no turning back. My hand lingered there, searching for comfort, but all I felt was the weight of my own failure.

"I'm sorry," I whispered into the hollow air of the half-finished room. "I got the best one I could get you… with what I had."

The apology tasted bitter, sour on my tongue.

"I'm sorry you're stuck with me." My throat tightened. The words broke before I could stop them. "Hopeless, clueless me. I don't even know what I'm doing. How am I supposed to look after you?"

The sob tore out of me before I could swallow it down. I bowed my head over the curve of my belly, hot tears dripping onto my shirt.

The flat-pack cot loomed over me, its scattered screws and wooden slats spread across the floor like proof, proof that I wasn't ready. Proof that I couldn't do this.

I pressed both hands to my stomach, desperate for the tiny flutters that reminded me this little life was real. My voice cracked, thick with shame.

"Feed you? Clean you?" My chest hitched. "When I can't even build a cheap-ass cot without falling apart?"

I leaned harder into the swell of my belly, as if pressing close enough could translate the storm in my chest into something it would understand.

"I'll probably kill you," I choked out, brutal and merciless. "Through being stupid. Careless. Not knowing what the hell I'm doing."

A sob rattled through me, jagged and sharp.

"Maybe my parents are right." The thought slipped free before I could stop it, soft and venomous all at once. "Maybe I should put you up for adoption. Maybe that's the only way you'll ever have a chance at something better than me."

The silence after was deafening. Just me, the broken pieces of a cot, and a baby kicking faintly inside a mother already convinced she wasn't enough.

My throat burned as the words spilled jagged, tearing me apart with every breath.

"I'm no good to anybody. Let alone a helpless child who needs real parents. Good parents. I can barely look after myself." My voice cracked, breaking into a bitter edge. "I'm always making stupid decisions. I mean, I can't even hold down a job. And my taste in men…"

A sound slipped out of me, a laugh that wasn't really a laugh. Hollow. Sharp. "God, my taste in men is fucking woeful."

The silence pressed in, heavy, suffocating. I leaned back against the wall, the paint cool against my skin, the weight of it all threatening to crush me.

How can I go through all of this, the sickness, the exhaustion, the pain, and then have nothing at the end of it?

And then I felt it. Small. Faint. Undeniable.

A kick.

My breath hitched. My hand flew to my stomach, smoothing over the swell like I could reach the life inside. The smallest reminder that this wasn't just my disaster. This was a person. A future.

I swallowed hard, my voice breaking on a whisper. "Can you tell me what you want?"

The room answered with nothing but stillness.

A bitter sigh escaped me. "No. I didn't think so."

The quiet didn't last long. My phone buzzed on the carpet, rattling like it was mocking me. I reached for it, thumb swiping across the screen, and my heart sank.

Lucas.

*Oh my God. Stop, Lucas.*

Another photo. Another smug grin. A towel slung low across his hips, water dripping from his skin like he'd just stepped out of the shower. Another reminder of everything he was, everything I wasn't. Another taunt I didn't need when I was already breaking.

My thumbs trembled as I typed, the anger barely holding back the grief.

**Me:** *"I swear to God I'm going to block your number, Lucas! Stop."*

But I didn't. Not yet.

Because deep down, I knew I wouldn't.

Instead of relief, the angry words I'd just sent tore me open. My chest caved. The sobs came fast, ragged, unstoppable. The phone slipped from my hand, landing in my lap like dead weight, its glow fading against the shadow of my tears.

*How did I get into such a mess?*

The question hung in the air, thick and suffocating, echoing off the bare walls. No answer came. Just silence. Just me. My failure. My shame.

And then, soft, subtle, but real, the flicker came again. Small kicks. A gentle reminder from the little life inside me.

My throat tightened as I pressed both hands against my swollen belly, cradling it like it might break if I let go.

No matter how broken I was, no matter how much I hated myself for every choice that led me here… I wasn't completely alone.

For the first time that night, the sobs eased into shaky breaths, the kind you cling to just to keep from drowning.

"I'll try," I whispered hoarsely, to the baby, to myself, to no one at all. "Even if I screw it up… I'll try."

# Chapter 15

## Lexi

A couple of days later, I found myself sitting across from Maddie at the local café. Sunlight streamed through the dusty windows, catching on the chipped edges of the tables, making the whole place look warmer than it actually was.

The smell of coffee beans clung to the air. I used to love that smell. Now, with pregnancy twisting my senses, it just made my stomach churn. I closed my eyes for a second, willing the nausea to pass. The last thing I needed was to vomit here, in front of Maddie.

They said morning sickness would only last the first three months. Lies. It wasn't just mornings, and for me, it had been coming and going the entire pregnancy. Just my luck.

When my stomach finally settled, I opened my eyes. Maddie tilted her head, her black curls catching the light, her hands already planted on her hips in that familiar way, like she was ready to poke at me until I cracked.

"It's not like you to call me and ask to see me?"

I shifted in my chair, fingers fussing with the seam of my sleeve like it might hold me together. "I know… well…"

Her face softened instantly. Maddie always had that kind of smile, the kind that looked like it could fix things just by existing.

"Oh no, I love it," she said quickly. "We used to talk about everything, Lexi. Every little thing. Every crush, every fight with your parents. You used to call me the second something happened."

She sighed, and the smile slipped into something sadder. "Then we left school… and we drifted."

The weight pressed hard against my chest. My words scraped out like glass. "Yeah, well, after Joshie…" I swallowed, forcing it out. "I just wanted to put all that behind me. Seeing you all just kept… dragging it back. The grief. The guilt. Everything."

Her eyes softened, glassy with understanding. Her voice dropped low. "I know… but maybe we can work at getting back to the way it was."

For the first time in years, something cracked open inside me, not pain, not bitterness, but something gentler. A genuine smile tugged at my lips before I could stop it. "I'd like that."

Her grin widened, that old spark of Maddie's coming back, warmth flickering through like sunlight on a cloudy day. For a heartbeat, it almost felt like we were kids again. But then her brows pinched, and she leaned in.

"So, what was so important? You sounded upset on the phone."

My stomach twisted. The tea in front of me suddenly tasted sour, the heat crawling up my neck. I rubbed my palms on my jeans, wishing I'd hung up instead of dialing in the first place.

"I really hate to ask this… I mean, I know I've only met him the once, and I don't really know him, but…"

Her eyes widened with curiosity, and that teasing grin of hers broke through. "But…?"

I let out a nervous laugh, sharp and brittle.

"Will you just spit it out, girl?" she giggled, shaking her head.

And there I was, teetering on the edge of words I didn't want to say. My heart hammered against my ribs, every beat threatening to give me away. Maddie's gaze stayed steady, patient, like she could see every hesitation I was choking on.

My fingers twisted together in my lap. Finally, the words tumbled free, shaky and small. "Would Ray… be able to help me this Saturday?"

Her expression softened instantly. Relief should have come with it, but instead, the knot in my stomach only tightened.

"I've been trying to put a cot together," I rushed out, desperate to explain before she could turn me down. "And I just can't do it. I've tried everything, Maddie, and I can't make the damn thing stand up without it collapsing the second I stand it upright."

My hand moved instinctively to the swell of my stomach, pressing gently, grounding myself. My voice cracked.

"This one needs a place to sleep. And I don't… I don't have the money to pay someone to do it."

The words hung between us, fragile and humiliating, like I'd just handed over proof of how useless I really was.

Later that night, I found myself scrolling aimlessly until Lucas's name lit up my phone again. Another picture. Another smug grin. This time, he had a busty woman clinging to each arm at the bar he worked at.

I tossed the phone onto the bed, my stomach twisting. God. Does he even see himself anymore? Or is this all he knows how to be?

Maddie's voice echoed in my head, her warmth, her patience, her hope for reconnection. And then the bitter truth pressed down again: Lucas had become everything I once feared boys were. Fun. Sex. No strings. No care.

And yet… a part of me still hated that I couldn't stop checking his messages.

# Chapter 16

## Lucas

The bar smelled the same as always, stale beer and a hint of cheap perfume that clung to the walls. Neon lights buzzed overhead like they were tired of their job.

I leaned against the counter, rag in hand, polishing the same stretch of wood I'd already wiped three times. Habit. Distraction. Something to do while I waited for the next laugh, the next drink, the next excuse to keep the emptiness at bay.

The door slammed open so hard the hinges rattled. My head snapped up.

A small, fierce-looking woman stormed in, heels hammering the sticky floor, eyes blazing like fire. She cut through the haze of voices and clinking glasses as if none of it could slow her down.

Her shoulders were squared, her jaw set, fists clenched at her sides. Surely, she's not after me. I've slept with a lot of women, but I'd remember her.

Especially with a rack like that. Yeah, no way I'd forget them.

"Tell me who the jerk was that did this to her," she demanded, voice sharp, furious.

I blinked, caught off guard, the rag slipping in my hand. "I'm sorry," I said, trying for casual. "I don't know what you're talking about."

Her glare didn't waver. If anything, it cut deeper. "I'm Jackie. My friend was here the other night. Some ass took her home and treated her like a piece of shit. And now…"

Her voice broke. Tears filled her eyes, and she pressed her hands to her face, sobbing louder than the jukebox humming in the corner.

Guilt hit me sharp, immediate, but I forced my shoulders loose, kept the smirk in my tone. "Who is your friend?"

Her head lifted, red-rimmed eyes blazing with hurt. "Her name is Sammy," she spat. Her voice shook, softer now. "What he did… what he made her do… he has no idea what he's done."

My stomach dropped. *Sammy*. The name cracked through me like glass shattering. I swallowed hard, jaw tightening, but I kept my mask on.

"I don't know any Sammy," I lied smoothly. "But maybe you can tell me what happened?"

Jackie sniffled, her shoulders sagging as some of the fire drained from her. "I'm so sorry," she whispered, raw. "You must think I'm crazy."

I shook my head quickly, my voice softer than I meant it to be. "No… not at all."

She sank onto a barstool, fingers twisting together like they were the only thing holding her together. "It's just that… Sammy came in here a couple nights ago."

I nodded, trying to stay neutral, trying not to give myself away while knives twisted in my gut.

"God, I feel partly responsible," Jackie murmured.

Her confession landed heavier than she knew.

"I was supposed to meet her here," she continued. "But I was late. Work." Her face crumpled. "I was supposed to cheer her up. She's been going through a nasty breakup. Fiancé, ex- fiancé, cheated. With two of his coworkers. Aweek before their wedding."

Her words painted the picture clear: a woman already broken before she even stepped into this place.

"She's spent weeks canceling plans, retelling the story, explaining to family and friends." Jackie's tone thickened with grief. "She's lost all faith. In men. In humans."

The rag in my hand felt like lead. The smirk was gone.

Jackie pressed on. "By the time I got here that night, she was gone. I thought she just got tired of waiting for me. I went home, texted her. The morning after…"

Her voice cracked. "I woke up to a message saying all men were evil. That she was done. That all she was to men was sex. That another one had treated her the same. And she was sorry."

The air in the bar turned heavy, pressing down until I could barely breathe.

"I rushed to her place," Jackie whispered, tears breaking free. "And she had tried to hurt herself."

Her sobs ripped through the space. My chest tightened. My whole body went rigid.

"But I got there in time. She's in the hospital now, recovering."

I rubbed the back of my neck, nerves firing under my skin. My mind circled one truth I didn't want to face: That night, Sammy had been with me.

Jackie's jaw clenched, anger cutting through her grief. "Just because some jerk wanted to get his rocks off."

Her words sliced me open. She didn't even know how close she'd hit.

"Oh god, I'm sorry," she said suddenly, sagging against the bar. "You didn't need all this dumped on you."

I shook my head quickly. "It's fine… bartenders are like hairdressers. We're here to listen." My voice dropped lower. "Is your friend going to be okay?"

"She will survive," Jackie replied, but her face didn't soften. "What damage has been done… we won't know until she wakes up."

The ache in my chest hollowed me out. "I'm sorry," I whispered.

"You have nothing to be sorry about."

But I did. *Fuck, I did.* She just didn't know it was me.

Jackie sighed. "I'm sorry I barged in here like that. Offloaded on you."

Maybe it was exactly what I needed.

"It's fine," I said with a practiced grin, forcing my hands onto my hips. "How about I get you a drink… on the house?"

She gave a tired laugh. "It's still early."

"It's been a big day," I replied evenly.

Her lips pressed thin. Then she gave in "One can't hurt."

I busied myself with a spotless glass, polishing it again to steady my hands. "I hope your friend makes a speedy recovery."

"Thanks," Jackie murmured. Her gaze cut sharp as a blade. "If you ever find out who the guy was… tell him he needs to think with something other than his dick. Because behind the boobs and the body is a person with feelings. A person who might already be going through shit he doesn't know about."

Her words landed like bullets, every one a direct hit.

I kept my face neutral. "I'll pass the message on… if I find out who he is."

*Message received. Loud and clear.*

Jackie managed a faint smile. "See, now if she met someone like you…"

I froze.

"You've been nothing but kind. You listened. That's all women want, to be heard, to be thought of, to know they're more than a body. And for a man to stay faithful." She rolled her eyes. "Some guys can't even do that."

I scratched the back of my neck, hiding the guilt crawling under my skin. "Yeah, well, it's easy to listen when you're behind a bar." I forced a grin. "But you've given me a lot to think about today."

"Good," she said simply.

Silence stretched, pressing heavy. I muttered under my breath, almost to myself, "Being a man and all…"

Jackie let out a quiet giggle. "You have potential."

I arched a brow, smirking through the churn in my gut.

"You got a girlfriend?" she asked.

My throat tightened. Before I could answer, she added quickly, "Oh, I'm not asking for me. Or my friend."

Her words lingered, light but edged. I forced a faint smile, even as guilt chewed at me.

She studied me carefully. "I'll be advising her to steer clear of men for a while. Was just wondering if someone has snapped you up yet."

I leaned back, wearing my lazy grin like armor. "Nope. Forever single."

She shook her head. "All that means is you haven't met the right one." She paused for a moment and looked at me with questioning eyes. "Oh, I see."

Her eyes narrowed, sharp, reading me like a book. "You have met the right one. Just not the right time."

The words stopped me cold.

"No, I am perfectly happy being single. Some men aren't out for a relationship you know. They're just happy living a single life." I said, trying to defend my singlehood.

She smirked knowingly. "If there were no feelings involved, you wouldn't be this defensive. You're hung up on a woman… who isn't hung up on you."

My arms folded before I realized it. "Nooo… I like my single life. No responsibilities. No one to answer to. Freedom."

Jackie laughed, gathering her bag. "Keep telling yourself that. One day you might believe it." She paused, eyes steady. "Grow some balls and go get her. Stop with the bravado. Tell her how you feel."

She gave me a final nod. "Thanks for the drink. And for listening."

I stood there, motionless, my grin fixed like a mask. Inside, her words echoed louder than I wanted to admit.

*Grow some balls and just go get her.*

If only it were that easy.

# Chapter 17
## Lexi

The flower shop smelled of roses and eucalyptus, the sweetness barely masking the faint musk of damp soil. I stood at the counter, fingers tangled in a length of ribbon, pretending I knew what I was doing. My back ached; my belly pressed taut beneath my apron.

For once, the low hum of the shop felt almost soothing.

Then a voice cut through it.

"So…"

I jumped, spinning around, hands automatically flying to cradle my stomach as if shielding it could make the appearance of my boss less dangerous. My heart thudded against my ribs.

Simone stood a few feet away, arms folded, one brow arched. Her heels clicked on the old floorboards as she leaned on one hip, watching me with that calculating look that always made me feel exposed.

My throat tightened. I knew that tone. Simone wasn't here for flowers, she was here for answers. I exhaled and pressed a hand to my belly to steady the panic rising in my chest.

"Oh my God, Simone, you scared me."

She didn't smile. She didn't move. Arms crossed, expression carved from stone, she repeated, "So…" as though the word itself already carried the answer.

I forced a brittle smile, searching for an escape. "Oh yes! I just finished the display. I organized today's deliveries and…" My eyes darted to the counter; I twisted the ribbon until my fingers ached. "Oh, and I ordered the pansies you wanted."

Simone rolled her eyes, unimpressed. Her voice cut. "No."

She stepped closer, gaze pinning me. "So, did you talk to him?"

*Lucas*. Of course.

The ribbon slipped through my fingers as I stalled, heart hammering. I fumbled with the bouquet like it might hold answers that weren't there.

"Look, Simone…" My voice cracked. "Lucas isn't one to stick around. I… I spoke to him, but…"

Guilt rose in my throat.

"He's not likely to call you back. I'm sorry. He's just… a dick. He'll be forever single, moving from one woman to the next. Better to forget him."

My bluntness was meant to protect, but it landed like a blow.

"So, you're telling me I'm not good enough for him?"

Panic clawed at me. I shook my head. "No… it's not that. It's who Lucas is. He's always been like that, since high school."

Simone's lips pressed thin. "Well, the company you keep says a lot about who you are."

Her words hit like a slap. Suddenly the shop, warm light and soft perfume, felt suffocating. The walls drew in. My hand tightened on my belly as if I could hold myself together by force.

Heat rose to my cheeks. I straightened. "Oh, Lucas and I are not friends."

Simone's brow arched. "Don't you see each other, like every week?"

The accusation made my stomach lurch. I shifted, searching for words that wouldn't make things worse. "Yes… but it's not what it looks like."

Her face hardened. "We just received a delivery of pots out the back that need unpacking."

I blinked, stunned. Anger flared through the shame.

"I thought we agreed I wouldn't do heavy deliveries this late in my pregnancy," I said, voice trembling but fierce, palm pressing harder to my belly. "I can't bend and lift like that. It's not good for the baby."

My supposed safe place closed in. The perfume of lilies and roses thickened until it felt like drowning. My back protested as I leaned on the counter, exhaustion prickling at the edges of everything.

Simone didn't even blink. Hands on hips, foot tapping an impatient beat, she smirked coldly. "Well, I just got my nails done. I wouldn't want to chip them."

She held out a hand and inspected her polish with obvious pleasure.

Nails. That's what mattered to her. Polish, not swollen ankles, not sleepless nights, not the baby kicking like a small, insistent heartbeat reminding me this wasn't just about me.

Just her damn nails.

Surrounded by symbols of new life, flowers, light, promises, I felt smaller than I had in years.

Simone spun on her heel and stalked to the storeroom, heels snapping on tile. Over her shoulder she called, sharp and dismissive, "Make sure they're done before the end of your shift, Lexi."

I watched her go, mouth dry, anger clawing up my throat. My hands balled into fists, nails bit into my palms.

The words slipped out before I could stop them, low and trembling. "I'm going to kill you, Lucas. Why do I have to deal with your messes?"

It was always him, his careless choices bleeding into my life, staining it in ways he never had to face.

A sharp pain tugged at my side. I bent slightly, clutching my belly as if my hand could soothe both of us. Exhaustion and fury collided; my breath left me in a shudder.

Still, I moved toward the storeroom, every step slow and clumsy, like an invisible weight pulled my limbs down.

The baby shifted, a firm kick, and the world tightened around that small, undeniable life. I wasn't just carrying my own burden anymore; I was carrying his, too.

The lump in my throat rose until it almost choked me. I wasn't only tired; I was done.

Done with Simone's cruelty. Done with Lucas's recklessness. Done being the one who had to hold everything together while everyone else lived carelessly and left me with the fallout.

But I kept walking, because what other choice did I have?

# Chapter 18
# Nelly

The hum of the big rig filled the gaming station, a low mechanical drone that only made the silence louder. Monitors glared back at me, their cold blue glow bleaching my skin corpse-white. My fingers tapped out a frantic rhythm on the mechanical keys, the only pulse this place had left.

"Where the hell are they?"

One o'clock sharp. That's our thing. Always has been. Today was supposed to be Serpent slaughter day, I'd been grinding for it, waiting for it. And the lobby…? Empty.

I logged out. Switched accounts. Checked again. There they were.

*They've joined another alliance.*

The thought clawed its way in, jagged and mean: *They'd blocked me and moved on.*

I slumped back, the cheap chair biting into my spine, betrayal settling cold in my chest. Same damn story. Different day. People leave. They always do.

Why didn't they say anything? They could have just said something.

Why did they block me? Why are they hiding from me?

My vision blurred. I bit my lip until I tasted iron, until the sting reminded me I was still here. Of course this happens. Every time. Nobody sticks around for me. Not for Nelly. There's always someone shinier, funnier, easier. Someone worth keeping.

My nails dug crescents into my palms. "Why does this always happen?"

I pounded the keys harder, faster, like I could bury the ache in pixels and code. But it bled through anyway. The truth always does.

I was still the one left behind.

Delete the accounts. Wipe the characters. Pretend it never mattered. Pretend I never cared.

The cursor blinked at me on the blank screen, smug little bastard, like it knew I'd lost again. Like it was waiting for me to admit it.

Why the hell did I think online would be any different from reality? Friends, alliances, "teams," just fancier words for the same old shit. They leave. They always leave.

Maybe it's me. Scratch that, it's definitely me. I'm not the kind of person people stick around for. No matter what I do, I'm always the first one cut loose. Dead weight in combat boots.

Hope… what a sick joke. Every time I think I've found something solid, something everyone else seems to have on autopilot, it crumbles like rot under the floorboards. The only constant is disappointment.

My throat burned as the words curled in my head, bitter as ash.

Friends are overrated.

The chair shrieked against the floor when I shoved back, loud enough to sound like a final verdict. My body felt drained, every step a punishment. I left the monitor glowing over the empty seat, like even it was lonely now.

Doc Martens dragged across the floor as I walked out, head down, hair falling across my face. A curtain. Not that anyone was watching. No one ever is.

The hallway outside was as empty as I felt. When I pushed through the door, the late sun spilled across the street, all golden and smug, as if the world had the audacity to keep shining. It slid right off me. Never touched.

On the corner, the clichés of high school hell clustered together: footballers puffed up like peacocks, cheerleaders shrieking laughter sharp enough to cut, like they were auditioning for a sitcom no one invited me to. Their script, their spotlight. I was just the shadow passing by.

Invisible. Perfect.

I kept my head down, thumbing through old messages just to look busy. Then a notification flashed across the screen, and my jaw clenched.

The boss. Of course. Always him. The peddler of rainbows, puppies, and plastic smiles.

Well, he got what he wanted, cheerful garbage to slap on billboards so the masses could choke on it. I'd call him back later. Or never. Same difference.

My thumb hovered over the screen as I quickened my pace, praying I could ghost past the pack of hyenas on the corner. But luck and I have never been on speaking terms.

"Hey, freak!"

The word cut clean, sliding under my skin like a rusted blade. My shoulders tensed, breath snagged, but I didn't look back.

"Thought you couldn't come out in the daylight?" one of the football meatheads jeered, his tone rehearsed, slimy.

Laughter erupted on cue, a laugh track to a show I never auditioned for. Footballers with their swollen egos, cheerleaders with their plastic grins, all of them playing the same old scene. And me? The eternal punchline.

I rolled my eyes, dragged my mask into place, the one that said *unbothered, undead, couldn't care less.* My boots scuffed the pavement, each step a funeral march.

"Better get back to your coffin before you burn away!" Same voice, same whipcrack laugh slicing across the street. The chorus followed, their mockery swelling as if it had been waiting just for me.

Heat crawled up my neck, not from the sun, but from the shame, the old, familiar kind that always did.

The phone trembled in my hand before I shoved it deep into my pocket, fingers curling tight like I could crush their voices if I held on hard enough. I gave them nothing. No flinch. No look back. Just silence.

That's my only weapon. Pretend it doesn't matter. Pretend I'm not already stitched together with old scars, every word a bruise layered on bruises that never fade.

But inside? It landed. It always lands.

And I wondered, just for a heartbeat, how many more I could take before I finally shattered.

The house was silent when I got home. Not the gentle kind. Not peace. No, this was corpse-silence. Heavy. Suffocating. The kind that seeps into your bones and thickens the air until even breathing feels like a chore.

I stood in the middle of my shoebox living room, staring at the wreckage like it was a crime scene, and I was both the victim and the killer.

Light slashed through the blinds in harsh little stripes, catching on the table. Empty bottles. A chipped glass clinging to stale whiskey. The orange pill bottle rattled when my knee brushed it. A razor blade gleamed in the sun like it was in on the joke.

My life, laid out in neat little props. Each one whispering its own accusation: pathetic, weak, broken.

I dropped into the chair, elbows smacking the table, head falling into my hands. The glow of my phone cut through the gloom, glaring at me like an interrogation lamp. His name flashed up, my boss. Of course.

*Go on, Nelly. Answer him. Let him ruin your day properly.*

Before I could talk myself out of it, I hit answer and placed the phone to my ear.

"What do you want?"

I snapped sharper than I meant, but too late to reel it back now.

"You don't speak to me like that, Nelly. I'm your boss." His voice was clipped, condescending, the kind reserved for chewing gum stuck to a shoe.

My jaw locked. I pressed my palm into my forehead, grounding myself. "It's my day off. Why are you calling?"

"You think days off matter right now?" He sighed deliberately, heavy with manufactured disappointment. "We lost the Baxter job. Your work wasn't good enough."

My stomach dropped. My eyes drifted to the razor blade, its glint cutting at me, mocking.

"The execs have been talking," he droned. "We're pulling some of your accounts. Your work's... different lately. Raw."

Raw. Like I hadn't heard that diagnosis before. Like it wasn't tattooed across every inch of me already.

I swallowed, throat burning, voice scraping out low. "It's who I am."

Silence. Then his reply, clipped and final, like a coffin lid shutting. "Maybe who you are isn't what we need anymore."

"*Underground,*" he called it. Like my art was some diseased rat I'd dragged up from the sewers.

"It's not what our clients want. With fewer accounts, you'll have time to... explore your style. Build your own clients. Once you do, we'll hand the rest over to Reece."

The words landed like a slap, sharp and humiliating. My throat tightened. "So... what, I'm fired?"

"It's called artistic differences," he said smoothly, as if practicing it in the mirror. "We just don't see a future here for you, Nelly. You don't fit our vision."

The silence screamed louder than his voice. My ears rang, pressing in, suffocating.

Click.

I killed the call. The phone hit the table with a thud, rattling the whiskey glass and pill bottle like they were applauding my failure.

The rage broke loose.

I shoved the couch back, its legs shrieking against the floorboards, and I let out a scream, raw, jagged, shredding my throat as it bounced off the peeling walls.

"Four years!"

My fists slammed the table, rattling everything on it. "I gave them four years, landed their biggest accounts, and now I'm disposable?!" My chest burned, lungs clawing for air. "They can't do this to me!"

My hands shook, knuckles bone-white, hair tangled in fists as if yanking hard enough might rip the thoughts from my skull. My pulse thundered like a funeral drum.

And then it came, the switch I despised most. When anger, grief, and humiliation piled too high, when the mountain crushed instead of letting me climb.

Everything went cold.

Easier that way. Easier than feeling every jagged edge slicing me open from the inside.

The room sagged around me, hollow, like I'd already faded out of it. Maybe I had. Maybe I was halfway gone already.

Because who would notice if I disappeared? Who would care?

No one. Not really.

And in that moment, the numbness wrapped tighter than pain ever could, cold, quiet, safe, like a coffin.

# Chapter 19
## Nelly

Pills scattered like confetti at the world's worst party. The whiskey bottle tipped on its side like a corpse bleeding amber. The razor blade, blood-soaked, gleaming in weak light, grinned at me like it already knew the ending.

*Which one, Nelly?*

The pills: quiet, almost polite. The whiskey: numb myself into oblivion. The razor: messy, brutal, poetic, maybe.

Which would be quickest? Which would hurt the least? Or maybe pain was the point. One last sting before the lights went out.

The questions circled me like vultures, pecking at what was left.

Then my phone shrieked, Sharp, insistent. My chest jolted like I'd been shocked back into the land of the unwilling. Lucifer, couldn't I even plan my own demise in peace?

The screen lit up.

*Lucas.*

Of all people.

I groaned, dragging the phone to my ear. "What the hell are you doing calling me? And how the fuck do you even have my number?"

His voice wasn't cocky for once. It was hesitant, clumsy. "I… uh… got it from Madz. I just… I need to ask you something."

I slumped back, exhaling hard. My head throbbed. "What?"

Silence. Awkward, fumbling silence. I could hear him breathing, probably scratching his jaw like he always did when his brain short-circuited.

Finally, he stammered, "I was just wondering… I ahhh… umm…"

My patience snapped like brittle glass. "Spit it out, Lucas."

My tone was sharper than the blade still gleaming on the table, and I didn't regret it.

And then he said it.

"I was just wondering if you can talk to me about being depressed."

My jaw locked, disbelief scorching hotter than anger. "What the fuck, Lucas? Who the fuck says I'm depressed? And who calls someone up to ask that?"

He stumbled over his words like they were broken glass. "Well… I… you're all goth and wear black all the time. You hate the world… you hate us… arghhh, I'm screwing this up. I just… something happened today… and I…"

I sliced through his babble, my voice dripping venom. "Oh, I get it. You wanted to phone the depressed goth girl. She'll know what to do. Just because I wear black and don't worship sunshine doesn't mean I'm your personal suicide hotline, Lucas."

Silence.

Then his voice came back smaller, cracked, like swallowing razor blades. "I just… needed advice. Someone to talk to. I made a mistake. And I…"

My stomach twisted. That tone, the one dripping guilt and regret, the kind I knew too well. My words dropped flat, dull as concrete. "For fuck's sake. This has something to do with Lexi, doesn't it?"

The phone burned hot against my ear. His stammered denial was as convincing as a wet tissue. "No… no, why would you think that?"

I shut my eyes, pinching the bridge of my nose until stars burst behind the lids. I didn't have the energy for this, his fumbling, his guilt, Lexi's shadow dragging behind it all.

"Well, you came to the wrong graveyard. I can't help you, Lucas."

I didn't wait for the reply. My thumb hit *end call*, the beep as final as a nail in a coffin. The phone clattered back onto the table, swallowed by clutter. Screen black. Patience gone.

My stomach knotted, anger and exhaustion tangling into one festering pit. Always Lucas. Always barging into my life, ripping open scars I'd stitched shut with rusted wire years ago.

I tipped my head back against the couch, eyes rolling to the ceiling like it might have answers. Bitter laughter bubbled up but lodged in my throat, jagged and humorless. "Why the hell is it always me they call when they want the answers?"

My hand dragged down my face, pulling me deeper into the dark. The silence thickened, suffocating, wrapping tight like a burial shroud. And for once, I wished everything, thoughts, heart, lungs, would just stop. I wished so hard for my heart to just stop. I was sure if I wished hard enough I could make it happen. Just stop!

But I couldn't. It keep annoyingly beating.

I sat up. Grabbed the razor blade. Leaned back in the chair.

I slipped my skirt up as I pressed the edge against the highest part of my thigh. Slowly. Carefully.

The first scrape sliced fire across my skin. The sharp, burning pain came crashing over me, drowning the noise, drowning everything.

And for a moment, just a moment, every other feeling melted away.

# Chapter 20
## Lucas

The sting of antiseptic clung to the air, sharp enough to burn the back of my throat. Machines hummed around me, their steady beeps marking out a heartbeat that wasn't mine.

Sammy lay motionless beneath the thin hospital blanket, her skin washed-out against the sterile white of the gown.

I shoved my hands deeper into my pockets, staring at the shallow rise and fall of her chest. My stomach churned, the same thought looping endlessly.

*I can't believe I did this to her.*

It pressed down harder with every second I stood there, guilt clawing at me from the inside out. I shifted on the polished concrete floor, dragging in a shaky breath that did nothing to steady me.

I shouldn't have treated her like that. I shouldn't have kicked her out, laughed it off like she didn't matter. I didn't know she'd do this, but not knowing doesn't excuse me.

My jaw locked. A low groan scraped out of my throat as I dragged a hand down my face. This wasn't just guilt. This was shame. The kind that seeps into your bones and won't leave.

What the hell am I supposed to say to her when she wakes up? *If* she wakes up. How do I apologize for being the kind of man who can make someone feel so disposable?

Maybe the best thing I can do for her is walk away before I hurt her again.

And Nelly, god, Nelly was right to be furious. She saw through me. She always has. She knew the game I was playing, the mask I wore. A mask built from every cheap line, every smirk, every one-night stand.

It hadn't always been like this. Back in high school, I thought I'd cracked the code: be caring. Be thoughtful, be the guy who listens. I thought that would matter. I thought *that* was what women wanted.

It wasn't. At least, not then.

So, I changed.

I became the guy they *did* want, the one who laughed, who never asked for more, who kept things easy. No strings. No responsibility. Just fun.

And for the first time, they started saying yes. They came back for more. Over and over, they wanted the Lucas who didn't care.

But standing here now, watching Sammy hooked up to machines, broken in ways I can't fix, the mask doesn't feel clever anymore. It feels rotten. It feels like the reason she's here.

And for the first time in years, I hate the man I've become.

I'd told myself for so long it was harmless, that I was just giving them what they wanted: fun, no strings, no mess. I thought I was the escape, the good time before real life dragged them back down.

But looking at Sammy like this, pale, fragile, bruised by the fallout of my carelessness, I couldn't keep lying to myself. This wasn't harmless. Not if this was the end result. Not if women walked away from me feeling disposable, broken, pushed to the edge.

My chest tightened as I studied her face, peaceful only because the drugs and machines forced her body to rest. Underneath, she was shattered. And I had been part of that.

I placed a letter on her side table beside a bouquet Lexi swore would "cheer up any woman." The flowers looked too bright against all this gray. Cheap comfort, but it was something.

This wasn't what I wanted, not really. Somewhere along the line, I'd traded the kid I used to be, the one who cared too much, for the man standing here now, hiding behind smirks and meaningless nights.

And for the first time, I saw the cost of it.

The cost wasn't just theirs.

It was mine too.

I couldn't keep doing this. Not if *this* was the cost.

# Chapter 21
## Lucas

Nelly's glare stayed fixed on the table, one arm wrapped tight around herself as if she'd disappear if she folded in small enough. The tapping of her nails against the wood sounded louder than anything else in the room.

Maddie fidgeted with her spoon, eyes darting between us, silently begging someone to fix it.

For once, I didn't want to be the guy who smirked and shrugged and let it roll off. My chest burned too much for that.

I leaned forward, my voice lower, softer. "Nellyfish… I wasn't trying to use you."

The nickname slipped out before I could stop it, Joshie's name for her. Her head snapped up, gray eyes flashing, but I kept going.

"I just… I don't know how to do this stuff. I don't know what to say when people are hurting. And I'm sorry for being an ass about it."

The table went quiet.

Nelly blinked at me like she was trying to figure out if I was messing with her. "Since when do you care?" Her tone was flat, bitter; the edges of it trembled just slightly.

"Since always," I said, surprising myself. The words came out rough, like I'd dragged them over glass. "I just hide it. I've gotten real good at that."

Lexi rolled her eyes. Maddie's gaze softened; her lips parted as if she wanted to step in, but she didn't. She let me keep talking.

I dragged a hand through my hair and exhaled hard. "Look, I screw up. Constantly. I chase the wrong things, I say the wrong shit, I make a mess out of pretty much everything. But I don't want you thinking I don't care about you. Because I do. You're part of this group, Nellyfish. You're one of us. And I don't want to lose that."

Her eyes narrowed, searching for the punchline, the smirk, the inevitable crack in the act. But I didn't give her one. I just sat there, palms flat on the table, my chest open like a wound I couldn't hide.

For the first time in a long time, I wasn't Lucas the player. I was just… Lucas.

Things settled for a moment, too long. A faint clink from someone stirring, the soft scrape of a chair. The room seemed to hold its breath with me, waiting to see if she'd stay on guard or let something else show.

She only smirked, leaning back with arms crossed, gray eyes flashing with challenge. "That's rich, coming from you."

# Chapter 22

## Lexi

The table had gone still, the kind of stillness that isn't peace but pressure, heavy and sharp like glass about to splinter.

My arms stayed folded tight across my chest, my belly shifting beneath them, the baby kicking like it could sense the storm in me.

Nelly sat rigid beside me, her eyeliner only making the scowl carved across her face more striking, more impenetrable.

Across from us, Lucas shifted in his seat. For once, he didn't wear that smug grin, didn't toss out some slick line to make it all go away. He exhaled, rubbed the back of his neck, then looked at Nelly with a softness I hadn't seen in years. His voice dropped low, almost shameful. "I'm sorry, Nellyfish. I'm glad you're not depressed."

The name hit like a ghost in the room, Joshie's nickname for her, and every time Lucas used it, Nelly blinked like she'd been sucker-punched.

Maddie leaned forward, worry creasing her brow. "Are you depressed, Nelly?" she asked, tentative, like she was scared of what Nelly might actually say.

Nelly's arms folded tighter, her chin lifting like a wall going up. "Stop with the nickname and we're so done talking about this. This is ridiculous. I'm gonna go."

She shoved her chair back, the screech of its legs slicing through the cafeteria.

Maddie's voice rose in panic, desperate. "Noooo, don't go. We'll stop." Her glare snapped to Lucas, sharp enough to draw blood. "Won't we, Lucas?"

Lucas scratched at his neck again, guilty as hell. "Of course, Nelly. No more."

I leaned back in my chair, letting out a sharp breath, my bitterness boiling over. I was happy to offer a topic change. "Well, thanks to you, Lucas. My boss is pissed off, and now I'm pulling double shifts and doing all the heavy lifting."

His face fell, boyish guilt flickering in his bright blue eyes. "She's that upset?"

"Upset?" My arms tightened across my chest, the heat rising against my throat. "She's ready to make my life hell."

He fumbled again, awkward, trying to fix it. "I'll call her and apologize."

I laughed, sharp and humorless, the sound cutting the air between us. "Unless you're planning to date her, Lucas, leave her alone. I don't want to be stuck working a shift while pushing out this baby. I'd at least like the day off."

My hand dropped to my belly, instinctively protective, as I glared at him. Because no matter how many apologies he tried to mumble, Lucas's messes always seemed to bleed into my life. And I was so damn tired of cleaning them up.

His brow furrowed, real confusion flickering across his face, like he hadn't even considered the fallout he left me with. "She's making it that difficult for you? I had no idea. How can I…"

I cut him off before he could finish, my words sharp, cracking like a whip. "What you can do, Lucas, is keep that dick in your pants when it comes to anyone I know."

The words landed heavy, but he didn't flinch. Didn't argue. He just nodded, almost too quickly, like surrender. His voice was quiet, stripped bare.

"I promise I won't do that to you anymore… Le Le."

The nickname hit me square in the chest. For the first time in years, his words almost sounded sincere. Like he meant them.

My hands rubbed over my thighs, restless, as I shifted in my seat. "It's been ages since you've called me that," I murmured, softer than I intended. "Oh my god… since school. When you were…"

His brows lifted, leaning forward slightly, eyes fixed on me like he was pulling at a thread. "When I was?"

I let out a slow breath, the words catching somewhere between a smile and a grimace. "When you were that sweet boy back in high school."

A grin tugged at his lips, that grin I hated. That grin I missed. "I'm still sweet."

I rolled my eyes, forcing the tears back down where they belonged. Damn pregnancy. I cried this morning because I ate the last of my favorite cookies. So, this has absolutely nothing to do with Lucas. "Before you turned into a man whore."

He planted his hands on his hips, his tone firm but not unkind, like he wanted me to really hear him this time. "You just don't spend any time with me. You really don't know who I am these days."

The words stung because they sounded too much like the truth. I shook my head, sharper than I meant to. "Yeah, somehow I don't think any of the Lukey from back then is left. I lost *my* Lukey the moment he stepped out of high school."

His eyebrows shot up, and then he tilted his head. Something in his gaze softened. The bravado slipped, just for a moment.

His voice dropped, low, almost playful but lined with something raw underneath. "Maybe we should hang out, and you can find out."

From across the table, Nelly groaned loudly, arms folded tight, eyes rolling like she couldn't stand another second of us. "Will you guys just fuck already. I mean, how many years have you been doing this dance? It's gotten to the point even I want you to fuck."

Maddie gasped, her laugh nervous and bubbling into the thick air. "Nelly!"

But Nelly only shrugged, unapologetic. "What?"

Heat rushed up my neck, my cheeks burning. The air turned heavy, suffocating, like the walls were closing in. My palm pressed against my stomach, rubbing where the baby pushed uncomfortably against my ribs.

The silence that followed was sharp as knives.

# Chapter 23
## Joshie

I hovered near their table, not sitting, not standing, not really anything. Just existing. Watching.

God, they were a mess. My mess.

The air between them crackled like a live wire, Lexi's hormones warring with her pride, Lucas wearing guilt like a cologne, Maddie trying to glue everything back together, and Nelly… poor Nelly, hiding behind that razor tongue like it could stop anyone from seeing how close she was to falling apart.

I wanted to scream. To knock their heads together. To remind them why they were there, *why I made them promise.* But all I could do was watch.

Useless. Powerless.

Lexi looked exhausted, her hand rubbing her belly like she could calm both herself and the life inside her. Lucas leaned forward, trying to bridge a canyon that had been years in the making. Nelly was already halfway to the door, her boots clicking like gunshots on tile.

*No, no, no…*

I reached out on instinct, some echo of the way I used to break up their fights, hands out, words ready. But my hands weren't hands anymore. My frustration burned through whatever this half-life was, shaking the air around me.

The light above the table flickered. The salt shaker rattled. Maddie's coffee trembled in its cup.

"Oh, for fuck's sake," I muttered, or thought I did. The world wavered with me, humming, trembling, then suddenly, it hit.

A faint, buttery scent. Popcorn.

I froze, horrified. Seriously? Out of all the spectral signs manifestation I could've conjured, lightning, thunder, a dramatic gust of wind, I smelled like a cinema snack.

Lexi wrinkled her nose. "Does anyone else smell… popcorn?"

Maddie frowned. "What the hell…"

Lucas sniffed the air, confused. "Is someone microwaving something?"

Nelly groaned, dragging her chair back. "Oh, great. Even the universe thinks we're a joke."

And maybe we were. But they were *my* joke.

I could feel the edges of myself unraveling, the scent fading with the trembling air. The anger drained, replaced by something heavier, sorrow, longing, love. They were all still fighting, but they were there. Still showing up. Still trying.

That was the point of it all.

I took one last look, Lexi's hand over her belly, Lucas watching her like she was his whole world, Maddie's tired smile, and Nelly pretending not to care.

The popcorn scent lingered faintly as the café settled again.

"Yeah," I whispered to no one but the ghosts of memory, "you idiots still need me."

And then I was gone.

# Chapter 24
## Lexi

The smell hit me first.

It wasn't strong, just faint, buttery, a little sweet, but enough to stop me mid-sentence. I frowned, glancing around the café. "Wait… does anyone else smell popcorn?"

Maddie sniffed the air, nose wrinkling. "I thought it was just me."

Lucas tilted his head, scanning the room like he expected to see a popcorn machine materialize next to the coffee grinder. "What the hell? Nobody's eating popcorn in here."

Across from us, Nelly groaned, dropping her head into her hands. "Fantastic. We're all collectively losing our minds. First, forced group catch up therapy, now shared hallucinations. Love that for us."

But something about it, the smell, the timing,

It wasn't random.

It was Joshie.

I froze, my chest tightening like someone had gripped it from the inside. "Do you guys remember…?" I started, my voice trembling before I could stop it. "On movie nights?"

Lucas's gaze flicked to mine. He knew. He remembered. His lips parted, his expression softening into something genuine. "And when Joshie used to sneak popcorn into assemblies and pretend it was 'for the teachers.'"

Maddie laughed, that kind of laugh that cracked and wobbled at the edges. "He'd always burn it, too. The whole place smelled like scorched butter for hours."

Nelly lifted her head, eyes distant, voice softer than I'd heard it in weeks. "He used to bring popcorn to everything. Said it made boring things smell like movie nights."

A silence settled over us, not sharp this time, but warm, like a blanket pulled tight over old wounds. The kind of silence where you could almost *feel* him.

I could still see him in my mind: slouched in his chair, grinning, eyes too bright for someone who carried so much inside. He always wanted to make things lighter. Even when he was heavy.

Maddie's hand slid across the table and brushed mine. "Maybe…" She hesitated, her voice small, hopeful. "Maybe he's still trying to make things smell like movie nights."

Lucas swallowed hard, clearing his throat like he was trying to shake something loose. "If it is him," he said, voice rough, "he really needs to work on his haunting aesthetic."

Nelly smirked faintly, eyes glassy. "Popcorn ghost. Figures. He'd be too nice to actually scare anyone."

I smiled through the ache, letting the scent settle in my lungs. For a moment, the noise of the café fell away. It was just us, and him, a whisper of warmth, laughter, memory.

"Hey, Joshie," I murmured under my breath, so quiet I wasn't sure if anyone heard. "We miss you."

The smell lingered just a little longer, then faded, soft and slow, like someone finally at peace.

"Well, would you look at that," Nelly muttered finally, scraping her chair back. "Time's up. I'm going to meet other friends." Her lips curved into something that wasn't quite a smile, more like a cut.

Maddie forced a small smile, but it didn't reach her eyes. "Okay… sounds like fun."

I shifted in my chair, pressing firmer against my belly as the baby kicked again, harder this time. My voice came out softer than I meant, almost apologetic.

"I'll go too. You still good for helping this afternoon, Madz?"

Maddie turned toward me, her nod steady, determined. "Yes. You'll get help this afternoon."

Relief loosened something in my chest, though only for a moment. I pushed back from the chair, standing with effort, stretching to ease the pull in my lower back. A groan slipped out before I could stop it. "Oh man. This one is killing me today. See you later, Madz."

I started toward the door, each step heavy with the baby's weight, and heavier still with everything else pressing down on me. Out of the corner of my eye, I saw Lucas stand too, that forced smile plastered across his face. The one that almost hid the tension running deep in him.

# Chapter 25

## Maddie

"Well," Lucas said lightly, pushing his chair back, "looks like I'll go too."

But I cut him off before he could move, my voice sharper than I intended. "Before you go, Lucas, I need to ask you something."

I hesitated, just for a second, and that was when Ray walked in.

He carried himself the way he always did: confident without trying, filling the doorway like it belonged to him. The moment his eyes found mine, my whole body softened, like all the tension I'd been holding finally let go.

"You ready to go, buttercup?" he asked, sliding into the seat beside me with ease, his tone warm and certain. "It's almost time."

I couldn't help the smile that curved my lips. With him, it wasn't just affection, it was safety. It was home. He grounded me in a way no one else ever had. And sometimes I caught Lexi looking at us like it bruised something inside her, like she'd never had that kind of steady comfort to lean on.

I fiddled with the hem of my sleeve, avoiding Lucas's eyes. My voice came out smaller than I intended. "I haven't asked him yet."

Ray folded his arms across his chest, solid and sure, giving me the gentle push I needed. "Well, come on then," he teased, though his tone left little room to back out. "He's not an asshole. He'll say yes."

Lucas leaned back with that cocky grin that had grated on me since we were teenagers. "Oh my god. Finally. Thank you. Someone who thinks I'm not all bad." He smirked. "What do you want to ask?"

I chewed my lip, hating myself for even having to put Lexi in this position, but I'd made the promise and couldn't back out now.

"I promised to do something, but I forgot Ray and I have an appointment, one we can't change." My eyes flicked between them, my stomach twisting. "I was wondering if you could help me out."

Ray gave me a soft nudge, his voice gentle but firm. "You'd be helping us out, bro. Mads hates to let people down. She'll wear that sad face all day otherwise."

Lucas shrugged, acting like it was nothing, though I caught the flicker of something real in his eyes, curiosity, maybe even nerves. "I'm sure I can help. Contrary to what everyone believes, I'm not a complete asshole. What do I have to do?"

Relief slipped out in a breath I didn't realize I'd been holding. "Great. Lexi needs help building a cot. I offered Ray to help her, but we've got this appointment. She doesn't have the money to pay someone, and she tried to do it herself but can't."

The moment the words left my mouth, I regretted them. *Lexi will hate this.* She can't stand him. What had I done?' I'd just thrown her to the wolves.

Lucas tilted his head, rubbing at his chin like he was sizing up a challenge. The pause was long enough to prickle my skin.

"You know she hates me, right?" His smile faltered into something closer to a frown, defensive, uncertain.

I straightened, holding his gaze. "Hate's a strong word, Lucas. More like… she can't stand what you do. You represent everything that's landed her where she is today."

The air between us thickened. He flicked his eyes around the room, avoiding mine. "And where is that?"

I folded my arms, my voice flat, firm, cutting. "Single. Pregnant. Lonely. Scared."

I hated myself for saying it out loud, for making Lexi's pain real in front of him, but he needed to hear it.

Ray chuckled low under his breath, though there wasn't much humor in it, more a release of tension than amusement.

Lucas shifted in his chair, rubbing the back of his neck. For once, he didn't fire back. "I don't know, Madz," he said carefully, softer than I expected. "She seems pretty strong to me. Feisty. Independent. She's taking it all better than I expected."

*Strong. Feisty. Independent.* Words meant as praise, but I knew what they really were: armor Lexi had been forced to wear. Armor she carried alone.

Ray muttered, arms folding now too, his frustration matching mine. "I think I gave him too much credit."

"You have no idea," I said firmly, staring right at Lucas. "Go and help her. If she'll let you. Spend some time with her. You two were inseparable in high school. Don't you miss that? Don't you miss her?"

Lucas's eyes dropped to the table, his whole face faltered. His voice came out quieter, almost reluctant. "More than I care to share with you two."

He scratched at his jaw, nerves twitching through his cocky mask. And for just a second, I saw a glimpse of the boy he used to be, the one who actually cared, before he buried it under women and bravado.

After a pause, Lucas finally said, "I'll go help her. I'd love if she'd let me in. I'd love to be there for her."

And for once, it didn't sound like his usual smooth one-liners, the kind he'd whisper to a woman in a dark booth just to get what he wanted. This time, his voice carried weight. Something real.

I felt my expression soften in spite of myself. "Maybe you can prove us all wrong," I said, my tone lighter, though a sigh tugged at the edges. I pulled out my phone, thumbs flying across the screen. "Here, I'll text you her address."

But Lucas shook his head, guilt flickering in his eyes. "Ahh… I already have it. I may have looked her up. I've almost gone over to hers a few times. Almost confronted her. Just… never…" His voice trailed off as his hand rubbed at the back of his neck, eyes fixed on the floor like a teenager again.

A long, tired sigh slipped out of me before I could stop it. "Just like back in high school. You never had the kahunas to tell her how you really felt."

Ray laughed beside me, the sound warm and full, his hand clapping Lucas's back with enough force to jolt him. "Man, when it comes to the ladies, you see what you like and you just go after it."

Then he turned to me, his grin softening into something that always undid me. "I knew what I wanted, and I wasn't going to let her say no."

Heat crept into my cheeks as I tilted my face toward him, lips curving into a smile I couldn't hold back. "And why would I say no?"

Ray's eyes glinted, smug but sweet, and my heart did that little flutter it always did. I leaned into him with a grin, my voice playful as my gaze swept over his solid frame. "Look at you… you beefcake."

He winked at me, cocky as ever, and I bit my finger with mock hunger, my laugh bubbling out, light and bright, the way I wanted him to see me. Carefree. Happy. Like I didn't have a care in the world.

But from the corner of my eye, I caught Lucas shifting in his seat, discomfort written all over his face. His jaw tightened, his shoulders stiff.

"Umm… yeah," he muttered, brushing off his jeans as he stood, like he couldn't get out fast enough. "That's my cue to leave."

He slipped away before either of us could stop him, the sound of Ray's chuckle and my own laughter chasing after him. And yet, even as I leaned into Ray's warmth, I felt the echo of Lucas's retreat, heavy in the space he left behind.

I sighed once Lucas slipped out the door, the weight of it easing from my chest. "I feel better now that's sorted," I murmured, mostly to myself.

Ray tilted his head, those dark eyes of his studying me like he could see straight through me. "So that's really been going on for years? Since high school?"

I nodded, pushing my chair back to stand. "He has it bad for her. It's kinda sad, honestly. He needs to do something about it, or just move on."

Ray let out a low whistle, folding his arms across that broad chest of his. "No wonder he's so messed up with women, the way you tell it. Holding a flame that long? That'll burn a man hollow. Have they ever…?"

"Nope." I shook my head, lips curving into the smallest smile. "Although he's awkwardly tried. He's not as smooth as you, baby."

Ray's smirk slid slow and easy across his face. "Well, buttercup, you were lucky enough to snag the best." He dipped down, pressing a kiss to the top of my head. "Now come on, or we'll be late."

I rolled my eyes, grabbing my bag. "Yeah, don't want scary Nurse Lucifer adding that to her naughty Maddison list. Doesn't show up on time. Doesn't lose weight…"

His jaw tightened instantly. He turned me gently, tipping my chin up until my eyes locked on his. "I'll have none of that," he said, smooth but fierce. "She brings up your weight again, I'll handle her myself. You've lost more than enough, baby. I'm proud of you. Anymore, and I'd be spoon-feeding you."

Heat rushed to my cheeks as I leaned into him, my lips brushing against his. "Come on then. Let's go see if we can make a baby."

Ray's grin turned molten, that spark in his eyes lighting me up from the inside. "I like the sound of that."

His big hand slid into mine, grounding me, steadying me, like it always did. Together, we walked out, our laughter twining in the air behind us.

And for a moment, just a fraction of a moment, I let myself believe I really was as lucky as he always swore I was.

# Chapter 26

## Lexi

A few hours later, the sharp rap of knuckles on my front door jolted me out of my thoughts.

I was halfway down the hall, one hand pressed against the small of my aching back, muttering under my breath, "Coming, Madz."

I pictured Maddie's easy smile waiting on the other side of the door, her warm laugh spilling into the room. But when I swung it open, the air caught in my throat.

"Oh my god." My voice dropped flat, heavy with shock and instant annoyance. "It's you. What are you doing here?"

Lucas stood there like he owned the space, casual, irritatingly handsome, that damn smirk tugging at his lips just enough to make me want to slam the door shut in his face.

"Nice to see you again too, Le Le" he drawled, far too pleased with himself.

And just like that, the walls I'd worked so hard to build trembled. My arms folded protectively across my swollen belly, my patience unraveling fast.

"How do you even know where I live?" I demanded, rolling my eyes before I could stop myself. "Argh, you know what, that's not even the point. You need to go, I'm expecting someone."

I turned on my feet, every step of my waddle heavier than the last, muttering, "Don't let the door hit you as you leave."

Behind me came the sound of his sigh, calm and steady, the kind of tone that made my skin crawl because it felt too composed. Like I'd hate whatever was about to come next.

"I'm the one you're expecting."

I froze mid-step, spinning back toward him. "What?"

He shifted, rubbing at the back of his neck, and for once, his cocky mask cracked. He looked… uneasy.

"Madz double-booked herself," he admitted, voice softer now. "She asked me if I could help you out." He hesitated, like he knew how badly it stung. "She felt really bad about it. Her and Ray had an appointment they couldn't cancel."

The words landed heavy. Maddie had sent him… of all people, *him*. And all I could think was: *God help me.*

"Please don't be annoyed with her," Lucas almost pleaded.

I clenched my jaw, frustration bubbling so high it felt like it might choke me. "I'm not annoyed at *her*," I snapped, glare sharp enough to cut. "I'm annoyed you're here."

Of course, Lucas only smirked, like my fury was just another game to him. "Look, I came here to help build a cot. I believe you've been having some troubles."

A groan tore out of me as I dragged a hand down my face. "God, I'm going to kill Madz. Of all people…" I laughed bitterly, shaking my head. "She asked *you*."

He chuckled, clearly entertained. "Actually, I'm very good with my hands."

I narrowed my eyes, heat rushing into my cheeks before I could stop it. "Oh, is that supposed to have some double meaning? Let me make this perfectly clear, if I let you help, it doesn't mean I'll repay you with sex."

Lucas lifted his hands in mock surrender, though the glint in his eyes betrayed him. "Do you think that's all I think about?"

I crossed my arms tighter, letting the silence speak for me.

He broke first, his laugh low, quiet. "Okay, that's fair. I do think about it… a lot. But come on, I'm a young, good-looking man in my prime. It comes with the territory."

Then, just for a moment, his grin softened, less polished, less performed. Almost real.

"But no. All I meant was I'm handy, and I can build this cot for you. If you let me. Le Le"

A sharp ache curled low in my belly, and I sucked in a breath, bracing one hand against the wall and the other over the swell of my stomach.

His voice dropped, steady, unexpectedly gentle. "You look like you could use a rest. Looks like the little one's giving you a rough time today."

I exhaled shakily, rubbing slow circles across my bump. The movement soothed, even if it didn't ease the pain.

"He... she... It's not letting up today," I admitted, voice quieter now, edges worn down by exhaustion. "I think it was moving all those heavy pots in the shop. It didn't like it."

For once, Lucas's smile wasn't cocky. It softened, almost warm. "Well, let me take this off your list. I'm more than happy to help."

I studied him carefully, suspicion still gnawing. He stood there like he always did, confident, sure of himself, as if forgiveness was just a given.

"And you aren't expecting anything in return?" I asked, narrowing my eyes further.

"Maybe some conversation and company while I build it," he said, grinning but not pushing. "That's it."

I let out a long sigh, torn between pride and sheer fatigue. My hand stroked across the swell of my stomach as if the baby could somehow give me strength. Finally, after a pause that stretched way too long, I gave in.

"Fine."

The word left my lips, and almost instantly, something shifted in the air.

A faint, buttery scent drifted through the hallway, warm, soft, familiar. Popcorn.

I froze. The smell wrapped around me, tugging at something deep in my chest, something that felt like memory and comfort all at once. The tension in my shoulders eased, and a strange calm washed through me.

*Joshie.*

It was him. I didn't have to see him to know it. That gentle whisper of popcorn told me everything, that I'd made the right choice, that he was here, quietly cheering me on like he always used to.

Lucas's fist shot into the air like a kid who'd just won a game. "Yes…"

Despite myself, I laughed, shaking my head as I rubbed at my aching lower back. "You do realize it's just building a cot, right?"

"I know," he shot back with that damn lopsided grin, the one that exposed the dimple I hated noticing. "But I've wanted to spend some more time with you."

He started down the hallway with that cocky swagger that made my chest tighten, and I hated myself for noticing.

"Where is this cot at?" he called over his shoulder.

"Don't think this suddenly makes us friends," I warned, folding my arms tight across my belly.

"Oh, we're the best of friends now," he teased, voice light, playful. "Once a man builds you a cot, you're besties for life."

I tried to hold it back, but another laugh slipped out anyway, making my belly jiggle, breaking through the wall I'd worked so hard to keep up.

I shook my head, muttering softly, so he couldn't hear me. "Idiot."

"Is it the room to the left?" he asked, already nosing down the hall.

"No, No, No" I said in a panic. "Right. The room to the right," I corrected quickly, shuffling after him in my not-so-graceful pregnant waddle.

But I was too late.

He stepped into my bedroom, voice dipping low, smirk sliding back into place. "Ohhh, Le Le… you've got yourself a nice bedroom."

"Lucas!" I scolded, rushing forward as fast as I could manage. My heart gave a stupid jump at his words, though I'd never admit it. "You shouldn't make a pregnant woman run, Lucas. Or you won't just be building me a cot, you'll be rushing me to the hospital."

I hooked my fingers around his ear and dragged him into the nursery, releasing him the second we crossed the threshold. "Here. This is the room you're supposed to be working in."

Lucas rubbed his ear with a dramatic wince. "Jesus, Le Le, you could've just asked. No need to go full savage on one of my best features."

The cot sat half-assembled in the corner like an accusation, screws scattered like confetti across the carpet. The crumpled instructions lay abandoned on the floor where I'd thrown them in frustration.

My whole body ached, back, belly, head, and the sight of him standing in the middle of my chaos only made my chest feel tighter.

I felt like a failure, and the one person I did not need seeing my failures was standing right there, seeing all of them. Seeing *me.*

He paused, assessing the situation, then looked up as if he could read my thought across my face. "Just to build a cot," he said, shoving his hands into his pockets, trying to look casual. But his voice had softened. "And maybe spend some time with you."

"God, why do you do this to me?" My arms wrapped around my belly as the tears came hot and heavy, spilling down my cheeks until my whole body shook with sobs.

The unfinished cot stood like a cruel metaphor, half-built, broken, waiting for someone stronger than me to finish it.

"Is the baby still giving you trouble?" Lucas asked quickly, concern sharpening the edges of his voice.

"It's just not giving up today," I muttered through clenched teeth, breath hitching as another sharp twist rolled across my stomach. "It's in this awful position, pushing on everything. My ribs, my bladder, my back. All of it."

He shifted, one hand steadying himself on the cot frame, though his eyes never left me. "Why don't you sit down while I finish this? Put your feet up."

I grimaced, shaking my head. "No. It doesn't like it when I sit. I get the worst backaches when I do."

He gave a small, nervous laugh, but his gaze softened, lingering in a way that made it hard to breathe. "Seems like the little one's already giving you trouble. Getting you ready for when it comes?"

I rubbed slow circles over the swell of my belly, trying to disguise the bone-deep weariness gnawing at me. Every step, every movement, felt heavier these days, like my body didn't belong to me anymore.

I swallowed hard and turned away, because the way he looked at me, concerned, soft, *real*, was almost too much to take.

"Le Le…" His voice was gentle, careful, almost like he was afraid I might break. "Are you okay?"

The words hovered between us, raw and tentative, filled with everything left unsaid for years.

I glanced around the room. The cot lay in pieces between us, wood scattered across the floor, screws and instructions dumped in a heap. Lucas crouched in the middle of it, broad shoulders bent over the mess, while I leaned against the wall, one hand braced over the ache in my belly.

The baby shifted again, a heavy, uncomfortable roll that made me wince.

And before I could stop myself, before I could even understand what I was saying, the words slipped free, soft and broken.

"What if I'll never be ready?"

His head snapped up, confusion darkening his face. "What do you mean?"

My throat tightened, the truth clawing its way out. "I don't think I can do it," I whispered. "I don't think I'm mother material. I don't even know if I wanted children. It was… it was an accident."

The word came out like a confession, heavy and ugly, echoing in the room.

Lucas blinked, stunned. "Are you kidding me, Lex?" His tone softened, but beneath it was steel. "You're going to be a great Mom."

Tears burned my eyes, and I shook my head, clutching my stomach tighter, as if I could hold myself together that way. "Please, Lucas… you don't even know me anymore. I'm lucky if I can take care of myself, let alone another human life that has no one else to depend on."

I expected the smirk. The joke. The cocky twist of words. But none of it came.

Instead, he stopped what he was doing, tilted his head until his eyes locked with mine, and his voice came out steady, certain.

"You'll surprise yourself, I just know it. And guess what?"

Suspicion tugged at me. "What?"

"You've got Madz and Nellyfish to help you," he said simply. "And you've got me. I'll be here to help you with whatever you need."

A laugh burst out of me before I could stop it, too loud, too cracked, like it didn't know what it wanted to be. The baby shoved hard against my ribs, stealing my breath, and I clutched at my side with a sharp gasp.

Lucas rolled his eyes, leaning back on his heels like I'd just ruined his big speech. "Why did you laugh?"

I crossed my arms tight over my chest, meeting his stare with a raised brow. "Mister Playboy's going to help me with the baby? What's next, changing nappies and heating bottles at three a.m.?"

His face shifted, the easy charm dropping like a mask. He bristled, arms folding tight across his chest. "And what if I did?"

His voice cracked, sharp with anger, but there was something trembling underneath it.

"You think you know me, but you don't. You think that because I enjoy a woman's company, that's all I am, that I couldn't possibly be anything else."

His jaw worked, then softened. Almost pleading: "I have nieces and nephews. I help my sister all the time. I'm prepared to see the best in you… why can't you do the same for me?"

The words hit harder than I expected, like a punch I hadn't seen coming.

For once, the grin was gone. No swagger. No bravado. Just him. Raw and exposed.

And me, standing there with one hand on my belly, the other brushing hair from my face, caught between disbelief and the dangerous tug of hope and a tang of guilt.

The cot finally began to resemble something solid, its pale wooden frame sturdier than I could've managed on my own.

Lucas wiped his forehead, focused, serious, tightening the last bolt like it mattered. Like he cared.

Watching him there on the floor, I wondered if maybe… just maybe… I hadn't lost all of the boy I once knew.

The silence stretched thick and heavy until I finally broke it with a shaky breath.

"I'm sorry, Lucas. You're right." My voice cracked, low and raw. "I shouldn't judge you off one thing. There must be more to you than that."

He straightened, folding his arms across his chest as he looked at me. His voice was calmer now, but steel ran beneath it.

"There is. That's why I came here today. So, you'd have a chance to see it. But you've got to stop seeing me as just Lucas, the guy who sleeps around."

He hesitated, the swagger slipping. "Anyway… I sort of slowed down. Stopped." He cleared his throat, like even saying it out loud cost him something. "I'm not doing that anymore."

I tilted my head, studying him, unsure if I could believe it. "Why would you stop? I thought you loved it. I mean…" A bitter laugh slipped out. "You message me all the time bragging about how much fun you're having."

His gaze dropped to the floor, his hand rubbing at the back of his neck. "Call it growing up," he muttered. A quick cough followed, like he needed to break the weight of his honesty.

I pressed my palm against the swell of my stomach, the baby rolling uncomfortably beneath my hand. "Looks like we'll both be doing a bit of that then," I whispered, giving him a soft smile.

Something shifted in him. His mouth curved into a smile, not the cocky one he wore like armor, but softer, warmer. A smile that pulled at something deep inside me I didn't want to name.

"Maybe we can work at doing it together?" he said softly.

Heat rushed into my cheeks before I could stop it. I turned my head quickly, pretending to study the cot instead of him. But my lips betrayed me, tugging into a reluctant larger smile I couldn't hide.

He cleared his throat, rubbing his palms against his jeans like he didn't know what else to do with them.

"Well," he muttered, sweeping his hand toward the crib in a grand flourish, "all done. Ready for action."

I stared at it, solid, whole, waiting for a baby I still wasn't sure I could be enough for. My chest ached as I traced the edges of the wood with my eyes. And standing there with Lucas, the air felt… different. Lighter. Dangerous. Safe. All at once.

"Oh, Lucas, it's perfect. Thank you," I breathed, my chest swelling with something dangerously close to gratitude.

Impulse betrayed me. I leaned forward and brushed a quick kiss against his cheek. His skin was warm beneath my lips, the contact fleeting but enough to leave me unsettled.

He smirked, cocky and playful, but when I pulled back, I caught it, him drawing in a deeper breath, steadying himself like that tiny moment had shaken him too.

The silence that followed stretched taut. I scratched absently at my arm, my other hand resting protectively on the heavy swell of my belly.

Lucas studied me with a furrow in his brow, rubbing his chin the way he always did when he was actually paying attention. It unnerved me, like he could see through the paper-thin walls I'd built.

"What's up?" he asked at last, his tone softer than I expected but edged with persistence.

My throat tightened. I hesitated, fighting myself, then the words slipped out anyway.

"It's just… it's becoming so real." My voice cracked to a whisper. "It's happening so fast. In a month it won't be just me anymore. Me…" The word fractured in my chest. I let out a sharp breath, trying to gather myself. "Me doesn't exist anymore. It'll always be us. Unless…"

I froze. The weight of the thought pressed down like a stone. My fingers fumbled at my sleeve, desperate to fold the truth back inside me.

"Unless what?" Lucas pressed, his voice low but insistent.

"Nothing," I muttered, coughing awkwardly, shaking my head. I will not go into that with him. Not the option my parents wanted me to take. My eyes dropped to the floor. If I didn't say it out loud, it couldn't be real.

But he didn't let it go.

"Lex." His voice cut through the air, firm but not cruel. "Look at me."

I drew in a shaky breath and forced my eyes upward, though my gaze faltered, hovering somewhere near his collar instead of his face. My shoulders curled in like I could make myself smaller, invisible.

His expression softened in a way I hadn't seen in years. A faint smile tugged at his mouth, not the arrogant kind, but something gentler, steadier.

"Everything is going to be alright with the baby?" he said quietly, conviction threading through his words. "You and the baby will be healthy and happy."

That's not what I meant, I thought, a lump rising in my throat. Sweet that he believed I was only worried about the baby. Sweet that he thought I was that selfless.

He always thought the best of me, even when I couldn't see it in myself. That's what a good mother should be worried about, her child. Not herself. But me? My fear ran deeper.

"You and this baby," he murmured.

Before I could pull back, his hands lowered, pressing gently against the swell of my belly. His palms were warm, steady, grounding, like an anchor holding me still when everything inside felt like it was breaking apart.

He rubbed slow circles, his touch genuine, almost protective. My breath caught, and for a moment, just a moment, I let myself lean into it.

"You and this baby are going to be just fine," he whispered. "You'll be amazing. And you'll be just what each other need."

The words burrowed deep inside me, both a comfort and a crushing weight. Because if he was wrong, if I failed, it wouldn't just be me who paid the price.

Then it happened. His hand pressed firmer against my belly, and the baby kicked… hard. His eyes went wide, lighting up like a boy at Christmas.

"Oh my god… is that the baby?"

I nodded, too stunned by the warmth flooding through me to speak. Too stunned by the fact that I wasn't ripping his hand away. That I actually wanted him to feel it. That I wanted him to stay.

"I've never felt anything like that before," he breathed, his grin boyish, almost innocent. "It's amazing. Makes it feel so much more real. Like you actually have a little human being in there."

Another sharp shift pressed against my ribs, and I winced.

"Oh, I know there's one in there," I muttered. "Don't need cute kicks to remind me."

His smile faltered, his brow creasing. "I guess not. The baby's taking its toll?"

"Yes," I groaned, pressing my palm to the underside of my belly. "And today is bad. And since you touched my belly…"

The words broke as a stabbing pain ripped through me, sudden and brutal. My breath hitched, sharp and panicked.

"ARGHHHHH!" The cry tore out of me, raw and ragged, my voice cracking under it. My knees buckled slightly, my hand clutching the edge of the cot for balance as my whole body trembled.

"Lucas!" My voice was high, desperate. "Something's wrong!"

His face drained of color, all that cocky bravado gone in an instant. His eyes went wide with terror, his hands hovering like he didn't know where to touch me, how to steady me.

"Lex…" His voice shook, but there was steel in it too. "Tell me what to do."

# Chapter 27

## Lucas

"Oh fuck… oh shit." The words slipped out of me, barely more than a whisper. I froze, mind blank, hands twitching at my sides like they didn't belong to me. Panic slammed into me hard, squeezing my chest until I couldn't breathe, scrambling every thought. "What do I do? What the hell do I do?"

And then I saw it.

The spreading stain on her jeans. Dark. Wet. Wrong. At first, I thought, maybe her waters broke, but then the color hit me. Deep. Dark. Red. My stomach dropped so hard it nearly knocked me off my feet.

"LUCAS!" she screamed, her voice jagged with terror. "THE BABY! THERE'S SOMETHING WRONG WITH THE BABY!"

Her cry ripped me out of my frozen state. My phone was in my hand before I realized it, fingers fumbling across the screen, clumsy and slick with sweat. My chest heaved as I stabbed at the numbers, thumb trembling so hard I nearly missed.

"Come on, come on," I muttered, breathless. My voice cracked as soon as the operator answered. "She's, she's pregnant, she's bleeding, it's bad, it's serious. Please, we need help. Right away."

My words tumbled out in fragments, rushed, desperate, but I didn't care how I sounded. I didn't know what I was doing. All I knew was I couldn't lose her. Not her. Not the baby.

Lex staggered, one hand pressed tight to her stomach like she could hold herself together by sheer will. Her face was pale and broken. My chest split wide at the sight of her, Lexi, strong, sharp-tongued Lexi, reduced to something fragile, terrified.

I shoved the phone into my pocket and caught her before she fell. My arm locked around her shoulders, her weight trembling against me. "I've got you," I whispered, though my voice shook just as much as she did. "I've got you."

Step by step, I guided her toward the door. Her breath came in ragged gasps, her body leaning hard into mine. All I could do was keep her upright. Hold her steady. Pray.

And then, she went limp.

Her eyes fluttered, her body sagged against me, and cold panic carved through my chest like a blade.

The last thing I saw before she collapsed was her face, pale and streaked with fear. The terror in her eyes… I'll never forget it. That wide desperate look, like she was already slipping away and couldn't hold on. It gutted me.

What if she'd been alone? What if I hadn't been here?

God, I was lucky. Lucky doesn't even cover it.

The harsh fluorescent lights smeared into blinding streaks as the gurney rattled down the corridor. The sting of disinfectant burned the back of my throat, sharp and sterile, like it wanted to scrub every ounce of feeling out of me. But I felt everything. My chest was twisted, my hands shook so bad I shoved them into my pockets just to hide it.

Lex gasped beside me, clutching her belly like pressure alone could hold it all together, could make the pain go away. I couldn't tear my eyes away. Couldn't stop hearing her scream, replaying in my skull like punishment.

"She just started screaming and moaning in pain," I blurted, stumbling over my words as I trailed the doctor. Too loud. Too frantic.

"She said something was wrong with the baby, she'd been uncomfortable all day. She told me she moved heavy stuff at work. Her boss, she said her boss made her..." My throat closed, guilt shredding me raw. "Oh my god, this is my fault too. Fuck!"

The doctor didn't flinch. His face was calm, clipped, like he'd seen this a thousand times before. "Was there any other fluid besides the blood?"

My stomach dropped. "Argh... I don't think so?" My voice cracked. His eyes snapped to me, sharp and demanding. "How much blood was there?"

I swallowed hard, panic scraping my throat raw. "I... fuck, I don't know."

For the first time in years, I didn't have a mask. No smirk, no cocky grin, just me, scared out of my mind, walking beside Lexi as we moved down a hallway that felt too long, praying to a God I didn't even believe in.

"I don't know..." The words tore out of me, thin and useless. I hated how pathetic they sounded, like admitting it made me even more of a failure.

Then Lexi screamed.

A sound so raw, so guttural, it ripped straight through me. I flinched, every muscle in my body twitching toward her like I could help, like I could do something. But I couldn't. My hands hovered uselessly, my chest tightening until I thought it might split.

"It all happened so quickly," I muttered, my voice wrecked. But the truth was, it was still happening too quickly, spiraling out of control faster than I could breathe.

The doctor's voice cut through the chaos like gunfire. "I believe your wife is experiencing a placental abruption."

"She's not my wife," I blurted before I could stop myself, sharp and stupid.

He didn't even look at me. "Wife, girlfriend, partner, that's not important right now. What matters is the baby isn't getting enough oxygen. We need to get the baby out."

The world tilted. My stomach plummeted like I was falling through the floor.

"Noooo!" Lexi's scream shattered me. Her voice was ragged, torn. "It's too early. Arghhhh! I still have a month to go!"

The doctor checked her chart with brutal calm. "According to your records, you're thirty-six weeks. The baby's lungs should be developed by now. It should be safe enough to deliver." Then, to the nurse: "Get her to delivery, stat. Administer oxytocin. Let's get this baby out now."

The words hit me like a death sentence.

*Get the baby out now.*

I stumbled beside the gurney, dragging a hand through my hair, heart pounding so hard it drowned out everything else. My skin burned, clammy with sweat.

"Fuuuck..." The curse ripped from me, low and desperate, the only word I had left.

Lexi clutched the bed rails, knuckles white, body wracked with pain. And me? I stumble alongside, a useless shadow weighed down with panic and guilt.

But I stayed. Because that was all I could give her. The sound of my voice, shaky but there.

Maybe if I didn't leave her side, she wouldn't completely fall apart. Maybe if I stayed, neither of us would.

# Chapter 28
## Nelly

The phone felt like lead against my ear, every word she spoke stacking bricks on my chest. I pressed harder into the wall, the rough brick biting into my shoulder blades like it wanted to keep me pinned.

"University or not, Nelly," Ma Ma said, her voice flat, carved in stone. "You've wasted your time. You've wasted our money. A real job doesn't vanish. A real job doesn't leave you begging for rent."

My breath snagged. I bit the inside of my cheek until the sting gave me something else to cling to. Blood spread across my tongue, warm, metallic, almost comforting.

She always cut through me like I was tissue paper, like everything I'd built was trash waiting for the bin. And the worst part? Some rotten part of me believed her.

"I'm trying," I whispered before I could swallow it back. The streetlight outside flickered, weak and failing, like even it couldn't stand to look at me. "I'm trying, Ma Ma."

Her sigh dragged down the line, long and tired, weighted with disappointment. "You've been trying your whole life, Nelly. Maybe it's time you admit you're not cut out for the real world."

Something brittle snapped. My laugh scraped out hollow, broken, like glass under a boot. "You think I don't already know that? You think I don't hear it every day inside my skull? I don't need you to sing backup to the chorus, Ma Ma."

The silence that followed was worse than her voice. Empty. Condemning.

I pulled the phone away, staring at the screen like it had stabbed me in the back. My reflection glared back: hollow eyes ringed with smeared eyeliner, lips trembling, skin pale under the jaundiced glow of the cheap fluorescent bulb.

Lucifer, I hated her voice. But mine? I hated it more.

The phone slid loose in my grip, heavy by my ear. For a second, I imagined hurling it against the wall, grinding it into dust in the cracks. But I didn't. I just stood there, swallowed by the night, listening to the cracked walls breathe around me, trying to remember what it felt like *not* to drown.

The silence stretched so long I almost hoped the line had died. But then came the sound, her sharp exhale, clipped, dripping with disgust.

"You chose this, Nelly. You could've been normal. You could've made us proud. You could have been a doctor like your sister. Instead, you drag this family down with your... lifestyle."

Not new. Never new. Same blade, same wound, ripped open again and again until scar tissue was the only thing holding me together.

My nails dug crescents into my palms as I pressed the phone tighter to my ear, like proximity might force her to finally hear me.

"I didn't choose this," I hissed, voice trembling into a growl. "You think I *wanted* to feel like a fucking outsider in my own family? In my own skin?"

The words echoed through my hollow little room, but she didn't soften. She never softened.

"Enough," she snapped, sealing me off like a crypt lid slamming shut. "You've always been selfish, Nelly. Always chasing shame instead of pride. No wonder your life is falling apart."

There it was, the death blow. The sermon carved into my skull on repeat: *Your life is a failure, and it's your fault.*

My forehead pressed to the cracked, cold wall, the phone slick in my grip. "You know what, Ma Ma?" My voice splintered sharp. "You don't have to worry about me disappointing you anymore. I'm done. Done trying. Done proving. Done everything."

I ended the call before she could respond. The screen went black like it wanted to vanish with me.

For a moment everything blurred. The table in front of the couch cut through the haze, waiting like an altar, pills scattered, whiskey bleeding amber, the blade gleaming like it knew my name.

Her words echoed like gospel in my head. Disgust. Disappointment. Condemnation. And Lucifer help me, some part of me believed every word.

My knees buckled. I pressed into the wall to keep myself upright while the world spun on without me, uncaring. The vision bloomed sharp in my mind: me on the street in a couple weeks, bag stuffed with whatever scraps I could carry, shivering under a busted streetlamp while strangers passed without a glance.

No home. No family. No one.

Just another shadow in the dark.

My chest clenched so tight I folded at the waist, arms locked around my middle. A sound ripped out of me, jagged and ugly, like glass shattering in an empty room.

The phone hit the wall with a satisfying crack before sliding to the floor, useless, like me.

I followed it down, knees tucked to my chest, arms wrapped tight as if I could hold my shattering pieces together by force alone.

The voices came anyway, crawling out of the dark corners of my skull, echoes of Ma Ma, confirming every rotten thing she'd said. Every truth I already carried carved into me like scripture: *Pathetic. Broken, Unfixable. Disappointment.*

And no matter how hard I pressed my forehead to my knees, I couldn't outrun them. Couldn't outrun me.

# Chapter 29
## Maddie

The doctor's office smelled faintly of lemon… no, not lemon exactly, more like disinfectant and paper. That strange sterile mix that reminded you your life was reduced to test results, charts, and appointments.

I sat stiff in the chair, Ray's warm hand resting heavy on my thigh, protective but weighted, while my heart hammered too fast in my chest.

The specialist smiled as she scrolled through the results on her screen. "Well, everything is looking good," she said brightly. "And by the looks of your blood test results, you've just started your next cycle. So, we can commence the FET (Frozen Egg Transfer) cycle this month."

Relief washed through me so fast it almost made me dizzy. My palms clapped together before I even realized I was applauding, like a child being handed a prize.

Ray gave one of his slow, steady nods, calm as always. But I felt the tension radiating from him, buzzing just beneath the surface.

"So how many eggs will you be putting in this time?" he asked, his voice low, careful. Always careful with me.

"I will only ever put two in," the specialist replied, folding her hands neatly. "Don't need you having a litter."

A laugh bubbled out of me, too sharp, too quick, as if humor could chase away the nerves. Ray just sighed, rubbing his forehead like the whole thing was pressing down on him.

"No, I think one would be enough for starters," he muttered.

"Yes," the specialist agreed briskly., "So, we'll see how it goes. When we know you're close to your fertile phase, we'll thaw out your little ones and call you in for transfer."

*Little ones.* The phrase caught me off guard, a lump swelling in my throat. *Mine. Ours.* Words I wanted so badly to claim. Yet every time they were spoken, part of me flinched, afraid my body would betray me again.

"How long until we know if it works?" I asked, unable to hide the tremor in my voice.

"Ten days after transfer," she said gently. "That's when we'll test you. We'll know then if it's been successful."

Ray leaned forward, steady as ever. "So, she could be pregnant in about four weeks?"

Four weeks. Just a month. Close enough to touch, yet still far enough to feel impossible. Inside my chest, hope and fear twisted like enemies locked in a fight, leaving me breathless.

The specialist's brows lifted, amusement flickering in her eyes. "Well, I'm impressed. Most men just smile and nod, or look really confused."

Pride flares in me, chasing back the shadows. "Oh, Ray's not like most men."

She smiled knowingly. "Yes, I can see that. But yes, in four weeks, you'll find out if you've been successful or not."

My hands clapped together again before I could stop myself, that spark of hope pushing through the wall of fear I'd been carrying for months.

Ray chuckled softly, the sound low and warm, his hand squeezing mine. That sound, it always pulls me back from the edge.

But then the specialist's tone softened, gentler now. "I commend you both. It's not easy to stay this positive after so many tries."

The words cut deep, brushing over scars I rarely touched. My throat tightened, and I forced myself to speak.

We aren't always this positive," I admitted quietly, the truth burning in my chest. "But… we have to try. We have to keep believing it's going to work."

Her eyes softened, sympathy shining through. "It's a rough road. Not everyone can hack it. But I can assure you, the gift at the end, if you're successful, is worth every struggle."

I nodded quickly, clutching onto those words like they were rope keeping me from drowning. *Worth every struggle.* Please, let that be true.

"Just keep doing your blood tests and calling in each day," she reminded gently. "We'll call you when it's time to come in for transfer. It was good to see you again."

We watched her leave, the door clicking shut behind her, leaving the room too quiet, too full of the things we didn't say out loud.

I let out a deep breath, my gaze falling to the floor. The sterile tiles blurred as I blinked hard against the sting in my eyes.

# Chapter 30
## Lexi

The hospital room felt colder than it should have, even with sweat dripping down my temples and soaking the back of my gown.

The fluorescent lights above were too bright, too harsh, stripping away every shadow until the world looked too white, too clean, too empty of comfort.

Then it hit, another contraction. Brutal and relentless, slicing through me like fire from the inside out.

"Arghhh!" I cried, clutching the sheets so tightly my knuckles burned white. My chest heaved, every breath stolen before I could catch it.

Lucas hovered at my side, pale and wide-eyed, like he was the one drowning instead of me. His hand lingered close but unsure, his words tumbling out fast and desperate.

"Can I do anything for you, Le Le? Do you need anything?"

I shook my head violently, my eyes blurring with tears I didn't want him to see. My voice cracked, raw from screaming.

"I just… I just need the pain to stop. Arghhh! They're coming too fast, Lucas. It hurts… it hurts so much!"

Another wave slammed into me, tearing me apart, leaving me gasping, broken sounds ripping out of my throat that didn't even sound like me anymore.

The doctor entered, calm and commanding, as if he'd walked through this storm a thousand times before. Yes, I know he has. But I haven't. His words made my stomach drop.

"It's time," he said firmly, already gloving up. "The baby's heart rate is dropping dangerously low. We've increased the oxytocin to keep things moving. Contractions are only minutes apart. She's nine and a half centimeters dilated."

His eyes flicked to Lucas. "Prepare yourself, son, you're about to become a dad."

Lucas's head snapped up, panic spilling from him in broken words. "Oh no, you've got it wrong, I'm not who you think I am." he stammered, shaking his head.

But the doctor didn't stop, didn't even look at him. His focus was fixed on me.

"You need to push now, Lexi. Strong and hard, you're about to meet your little one."

The next contraction ripped me open, hotter and harder than the last. The sound tore out of me before I could stop it, raw, jagged, helpless.

"ARGHHHHHH!"

Lucas's hand slid into mine, and for the first time in years, I didn't pull away. His grip was warm, steady, grounding, and I clung to him like he was the only thing keeping me from completely breaking down.

Inside my head, the thoughts spiraled, messy and relentless.

*Do I want him here?*

*Do I trust him enough to let him stay?*

The doctor's words echoed like a drumbeat: *"You're about to become a dad."*

Lucas's voice echoed too. *"I'm not who you think I am."*

Now it was on me. The choice. To let him stay and stand with me in this terrifying, life-altering moment… or send him away and face it all alone.

Another contraction ripped through me like fire, tearing me apart. I screamed, clinging to Lucas's hand so tightly my nails dug into his skin. Maybe too hard, but I didn't care. I couldn't let go. I couldn't let *him* go.

I needed him. God help me, I needed him here. What did that say about me?

Fear swarmed my chest, sharp and suffocating.

*Was my baby going to be okay?*

*Was I going to be okay?*

*Could I even do this?*

The doubt roared louder than the pain.

"It doesn't matter," I gasped between breaths, my voice broken as the next wave slammed into me. Sweat soaked my hairline, dripping into my eyes. "Stay, Lukey. Don't go. I need you here."

His grip tightened around mine, strong, protective. His other hand came over the top, cocooning mine, as if he could shield me from everything with just that touch.

"I'm here for you, Le Le," he said, his voice steady but trembling underneath. "I'm not going anywhere."

For a fleeting second, the weight in my chest loosened. His words felt like a tether, pulling me back from the brink.

But then the doctor's urgent voice sliced through the haze. "Push, Lexi. You need to push harder and longer."

Tears burned my eyes, my whole body trembling with exhaustion.

"I can't," I sobbed, my voice breaking under the weight of it. "I'm exhausted."

"You *have* to," the doctor pressed, firm but not unkind. "The baby needs oxygen. You need to get this baby out now!"

Hours ago, I would've slammed the door in his face. Hours ago, the thought of Lucas standing this close, seeing me like this, holding my hand as my legs were spread wide open with everything on display, it would've made my skin crawl with anger.

But now?

I guess they're right, when the pain cuts this deep, when the worry eats you alive, self-preservation doesn't just slip, it shatters.

Now his voice was the only thing keeping me tethered.

Every contraction stole another piece of me, wrung me out until there was nothing left but sweat, tears, and the sound of him whispering in my ear.

"You can do this. Just one more push, beautiful. Just one more."

I clung to that voice like it was a lifeline. Everything else faded away. The room went dark, and all I could see… all I could hear… was Lucas.

The shame of being sprawled out, stripped of all dignity, of nurses and doctors barking instructions, their hands pulling and prodding, it should've consumed me. But his words drowned it out. They wrapped around me, steady and unyielding, cutting through the humiliation and the fear.

"Come on, Le Le. Just one more push. The baby needs you."

And God help me, I listened. His voice cut through the chaos like it was the only thing keeping me tethered. I didn't fight him, didn't question him. I just clung to every word and gave him everything I had left, every shred of strength, every last breath of energy, because somehow, with him beside me, I believed I could.

I bore down, screaming through the fire tearing me apart, gripping his hand until my nails bit into his skin, drawing blood. My vision swam, black-and-white spots dancing in the sterile glare of the lights.

Somewhere in that chaos, I realized something that terrified me almost as much as the contractions themselves.

I didn't want him to leave. I needed him.

For the first time in years, I didn't want to push him away. Because without Lucas right here, whispering that I could survive this… I wasn't sure I could.

# Chapter 31
## Lexi

All I could smell was sweat, my sweat, and I could feel the tremor in my own limbs as the tears threatened to spill. The doctor's words replayed in my head: *"You did a wonderful job."*

But all I could hear was the silence where a baby's cry should've been. The silence grew louder as the doctor walked off with the baby to check it over.

I didn't even want this. So why am I so worried about it now? The admission clawed its way out before I could lock it down. My eyes stayed fixed on the ceiling because if I looked at him, I'd shatter.

It's true. I didn't want this at first. I wasn't ready. I was angry. I hated being pregnant. I still don't know if I can do this. And now… now all I want is to hear it cry.

*It.* I didn't even know if it was a boy or a girl. What sort of Mother was I? My chest caved as the thoughts broke into sobs.

Now look at me. I'm lying here thinking about myself when it should only be about the baby. The tears spilled hot down my temples, soaking into the thin pillow. My thoughts turned sharper, edged with self-loathing.

That makes me a bad Mom, doesn't it? A real Mom would've been ready. A real Mom wouldn't be lying here wondering if she'd already ruined it before it even started. A real Mom would already know if she had a son or a daughter.

The weight of the confession crushed me, pressing me deeper into the bed until I felt like I could disappear into it. My hand drifted weakly to my belly, empty now, as though I could still protect something that was no longer inside me.

I finally dared a glance at Lucas. His face was tight with something I couldn't read, anger, sadness, maybe both, but his hand never left mine. With his free hand, he lifted it to my face and wiped away the tears.

"I don't even know," I whispered, my throat tight and dry. "Was it a boy or a girl?"

For a second, Lucas let out this strange laugh, nervous, disbelieving, almost like he couldn't process the question. "I didn't see. And he didn't say." His mouth curved into a small, apologetic smile. "Guess you'll have to wait a little longer to find out."

The way his eyes softened nearly undid me. It was the kind of look I hadn't seen from him since high school, the boy I'd once known still buried in there somewhere, peeking through the cracks of the man who'd tried so hard to hide behind smirks and bravado.

"Is there anyone you'd like me to call?" he asked gently.

I swallowed, my voice breaking again. "Can you call my parents? Take my phone. Tell them I'm here, that the baby is here." I hesitated, then added, "And Nelly… and Madz, too."

"Sure," he said softly. "I'll do that. I'll be back in a few minutes."

I watched him leave, his tall frame slipping through the door, and for the first time since the contractions had started, the silence swallowed me whole.

The beeping monitors pulsed like a second heartbeat in the room. The smell of birth hung heavy in the air. My body ached everywhere, raw, trembling, hollow, and all I could do was wait.

Wait to know if my baby was okay. Wait to know if I was. Wait to know if I had a daughter or a son.

When the door opened again, his presence filled the empty space like it always did, loud, unmissable, even when he said nothing.

His hair was messy from running his hands through it too many times, his shirt wrinkled from leaning against walls, pacing. But his face, God, his face, held something steady. Relief.

"Well," he said with a small smile, "I called everyone. They're all on their way in."

I shifted weakly against the bed, clutching the thin blanket in my hands. Every muscle screamed, every nerve hummed with the storm I'd just survived. "Argh… I wish they'd hurry back with the baby," I whispered, my voice cracked and fragile. Tears stung as my chest tightened. "I just want to know what I had… and that everything's okay."

Lucas planted his hands on his hips, tilting his head like he could just shrug off my fear. "I'm sure he won't be too much longer. What's a little more suspense in this exciting day?"

I shot him a glare through the fog of exhaustion, half furious, half amused. "I'm glad you think me painfully pushing out a baby the size of a watermelon is exciting."

That lopsided grin of his spread across his face, boyish and unguarded. "Come on, you have a baby now. That's exciting, Le Le. You are a Mommy."

The word hit me like lightning. *Mommy.*

Hearing Lucas say it melted something inside me I hadn't even known was frozen. My heart twisted so sharply I almost winced.

I hadn't even held the baby yet, hadn't looked into its face, hadn't heard it cry, and still, I already loved it. Fiercely. Terrifyingly.

How could that be? I didn't think I was capable of this. I didn't think I had it in me. Could I really be a Mom?

Lucas' eyes lit with a spark I hadn't seen in years. "Ohhh, I can't wait to have a hold." Then he faltered, rubbing the back of his neck, his voice dipping sheepish. "Ahh, that's if you'll let me?"

Despite everything, I found myself breathing the words without hesitation. "Of course I'll let you hold the baby, Lukey."

The shock of saying it out loud, of meaning it, sent a shiver down my spine.

Before he could answer, the door swung open. The doctor stepped in, cradling a bundle wrapped in a soft yellow blanket. My whole body tensed, then sagged with relief.

"Well," the doctor said with a smile that warmed the sterile air, "everything has checked out perfectly." His tone was steady, reassuring, the kind of voice that wrapped around you like a blanket.

"Ten fingers, ten toes. Lungs and heart are healthy. Reflexes are strong. And" …he chuckled as the baby squirmed and cried in his arms…"we've got quite the healthy cry. I think someone's already asking for a feed."

Tears stung my eyes, blurring the bundle in his arms. My chest rose on a shaky breath. "That's… that's great. Thank you, Doctor."

"And you," he added, glancing at me, "are recovering well too. Tired, of course, but strong."

I swallowed hard, forcing the question out. "Doctor… what is it? What did I have?"

His brows shot up, surprised I didn't already know. "Oh, you didn't find out? Most parents do these days."

He smiled, warmth radiating in every word as he stepped closer, lowering the tiny bundle toward me. "Congratulations, Mom and Dad," he said softly. "You had a..."

The world seemed to hold its breath.

"... a girl."

For a moment, time fractured. My brain tried to catch up with the words, but Lucas was already clapping his hands together like an excited kid, his joy lighting up the room with a warmth I didn't know I needed.

My lips trembled, the words spilling out on a shaky whisper. "I... I have a daughter." The phrase felt fragile, like it belonged to someone else, but so right it hurt.

"You sure do," the doctor said, his smile kind, his voice steady. "And a beautiful one at that. Here, Mommy, have a hold."

Panic surged through me so fast my chest constricted. My arms shook against the sheets. I shook my head quickly, my gaze darting to Lucas like he was my lifeline. "Oh no... no. Let Lucas hold her first."

His eyes widened, then softened. His whole face broke into a smile so bright it softened the exhaustion etched across him. "I would love to hold her, if you're sure, Lex," he breathed, almost in awe.

I nodded slowly. "I am sure."

The doctor passed the tiny bundle into his arms, and Lucas cradled her against his chest as if she was made of glass. He rocked her gently, every inch of his expression melting into something I'd never seen before, pure wonder, raw and unguarded.

"Congratulations, you two," the doctor murmured, slipping out quietly. The door clicked shut, leaving behind a stillness that felt both fragile and sacred.

I couldn't take my eyes off them, Lucas and the baby. *My baby. My daughter.* He gazed down at her like she was something holy, as if the whole world had narrowed down to the weight in his arms.

My throat burned as I forced the words out, hoarse and raw. "So… is she really okay?"

He lifted his head, meeting my eyes with a softness that threatened to undo me, then looked back at the tiny girl tucked against him. "She's better than okay, Le Le," he said, his voice cracking as his thumb stroked her cheek. "She's absolutely gorgeous."

A faint smile ghosted across Lucas' lips, tender and proud. "You did an amazing job at baking her, Le Le."

The soft warmth of his words barely had time to settle before a sharp knock rattled the door. My body jolted, weak and sore, the ache of labor still clinging to every inch of me.

Lucas shifted in his chair beside the bed, rocking my daughter carefully, protectively. Seeing him like that, gentle, watchful, steady, was a strange comfort against the dread curling in my chest.

He looked over at me, his voice quiet but certain. "Oh, Lex, your parents are here."

My chest tightened. I wasn't ready. God, I wasn't sure I'd ever be ready.

The door swung open and in they came. My mother's arms were folded tight across her chest, her mouth pressed into that familiar thin, disapproving line that had haunted me since I was a little girl.

My father followed, broad, heavy, the scowl carved into his features already aimed at me like a blade. And behind them, a woman I didn't know trailed in, clipboard in hand, her pen poised like judgment dressed in ink.

Lucas rose quickly, polite out of instinct. "Hello, Mister and Mrs…" He faltered as the tension thickened in the room.

"Lucas is here?" My mother's voice cracked sharp, brittle, and cold.

Dad's gaze cut to him, then to me, then back again, narrowing like he'd already made up his mind. His voice was low, biting. "So, is he the one? The father? The one that knocked you up and left you?"

Lucas shook his head fast, stammering. "Oh no…"

"No, Daddy," I said quickly, my voice fragile but firm. "He's not the father."

But my mother only scoffed, her words dripping with contempt. "So, you've already moved on to the next. You never did waste your time."

Heat burned behind my eyes, shame and fury knotting in my throat. Lucas stiffened where he held the baby, his arms drawing her closer as if he could shield her from words that weren't even hers to bear.

Before he could speak, I forced the words out, sharp and shaking. "No. Luckily, Lucas was there when I went into labor."

Dad sneered, unimpressed, his lip curling. "I thought you had better taste. I thought you got him out of your system back in high school."

Lucas' jaw tightened, his face darkening as he rocked the baby gently, silent but seething.

Still, my mother didn't stop. Her voice cut through the air, colder than the sterile walls around us. "Well, you should never have been in this situation in the first place. You should never have been so careless as to get yourself knocked up."

Her words landed like stones, each heavier than the last. My breath hitched, my arms wrapping tighter around myself as if I could shield the hollow ache inside me.

They hadn't even asked if I was okay. They hadn't asked to see their grandchild. They came only to tear me down, to remind me I wasn't enough.

Out of the corner of my eye, I saw Lucas's patience fray. His jaw flexed once before his voice cracked through the tension, sharp and sudden. "Who is the other lady?"

He nodded toward the woman standing half-hidden in the corner, clipboard clutched to her chest like she'd been waiting to strike.

The stranger cleared her throat lightly, but Dad beat her to it. His voice was low, deliberate. "Lexi knows who she is."

The words landed heavy. Lucas's brows pinched as he rocked my daughter gently. "You don't have a sister?" he asked, cautious. "Is she an auntie?"

And just like that, the bottom dropped out of my stomach. Ice flooded my veins, so sharp it hurt to breathe. I knew exactly who she was.

I couldn't look at her, or him. But Lucas kept staring, his face caught between confusion and concern, the baby tucked protectively in his arms.

My stomach twisted. Dread rose until it clogged my throat. *What's he going to think when he finds out? When he knows who she is, what she's here to do?*

"Le Le?" His voice broke through, soft but edged with hesitation, suspicion… maybe even fear.

I forced my eyes up, meeting his. The look on his face nearly broke me.

The shuffle of shoes on linoleum made my head snap to the side. Dad stepped closer, towering over me with that same stony glare that had haunted my entire childhood. Mom followed, arms crossed so tightly I thought she might crack a rib.

Then the woman with the clipboard stepped forward. Sharp suit. Hair pulled so tight it looked painful. A stranger, but not really. I knew the type: cold, businesslike, the kind who looked at lives like problems to be processed.

She cleared her throat, her tone flat and practiced. "As per our phone meeting, Lexi, I'm here to finalize the paperwork and advise you that the family is ready and waiting. It's all set to go, as discussed."

*Paperwork. Family.*

The words sliced through the air, sharp and merciless. I couldn't breathe.

Beside me, Lucas stiffened. His arms tightened around my daughter. "Paperwork? Family?" His voice grew sharper. "Go as discussed? Lex… what's going on?"

My lips trembled. My chest burned. But nothing came out.

Before I could speak, Mom's voice cut through like a blade. "We discussed this, Lexi. This is the right decision, the only decision. You're not made for this life."

My heart twisted, hot and sick. She wasn't talking about motherhood. She was talking about me. Always me, the failure, the disappointment, the one who never measured up.

Dad's voice boomed next, shattering the air. "You know your Mom is right. You can't even hold a job for more than a year. You can barely feed yourself, let alone another mouth."

Each word hit like a slap. And here they stood, with proof, this woman with her clipboard, to take my baby away.

My daughter.

My throat closed. My arms ached. I could only stare at Lucas, terrified he'd look at me the way they did: unfit, incapable, unworthy.

The woman's voice was calm, rehearsed. "Sign the paperwork, and I can take the baby to a family who will love and care for her. You won't ever have to worry again."

My breath caught. My mouth opened, but no sound came.

Beside me, Lucas went rigid. His eyes widened, fury flashing hot and bright. "You're going to put her up for adoption?" His voice cracked, raw disbelief.

"I…" My throat burned. "They… how…" I couldn't finish.

"She's your daughter," His voice softer but edged with iron.

The agent smiled faintly. "Oh, you had a girl. The family were hoping for a girl."

That was the moment Lucas changed. His jaw locked, knuckles white around the baby. His voice was low, lethal. "You're not taking her."

Dad stepped forward, his tone authoritative. "I'm sorry, son, but you have no say. You aren't the father."

Lucas's head snapped toward him, eyes blazing. "And you're not the father either. You're crappy grandparents who haven't even asked to see her. Not once."

Mom's arms crossed tighter. "You have no idea what you're talking about. This is none of your business."

And me? I just lay there, trembling, because for the first time, someone was standing up for me, for *her*.

Lucas stood taller than I'd ever seen him, clutching my baby like she was the most precious thing in the world.

His voice cracked with urgency. "Don't let them do this. You can't let them take your daughter."

The words pierced me, cruel in how much I wanted to believe him. But fear screamed louder.

"But they're right, Lucas," I whispered, tears choking me. "I'll be a terrible Mom. They know it."

Lucas's eyes softened, but his voice stayed fierce. "You will be amazing. I just know it. And you've got Madz and Nelly to help you. And you've got me." His voice wavered, raw. "I'll be here for you, Le Le. Whatever you need. "Please... don't do this. You'll regret it for the rest of your life."

Tears blurred everything. "You have too much faith in me, Lucas."

My body trembled, broken and weak. I didn't know what terrified me more, failing as a mother or believing him.

Mom's voice cut in again, cold and certain. "You know what the right decision is, Lexi. You know who you are."

Before I could speak, Lucas thundered, "Will you just shut up!"

The room fell silent. The sterile hum of machines grew deafening.

Mom's lips stiffened. Dad's face turned red with restrained fury.

But Lucas didn't back down. He turned to me, his eyes soft again. "You haven't even held her yet," he said gently. "Hold her, and you'll change your mind. She's gorgeous, and she's all you, Le Le."

His words wrapped around me like a lifeline, tugging against every chain my parents had locked on me since childhood.

He stepped closer, his voice dropping low. "Please," he whispered. "Just hold her."

Before I could answer, Dad's voice thundered again. "It will only make it harder when you give her up."

Something twisted violently inside me. My hands gripped the blanket, my entire body screaming to obey, to be still.

But another voice, small, shaky, mine, slipped out. "Okay…" My voice cracked. "Let me see her."

Mom's glare snapped to me, sharp and venomous. "Don't be stupid, girl. This will only make things harder."

I flinched but didn't look at her. For the first time, I wasn't sure my mother's voice was the one I needed to hear.

Lucas turned slightly, shielding the baby from their judgment. His jaw was clenched, but when his gaze met mine, the anger melted away. With infinite care, he eased the swaddle into my waiting arms.

And then… she was mine.

The weight of her landed in my chest as much as in my arms, solid, terrifying, perfect. She was impossibly small, her warmth seeping into me. Wisps of soft hair brushed the blanket, and when her eyelids fluttered open, something in me broke wide.

I'd spent months telling myself I wasn't enough. But holding her, I couldn't deny it. She was mine.

Lucas's voice was quiet, reverent. "See, Le Le. She's gorgeous. She's got your nose, your chin. And look at that hair." His laugh came soft, awed. "I love her already. And I'll be here for you both, every step of the way. Whatever, whenever you need me, just a phone call away."

Tears blurred my vision as I looked down at her face.

Mom's bitterness cut through the air. "So, you say. Why should she believe you now?"

Lucas didn't even look at her. "Because I'll prove it," he said evenly. "I'll be here for her, and for you, Lex. And I know Madz and Nellyfish will too."

Mom scoffed. "Everyone says that when it's easy. What about when it gets hard?"

Lucas leaned closer, his hand cupping my face. His eyes locked on mine. "Then that's when it matters most," he said firmly. "And I'll make sure I'm there. I promise, Lex. I'll be here."

My chest cracked open under the weight of it, his words, her warmth, and the ache of everything I'd been told I wasn't.

A tear slipped free before I could stop it, sliding hot down my cheek. I brushed my finger gently against the curve of her tiny cheek, my lips trembling as the truth fell out of me in a whisper.

"She's cute."

The understatement almost made me laugh, but my throat was too tight, my heart too full. For the first time in months, maybe years, I felt something stronger than fear.

Love.

Lucas' expression softened into a real smile, tender and unguarded. "She's more than cute, she's adorable," he murmured, leaning closer to study her face, his own only inches from mine. His hand hovered above the blanket, cautious, as if waiting for permission to touch what already felt too fragile for this world.

"And look…" His words trailed as he reached for my hand, his palm warm against mine. Gently, he guided my finger until it brushed against hers.

The baby's fist closed around my pinky, impossibly small, impossibly strong. My chest cracked impossibly wider. A rush of warmth surged through me so fierce it hurt, spreading through every vein like fire. She yawned, a soft, perfect sound, her eyelids fluttering as if even breathing was still something she was learning. Curious. Alive. Mine.

Tears blurred my vision as the question thundered through me, drowning out the hospital lights, the monitors, the world. Could I actually do this? Could I really be her Mom?

"Name her," Lucas whispered. His smile was small, full of wonder, and his eyes shone like he already believed I could.

But before I could even form words, the adoption agent's voice shattered the moment. "It's time." Her tone was brisk, clinical, like she wasn't talking about flesh and blood. She hugged her clipboard tight to her chest, her pen tapping against it like a countdown. "Sign the paperwork, and we'll take her."

The room spun. My arms tightened instinctively, curling the baby closer against me, shielding her from the sharpness of that voice. My whole body trembled, but I didn't let go. I couldn't.

Lucas went still. His jaw worked, his shoulders slumping with a grief I felt mirrored in my own chest. He turned his face away for a second, gathering himself, and when his eyes came back to mine, they were raw, pleading.

"No, Le Le," he said, his voice rough, breaking. "Don't. Please don't."

My throat closed up, air snagging in my lungs. I looked down at the tiny bundle in my arms, at the baby who had already claimed me with one small grip of her hand. The pen in the agent's fingers clicked impatiently, ready to sign her away like she was nothing more than paperwork.

But in my arms, she was everything.

When I looked down at her, my daughter, every doubt fell silent. Her tiny chest rose against mine, her fist still curled around my finger, and my heart screamed the answer before my mouth did.

"I can't do it," I whispered, my voice trembling but sure. Then louder, steadier, "I want to keep her."

The adoption agent faltered, her professional mask cracking just enough to show surprise. "Are you certain?" she asked, cautious now. "We have the perfect family waiting. They're ready to give her everything she could ever need."

"Yes," I said firmly, clutching the baby closer until I could feel her heartbeat against mine. "I'm sure."

And then it came, faint at first, curling through the sterile air of the hospital room. The soft, buttery scent of popcorn. Warm. Familiar. Home. So out of place.

My breath hitched. The smell wrapped around me like a blanket, and a wave of calm swept over my trembling body. It wasn't just coincidence, I *knew* that smell. Joshie.

It was him. His way of saying, *You've got this, Lexi. You're doing the right thing.*

The certainty rooted deep, stronger than the fear. I pressed my lips to my daughter's head, tears burning but no longer from doubt, they were full of love. Real, fierce, unstoppable love.

"You're making a mistake," Mom snapped, her arms folded like steel across her chest. Her glare burned into me, full of anger and disappointment, like every judgment she had ever piled onto my shoulders was being thrown all at once.

The weight of it almost broke me… almost.

But then Lucas' voice cut through, sharp and protective, a fire I'd never heard before. "No, she isn't," he snapped, eyes blazing. "And unless you're here to support her, then shut up and get out."

I froze, staring at him. My parents had never defended me. They'd never believed in me, never stood up for me, always willing to believe the worst in me.

But Lucas… Lucas had. He believed the best in me. He stood his ground without hesitation, his arms wrapped protectively around the air between me and them, like he'd fight the whole world if he had to.

Something raw and terrifying curled in my stomach, aching deep. No one had ever been there for me like this. No one had said *stay* when everyone else said *give up*.

And now, with my baby in my arms and Lucas standing like a shield by my side, I saw him differently. I felt drawn to him. Maybe more than I should.

Mom's voice cut through the room like a hot blade through butter. "Well, you've made your decision, Lexi. Now you're going to have to live with it. Come on, honey, let's go."

Her heels clicked against the linoleum as she spun on her heels, arms crossed so tightly it looked like she was holding herself together with anger. She didn't even glance at me, or at the baby in my arms. Not once.

Dad lingered at the foot of the bed, his face carved from stone, jaw tight, eyes burning into me with that same cold disappointment I'd grown up under.

"We told you what the right thing was to do," he said flatly. "Don't expect us to bail you out. You've made your decision." Then he followed after her, the door shutting behind them with a dull, final click.

For a moment, the silence they left behind was deafening.

Then Lucas snapped, his voice ricocheting off the sterile walls. "She won't need your help. She has us."

My chest squeezed, panic rising as if their absence had left me exposed. "Lucas... stop," I whispered, clutching my daughter closer, her tiny body soft and warm against my chest. My voice cracked under the weight of everything I couldn't say.

He looked at me, and in an instant his fury melted into regret. His shoulders dropped, his hand dragging over the back of his neck.

"I'm sorry," he muttered, softer now. "They just... got under my skin. I don't understand how parents can be like that. I don't remember them being like that."

"They've always been like that," I said quietly, my gaze fixed on the little face nestled against me. Her lips twitched in her sleep, her tiny breaths warm against my skin, and my throat tightened. "But I'll just... try to be different for her. I don't want her to grow up feeling the way I did. I don't want to be like them."

Lucas leaned in, his voice gentler than I'd ever heard it, certain, steady. "You won't. I know you won't."

I traced my fingertip along her cheek, unable to believe skin could be that soft, like velvet against me. She shifted slightly, her tiny lips parting in the faintest sigh, and my heart twisted so hard it almost hurt.

"She does have my nose," I whispered, a shaky smile breaking through my exhaustion.

"She does," Lucas said, his grin spreading wide, boyish, proud. "A cute little nose too."

The lump in my throat swelled, thick and unrelenting. My chest rose with a shudder, heavy with fear, with doubt, but underneath it all, a flicker of something I hadn't let myself feel in a long time.

Hope.

I bent my head, my voice breaking into a vow meant only for her. "I'll try my best to do this for you."

"You won't be doing it alone," Lucas said quietly, his voice steady in a way that caught me off guard. He didn't hesitate, didn't smirk, didn't joke, just truth. "I'll be here. To help you be a Mom. In whatever way you want me to be. I meant it Lex."

My eyes burned, but this time the tears weren't born from pain or shame. They came from that fragile, terrifying possibility that maybe I wasn't as alone as I'd always believed.

I held my daughter closer, her warmth sinking into me, and for the first time since all this began, I let the smallest breath of relief slip free.

# Chapter 32
## Maddie

The living room was so still I could hear the fridge humming in the kitchen, a low, steady sound that only made the silence heavier. Afternoon light bled in through the curtains, stretching across the floorboards in faded strips. It wasn't the kind of light that lifted a mood; it pressed down, dull and suffocating.

I sat curled on the couch, my phone clutched so tight in my hand it might as well have been glued there. My thumbs hovered uselessly over the screen, frozen, because what could I even say next? My chest ached with the weight of words I couldn't let out.

Ray's footsteps broke the quiet, steady, familiar, and then he was there, leaning closer, his voice soft with concern. "What's up, sweetheart?"

I looked up at him, and even though I tried to mask it, I knew he could see the tremor in my eyes. I swallowed hard, my voice catching on hesitation. "I just got off the phone with Lucas."

Ray frowned, leaning against the armchair like he was bracing himself. "Oh yeah? Did cot building not go well?"

I shook my head quickly, too quickly. "It's not that…" My lungs tightened as I forced the breath out, lips pressing together before the words tumbled free. "Apparently… she had the baby."

The look on his face almost made me falter, surprise flashing into a smile, warm and automatic. "Oh, that's great."

But then it hit him, the same thought that had hit me the moment Lucas told me. His smile slipped, worry clouding his features. "Wait, wasn't it early?"

My chest tightened as the words slipped out of me, quieter than I intended. "Yeah. There were complications, and they had to bring on the labor." Even saying it made my stomach twist.

Ray's reaction was immediate, like I'd dropped a stone straight onto him. His shoulders stiffened, his voice rough. "Is she okay? Is the baby okay?"

I forced a smile, thin, fragile, desperate to hold back the tide of worry in his eyes. "Oh yes," I said quickly, rushing the words out before I could falter. "They're both okay. And well."

And it was true. At least, Lucas had said it was true. But even as I said it, relief felt slippery in my hands, like trying to hold water. Because the weight in my chest told me there was more: more fear, more pain, more than I could put into words.

The room seemed to know it too, sinking heavier around me. I sat forward on the couch, elbows pressed to my knees, my phone still clutched in my hand like I couldn't let go of it. The light from the window hit the screen, glaring, but I didn't move it. I couldn't look at Ray.

He stepped closer, his voice softer now. "But you look upset, baby."

The breath I dragged in was sharp, heavy, almost painful. I let it out slowly, my shoulders sagging under the truth I hadn't spoken yet. "I just texted Nelly," I murmured, staring down at my lap. "We're going to go to the hospital and see them. Meet the baby."

Ray tried to brighten, bless him. "That's great..." he said gently. But I knew him too well. I could feel his eyes on me, see the crease between his brows. He could see right through me.

His tone shifted, steadier, concerned. "But you don't look happy?"

My fingers toyed with the hem of my shirt, tugging and twisting as guilt pooled in my stomach. My voice came out broken, hushed. "I know I should be happy for her. That this is supposed to be one of the happiest times in a woman's life, holding her baby for the first time, showing her off to her friends. I should be the good friend, telling her how gorgeous the baby is, how cute she looks, how amazing she is and…"

The rest of the sentence cracked apart in my throat. My breath caught, trembling, and I sucked in air like maybe that would hold me together. But it didn't. It only made the ache sharper.

I was torn in two places at once, half for Lexi, who had just stepped into motherhood with all its chaos and beauty, and half for myself. The words slipped out before I could stop them, low and trembling. "But with us going through treatment…"

Ray caught it immediately. His hand found mine, warm, steady. He didn't need me to finish the thought. He said softly. "I know, baby."

And that was all it took. My throat closed, my eyes burning hot as tears spilled faster than I could blink them back. "It's hard," I admitted, my voice breaking as the dam gave way. "All I can think about is, when will it be my turn? When?" The last word tore out of me like a sob.

My hands shook as I pressed them into my lap, fingers twisting until my knuckles went white. "What if it never happens? What if this is it for me? What if all I ever get is holding other people's babies… and pretending that's enough?"

The silence after my confession felt deafening, broken only by the faint hum of the fridge in the next room. My chest heaved as I tried to pull the words back, but they were out now, bare, exposed. "What if I never have my own?"

Ray moved in close, his presence wrapping around me like armor against the fear I couldn't fight alone. His big hands framed my face, forcing me to look at him. "Aww, baby," he murmured, his voice breaking in that soft way only he had with me. "We will get our baby. We're just waiting a little longer for our miracle to happen. And you know why?"

I blinked through tears, my voice a whisper. "No… why?"

"Because ours is going to be extra special," he said, his lips tugging into that crooked smile that always undid me. "It's taking a little longer because God knows we're meant to have the one every other mother is going to be jealous of."

A laugh bubbled out of me, fragile and cracked, but real. I clung to it, to him. "Stop," I said, swiping at my wet cheeks.

"There's that smile," he teased gently, brushing his thumb across my face. His gaze softened, melting me all over again. "I love that smile."

And for the first time that day, the ache in my chest eased just enough to let me breathe.

"It did make me feel better," I admitted, though the words wobbled on my tongue. I drew in a long, shaky breath and forced myself to straighten, to pull my shoulders back like I still had strength left in me. "I'll go pick up Nellyfish. Put on a brave face. Smile. Go cuddle, no doubt, what is an adorable baby, and say all the right things."

Ray leaned in and pressed a kiss to my cheek, his voice soft and certain. "That's my girl. And when you get back, I'll have a movie and ice cream waiting. We'll chill tonight, just the two of us."

For a moment, the heaviness inside me lightened. My lips curved into a faint smile. "Sounds good, handsome."

I grabbed my bag, pausing in the doorway long enough to take one last look, one last smile, before whispering, "Here goes nothing." And then I stepped out, closing the door behind me.

# Chapter 33
## Lexi

The room was quiet except for the steady hum of the monitors and the faint shuffle of shoes somewhere beyond the door.

My arms ached, heavy and trembling, but I couldn't bring myself to let go of her, my baby, my daughter. Wrapped snug in a yellow blanket, her chest lifted in tiny, shallow breaths. I rocked her gently, even though every muscle in my body screamed from the effort.

I felt split apart, hollowed out and raw, but I couldn't stop staring. She was mine. She was here. She was gorgeous.

Lucas lingered near the end of the bed, arms folded like he was trying to look casual, but his eyes gave him away, soft, unsteady, genuine. When his gaze landed on me, something inside me twisted.

"It suits you," he said quietly.

I blinked, frowning, my voice scratchy and weak from hours of crying and screaming during labor. "What does?"

His lips tugged into the smallest smile. "Being a Mom."

A tired laugh broke out of me before I could stop it, brittle and sharp around the edges. I shook my head, brushing my thumb across the soft curve of her cheek. "I sent the adoption lady away, Lucas. You can stop."

The words came out more defensive than I meant them to, like I needed to remind him, or maybe myself, that the choice was already made.

But the way his eyes stayed fixed on me, steady and unflinching, made me wonder if he saw more in me than I dared to believe was there. He didn't smirk, didn't wriggle out of it like old Lucas would have. His gaze stayed on me, steady, unguarded.

"I mean it."

I shifted, pulling my daughter tighter against my chest, brushing my lips over the soft fuzz of her head. Her warmth seeped into me, grounding me when my body felt like it could collapse into the bed and never rise again.

My eyelids were heavy, my chest aching, but I forced the words out anyway. "I've just been through labor, Lucas. I look like hell. I feel like I could sleep for a week. You don't have to waste your time being nice."

My throat thickened, the words tumbling out softer now. "I won't be giving her away. You don't have to worry."

"That's not why I was saying it," he murmured, his voice low, steady.

I squinted at him, narrowing my eyes as if I could peel back his layers and see what he was really thinking. "Well, if you're saying it in the hopes of getting lucky, let me make this very clear, you're not getting post-labor sex, Lucas!"

His eyes widened for a moment, then, of course, he laughed, dragging a hand across his jaw. "As if, Le Le. Can you imagine how big…"

My glare cut through him like a knife. My body stiffened, my face hot, the baby stirring faintly at my chest as if even she disapproved.

He threw both hands up in surrender, his laugh softer this time. "It was a joke."

I wanted to stay furious, to hold onto the anger because it was safer than anything else he'd made me feel in the last 24 hours. But the way he looked at me, genuine and almost boyish, shattered me just a little more.

"I was just being nice," he said, his grin crooked, his voice carrying that teasing warmth he always wielded like a weapon. "I know you don't think I'm capable of it. But you'd be surprised."

I rolled my eyes, but the corner of my mouth betrayed me, tugging upward. My whole body ached, my heart still raw, but his words smoothed over some of the jagged edges.

"Fine," I muttered, sinking deeper into the pillows, clutching my daughter close. "I'll forgive you this one time."

The door creaked open, breaking the fragile quiet, and a burst of footsteps shuffled in.

Maddie's voice came first, bright, bubbling, impossible to ignore. "Oh my god, the baby is finally here!" she squealed, her excitement spilling into the room before she even reached the bed.

Trailing behind her was Nelly, slow as ever, her storm-cloud presence filling the doorway. Her eyes immediately caught Lucas beaming down at the baby like he'd won the lottery, and predictably she rolled her eyes so hard I thought they might get stuck.

Lucas grinned wider, soaking in the moment like it was his. "Sure is," he said proudly, leaning closer to the bundle in my arms. "And sooo friggin' cute."

I wanted to scoff at his dramatics, but the warmth in his voice was hard to ignore.

Maddie was already leaning over me, her hands clasped tight to her chest, her eyes sparkling like she was about to burst. "Congratulations, Lexi," she breathed, her voice soft but brimming with joy.

Nelly stayed where she was, arms crossed like she'd been forced into this. "Yeah, congrats, Lexi," she muttered, her tone flat as day-old soda.

I managed a small, tired smile, my voice breaking with exhaustion but edged with pride I couldn't hide. "Thank you."

Maddie tilted her head, her excitement bubbling again. "What did you have?"

Before I could even open my mouth, Nelly's dry sarcasm cut across the room. "A human being."

Maddie groaned loudly, spinning toward her like an exasperated mother. "What did I say in the car, Nelly?"

Nelly smirked, her eyes rolling yet again before she finally sighed, relenting. "Fine."

The corner of her mouth betrayed her, twitching into the smallest smile.

"Better," Maddie declared, satisfied, before turning back to me with soft, expectant eyes. She lowered her voice like it was a secret meant only for us. "So… what did you have?"

I looked down at the tiny bundle in my arms, my heart twisting as I traced her delicate features. The words caught in my throat, fragile but full of wonder.

"A little baby girl," I whispered.

Maddie's eyes lit up instantly, wide and shimmering, her whole face glowing with joy as she leaned closer. "Oh my god, a girl! And what is her name?"

Lucas shifted at the edge of the bed, his grin stretching so wide it almost hurt to look at. "Yes," he chimed in, his voice bright with anticipation. "Tell us… what's her name?"

I rocked the baby gently against my chest, her tiny body pressed into me as if she belonged there all along. But the question twisted my stomach into knots.

The weight of her in my arms was nothing compared to the weight of this choice. My throat tightened, my breath catching. "It feels like such a huge responsibility," I admitted, my voice breaking with the truth.

Nelly crossed her arms, a smirk tugging at her lips. "Well, yeah. Pick the wrong name and you screw a kid up for life."

Lucas shot her a sharp look, his jaw tight. Maddie's glare followed, sharper still, daring Nelly to say another word.

Nelly sighed, throwing her hands up in surrender. "Fine. I'll shut up."

The air shifted again, softer, real, threaded with rawness and reality. Maddie's eager eyes locked on mine, Lucas leaning forward with that hopeful smile tugging at his lips.

My chest rose and fell as I dragged in a shaky breathe. "I've been thinking about it for a while," I whispered, lowering my gaze to the tiny fist curled against her blanket. "If I ever had a girl… I wanted to call her…Summer"

The name slipped from my lips, fragile and trembling, but it felt right. It felt hers.

Maddie gasped, clutching her chest as tears welled in her eyes. "Oh, Lexi… I just love it. It's perfect."

Nelly gave the smallest shrug, her usual sarcasm muted, replaced with a softness I hadn't expected. "That's… actually pretty cool."

"Thanks, guys," I murmured, my lips pulling into the faintest smile before my gaze dropped back down to my daughter. My chest swelled so much it almost hurt. "Madz, you want a hold?"

Maddie froze like I'd asked her to take hold of a live grenade. She shook her head quickly, panic flickering in her eyes. "Oh no, I couldn't. You just had her… I wouldn't want to take her from you already."

"It's fine," I said, reassuring, though my body still ached from every muscle being torn in two. "Lucas has already had a hold."

I shifted forward slowly, carefully, ignoring the tug of pain as I passed the baby into Maddie's waiting arms. She fumbled at first, her hands trembling, but then the bundle settled against her chest, and I saw her body soften around the tiny weight.

"Maddie…" I said gently, warmth blooming in me as I watched her. "I know how much you love babies. How clucky you get."

Her lips parted, her eyes never leaving the little face swaddled in yellow. "I… ahhh." Her voice wavered, thin, like she was holding back more than words.

I leaned back against the pillows, a smile tugging at me despite the ache in my chest. "See? You're a natural."

But I could see it in her, the way her shoulders lifted with shallow breaths, the shimmer in her eyes. She was fighting something. It flickered for a moment before she plastered the smile back on.

Lucas leaned in then, his grin soft and glowing, his gaze fixed on my baby with that boyish awe. He tipped his head toward Maddie's arms. "Isn't she just the cutest?" he said softly. "She's got her mom's nose…"

Before the moment could settle, Nelly's voice cut sharp across the room. She leaned against the wall, arms crossed, her smirk dark. "You gonna obsess over her for years too?"

My head snapped up, my stomach twisting. Confusion and dread tangled in my chest. "What?"

My voice cracked, uncertain, my eyes narrowing on her. "What do you mean by that, Nelly?"

Maddie's head snapped toward Nelly, her eyes wide with warning. "Nelly!!"

But Nelly only shrugged, unbothered, her tone flat. "I'm saying all the wrong things," she muttered, already pushing off the wall. "I'm going to get coffee, have a smoke, and wait for you outside."

Her gaze flicked to Lucas, then to the baby in Maddie's arms, softening for only a heartbeat. "Congrats again, man. She's pretty cute for a mini human."

And just like that, she was gone, her boots tapping a steady rhythm against the linoleum until the door swung shut behind her.

Heat flushed my cheeks as I turned to Lucas, irritation prickling under my skin. "Lucas?" My voice cracked with both exhaustion and frustration.

He looked up at me, startled, coughing into his fist like he'd been caught. "What???" he called after Nelly, his tone sharp but carrying that familiar playful lilt. "You need change, Nelly. I can help you with that!"

Before I could get another word out, he jogged after her, leaving me with Maddie.

I rolled my eyes so hard it almost hurt. "What the hell, Madz?" I muttered, folding my arms across my chest, my heart still racing with irritation.

Maddie just smiled faintly, her eyes locked on the baby curled against her. She rocked gently, as though the tension had no weight at all. "You two are hopeless, you know that?"

I stiffened. "What do you mean?"

Her gaze never left the baby at first, her voice calm but threaded with something sharper. "You're a smart girl, Lexi. You know exactly what Nelly was getting at." Finally, she lifted her eyes, steady and unyielding. "It's about time you stopped torturing the boy."

My stomach lurched, the words cutting deeper than I wanted to admit. I swallowed hard, shaking my head quickly, clinging to the denial. "I don't know what you're on about," I muttered. But the warmth crawling up my neck betrayed me, and Maddie's small, knowing smile told me she'd seen it all.

She shifted her attention back to Summer, her voice quieter now, deliberate. "I know it must feel nice, having a guy hang off your every word. To have someone who's been pining after you for years." She adjusted the baby gently, brushing her thumb across her tiny hand like she was grounding herself.

"But it's hurting him, Lex. He needs to know either way. If there's no chance, he deserves to move on."

I crossed my arms, hugging myself tight, trying to hide how sharp her words cut. "He's a player, Madz. He's not short on women. There's no way he's been pining after me."

Her head snapped up, gaze locking on mine with a force that made me shift uncomfortably. "Why do you think he became a player?" she asked, her voice low but pointed. "He wasn't always like that. He was the sweet one, the thoughtful one. And then... everything changed."

A bitter laugh slipped out of me, harsh and hollow. "I don't know... because he's like every other guy." My arms squeezed tighter over my chest, like armor I couldn't take off.

"Like every other guy you always went for," she shot back without hesitation. Her words landed sharp, slicing straight through the wall I was trying to hold.

Heat rushed to my cheeks, anger and shame twisting together. "So, what... you're saying it's all my fault?"

Maddie shook her head slowly, her tone softening but steady. "No, Lex. But you need to see it for what it is. He did everything he could to make you notice him. And when that didn't work, he turned himself into the kind of guy you always picked, the assholes you date, hate, and then swear off. He became what he thought you wanted, even if it meant you'd hate him for it. Because at least then… he still had your attention."

My breath hitched, the air suddenly too heavy in my chest. My voice came out small, almost broken. "He… he said that?"

"No," Maddie sighed, rocking Summer gently as her gaze softened. "But he didn't have to. We all saw it. Nellyfish, me, even Joshie. We knew exactly what was happening, even if you pretended not to."

I swallowed hard, my throat tightening like it didn't want to let the words out. "Then why didn't you say anything?"

"It wasn't our place," Maddie said softly, her eyes never leaving mine. "But surely you knew. It was so damn obvious."

A shaky breath rattled through me, my gaze dropping to my hands knotted in my lap. The blanket between my fingers twisted tighter and tighter until my knuckles turned white. The truth prickled under my skin, uncomfortable and undeniable.

"I thought… I thought he had a crush, sure. But just that. Nothing serious." My voice cracked, uneven. "I had no idea he still… liked me. I thought he was just being a sleazy player. That he wanted to sleep with me and nothing more."

Maddie's gaze stayed firm, her voice calm but insistent. "Well, you've got him all wrong. And you know it."

She shifted Summer in her arms, rocking her gently, as if the motion steadied her own heart too. "You need to talk to him, Lex. You need to tell him if there's even a chance. Otherwise, he'll keep hanging on. And it's been too long. It's starting to do him some damage. He deserves to know."

Her words pressed against me, pushing at every defense I had left. My stomach knotted hard, and I shifted on the bed, restless, my fingers picking at the edge of the blanket like it could distract me.

Talk to him?

The thought made my chest ache. Because what if she was right? What if I had been blind all this time? What if the player act, the cocky grin, the endless women, the arrogance, was never who he really was, but just a mask? A mask to hide the truth he didn't know how to show.

And the truth that terrified me most wasn't about him. It was about me.

What if I'd been pushing him away all these years… not because I didn't believe him, but because deep down, I'd been too scared to believe in someone who might actually stay?

But what if she was wrong? What if I let him in and it destroyed me all over again?

The thought coiled tight around my ribs, squeezing until I could barely breathe. I'd been shattered before. I couldn't afford to be shattered again, not now, not with a baby depending on me.

The room felt heavy, thick with everything Maddie wasn't saying. She kept rocking Summer, her movements calm, steady, but her eyes… God, her eyes never let me go. Gentle, yes, but unrelenting, like she was holding up a mirror I didn't want to look into.

I turned away, blinking fast, swallowing against the lump in my throat. My chest ached with the weight of it all, her words, his face in my mind, the what-ifs that clawed at me like they had teeth.

I wanted to deny it, to laugh it off, to build the wall brick by brick. But deep down, under all the fear and all the anger I'd carried. I needed to know.

And worse, deep in my bones, I knew Maddie was right.

# Chapter 34

## Lexi

The cafeteria buzzed with noise as we tucked ourselves into our usual small corner table by the window.

Maddie picked at the crumbs of her muffin, Nelly lounging back with her arms crossed like nothing could affect her, Lucas sat across from me, and I cradled Summer against my chest, swaddled in soft pink.

Maddie licked the sugar from her fingers, leaning back with a grin. "Mhmm, that apple and cinnamon muffin was delicious," she said, her whole face lighting up. "I swear, it tasted better than usual today."

Nelly rolled her eyes, her voice dry but playful. "No, that's just you and food. You always think the mud cake's better every time you eat it too. Nothing changes."

Maddie laughed, cheeks flushed, and I found myself laughing with her. The sound came out soft, fragile, but real.

I lowered my gaze to Summer, her tiny body warm against my chest. Breathing her in made the noise and chaos of everything else fade.

"Oh, I know," I admitted with a tired smile. "Since being pregnant, having her… and breastfeeding… I'm eating so much more. I get so hungry, and things just taste better when you're hungry."

Lucas leaned forward, his chuckle low and easy. "Yeah, and I'm always the one getting sent to the shops to grab snacks."

I shot him a sidelong look, arching a brow. He just laughed, unbothered, his eyes flicking down to Summer in my arms, so soft, so steady, that it made me go gooey inside every time he looked at her.

"And this little princess does nothing but eat too," he teased, his lips curving. "Just like her Mommy."

The word *Mommy* caught in my chest, sharp and sweet all at once. His voice wrapped around it like he meant it, not as a joke, not as a throwaway, but as something real. And God, it hurt. Not because it was cruel, but because it wasn't. Because it was dangerous. Because it was everything I wanted and everything I was terrified to believe in.

It had been four weeks now since Summer came screaming into the world, four weeks of sleepless nights, her cries clawing me out of shallow dreams, my body aching and my mind fraying at the edges. More than I thought I could survive.

But somehow, with him sitting next to me… it felt bearable.

Lucas had kept his word. He'd stayed. He'd shown up. Every single day.

When I first brought Summer home, he'd taken a whole week off work just to help me settle into the terrifying rhythm of motherhood. And even after that, he never really left. Whenever he wasn't working, he was here, walking through my door like it was the most natural thing in the world, like he belonged.

He rolled up his sleeves without me asking, no fuss, no questions. He knew exactly what to do: how to change a nappy without fumbling, how to test bath water with your elbow and how to check the temperature of her bottle by dabbing it on the inside of his wrist. He told me his sister had taught him when he helped with her kids.

He was a natural.

And me? Half the time, I felt like I was falling apart. Like I had no business being someone's Mom.

My hands shook, my chest tightened, shame curling sharp and ugly in my gut.

But then Lucas would step in, calm, patient, never making me feel stupid, somehow, I could breathe again.

If he hadn't been here, I don't know if I would've lasted. Some days, I still believed my parents had been right, that maybe adoption would've been the better choice. But Lucas had been my anchor. Even when he wasn't there, I didn't unravel the same way anymore. I could breathe. I could keep going.

And I owed that to him.

But how do you ever repay something like that? That kind of quiet, relentless kindness?

The absurd thought of how much Lucas had changed, bubbled into laughter before I could stop it. Lucas turned his head, one brow raised, that familiar smirk tugging at his lips.

"What are you laughing at, Le Le?"

"Nothing," I said quickly, still grinning, though heat crept into my cheeks. "Just… thought about something."

His smirk widened. "Oh, let me guess. Was it the time when your darling daughter projectile-vomited all over the back of my shirt?"

That did it. I burst into laughter, clutching my side until I could barely breathe.

The image replayed in my mind, Lucas frozen in horror, his broad shoulders streaked with sticky white milk, while Summer had looked smug and perfectly content.

He shook his head, mock-offended, but the glint in his eyes gave him away. "Glad my suffering entertains you."

"It really does," I said between giggles.

Across the table, Maddie clasped her hands together, her face glowing. "That sounds cute," she said warmly.

Nelly wrinkled her nose. "Yeah, *so* cute. Curdled, smelly milk all over him." She bent forward dramatically like she was about to gag. Maddie and I broke into another fit of laughter.

The sound softened the air. Even when Summer stirred against me with a faint whimper, the moment stayed light.

Maddie tilted her head, her voice gentle. "So… things are going well? Settling in as a Mom?"

Before I could answer, Lucas leaned forward, his voice rich with conviction. "Le Le is doing great. She's a wonderful Mom. And Summer is perfect. Sleeps really well and…"

I cut him off, shaking my head, smiling faintly "Lucas is being very polite."

He shot me a look, steady, insistent. I avoided it, turning back to my daughter, brushing her cheek with my fingertip.

"We're managing," I murmured. "Lucas has been a great help. We couldn't have done it without him."

His expression softened, his gaze catching mine with a weight that made my stomach flutter.

"Oh, you would have worked it out," he said quietly, almost shy. "I was just happy to help." Then his eyes dropped to Summer, his smile widening with something close to wonder. "And I mean… she's as cute as a button."

The warmth in his voice made my throat tighten.

I smiled at him, teasing. "Why thank you, Lucas. But I prefer sexy."

His cheeks flushed; his hand went to the back of his neck. "I was talking about Summer," he mumbled.

I laughed, lighter than I'd felt in weeks. "I know you were, silly."

He inhaled sharply, steadying something inside himself.

"I was just joking," I added softly.

"I see," he said, clearing his throat, shifting in his chair. "You're starting to get a sense of humor?"

"Occasionally," I teased, rocking Summer. "I can tell a joke."

His grin returned, slow and crooked, "Careful, Le Le. If you start laughing with me too, you might actually start liking me again."

The air shifted, heavier now. For a split second, I couldn't decide if that terrified me… or thrilled me.

From across the table, Maddie leaned in, her lips curling into a knowing smile. "So, I see you two are getting along better."

Before I could reply, Nelly snorted, rolling her eyes. "What Madz is really asking," she drawled, "is… are you guys fucking now? Since you already look like one big happy family?"

The words slapped through the air. My breath stalled, my arms tightened protectively around Summer. Lucas shifted beside me, his hand flying to the back of his neck, his ears crimson.

But Nelly wasn't done. Her grin sharpened. "So, he's acting like this, attentive, sweet, father of the year and he hasn't even got his dick wet? Makes you wonder what he'll be like when he finally does."

The scrape of Lucas' chair against the linoleum was so loud it made me flinch. He half-rose, voice cracking sharp. "NELLY!"

She only shrugged, smug. Maddie smothered a laugh behind her hand, caught between shock and amusement.

My face burned. I rocked Summer gently, wishing I could disappear into her softness.

But Lucas wasn't letting it slide. "Shut up! Enough! You need to stop with these jokes. I've stopped that lifestyle. I'm not doing that anymore."

Nelly arched a brow, her smirk fixed. "Oh, I don't even mean about you sleeping around," she shot back smoothly, her eyes cutting to me. "I mean about Lexi."

The air shifted instantly. Her words dropped like a grenade.

Lucas slammed his hand on the table, his voice threaded with steel. "Shut up," he snapped, pointing at her. "Just because you can't have any girls show you interest doesn't mean you can keep sticking your nose in my love life."

My breath caught.

*Love life?*

The words hit harder than anything else he'd said. My pulse thundered. Did he just mean me?

But before I could process it, his voice came again, harsher, cruel in a way I'd never heard.

"Couldn't get a guy, so you turned to girls. Now no girls want you. Don't go ruining my life because yours isn't turning out the way you wanted it to."

The words shattered the air. Summer whimpered, fists curling into my shirt as if she felt it too.

"Lucas!" Maddie's voice cracked, sharp and furious.

"Lucas!" I echoed, my own trembling with disbelief, my chest burning with anger, shock, heartbreak, all tangled together.

His eyes widened, regret flashing instantly across his face. "Shit!" he muttered under his breath, raking a hand through his hair like he wished he could claw the words back. But it was too late. The damage was done.

Across from us, Nelly's face broke apart. Her usual mask of sarcasm and sharp edges crumbled, leaving nothing but raw hurt.

She didn't argue. She didn't fire back like she always did. She just shoved back from the table, her chair screeching against the linoleum, and bolted.

Her hand flew to her mouth as tears streamed down her cheeks. Her shoulders shook as she disappeared through the doorway, the sound of her footsteps echoing until it faded completely.

The silence she left behind was suffocating. Maddie's glare snapped to Lucas, her arms folding tight across her chest. The disappointment in her eyes was louder than any scolding words could have been.

I couldn't even look at him.

My arms tightened protectively around Summer, my heart racing as if I could shield her from the

cruelty that had just spilled into the world, from the side of him I didn't recognize and wasn't sure I wanted to.

The silence that followed was brutal.

Lucas rubbed the back of his neck, shifting in his seat like he couldn't escape his own skin. "Fuck, I know," he muttered, voice low, dripping with shame. "You girls don't have to say it. I fucked up. I'm sorry."

I clutched Summer tighter against me, her tiny body squirming as though she could feel the storm still crackling in the air. Anger simmered hot in my chest, mixing with hurt that I didn't know how to untangle. My voice shook when it finally broke free.

"I don't think we're the ones you should be apologizing to," I whispered, trembling with fury.

His eyes flicked to me for a second, haunted, guilty, before he dropped his gaze to the floor. He nodded once, jaw clenched. "You're right."

The scrape of his chair against the linoleum was harsh, grating. He stood without looking back, his shoulders slumped like he carried a weight too heavy even for him. "I'll go after her," he said, and then he slowly skulked out of the cafeteria.

The cafeteria felt colder without him, but no calmer. I rocked Summer gently, rubbing small circles against her back, trying to soothe her as much as myself.

My chest burned, torn open by too many emotions, shock, anger, sadness. And underneath it all, that slip of the tongue… *love life…* still clawed at me, dangerous and fragile all at once.

Across from me, Maddie stayed silent at first. Her arms were crossed tight against her chest, her expression sharp enough to cut through the thick air. She didn't soften when our eyes finally met.

Her words came steady, unflinching. "This is partially your fault too, you know."

The bottom dropped out of my stomach. I blinked at her, stunned. My grip on Summer tightened instinctively, as if she were my shield. "Excuse me?" My voice cracked sharper than I intended, part disbelief, part defense.

But Maddie didn't back down. She leaned forward, her gaze unwavering. And in that moment, I wasn't sure if I wanted to fight her… or admit she might be right.

"I didn't say anything," I snapped, heat rushing through me before I could stop it.

Maddie's tone softened, but only slightly. "Exactly, Lex. You *haven't* said anything. You *haven't* had the talk with him yet, like I told you to."

My gaze dropped to Summer, her tiny lips parted as she breathed against my chest. The steady rhythm of her rise and fall was the only thing keeping me anchored.

My throat burned as I whispered, "It's been a tough few weeks. Trying to work out how to be a Mom. The lack of sleep. The constant feeding. The crying. The right time never really came up."

And it was the truth. Every single day had been survival mode, wake, feed, change, soothe, repeat. No space for anything else. Certainly not for ripping open wounds that had been festering for years.

Maddie leaned forward, her eyes sharp with conviction. "There will never be a right time for this chat, Lex. Not with him. Not when it's already long overdue."

Her arms folded tighter, her voice carrying the weight of someone who cared too much to sugarcoat it. "It's like ripping off a bandage, quick, brutal. But it's better than letting it sit there, festering, until it explodes. Because things like this…" she gestured toward the doorway where Lucas and Nelly had stormed out. "...this will keep happening until you do."

Her words hit hard, because they were true. But they felt unbearable, pressing down on a chest already cracked with guilt.

"I didn't cause this," I whispered fiercely, though my voice shook, betraying me. My grip on Summer tightened like I could shield both of us from her judgment. "I didn't make him yell at her."

Maddie's gaze softened just slightly, but she didn't let me off the hook. "No... but Lex, you lit the match."

She leaned closer, her tone calm but sharp, her hands braced on her hips as if she were deliberately holding me accountable. "You may not have made him yell," she said, "but Nelly's sick of watching Lucas hang around like a lovesick puppy. And what he just did? He lashed out because he didn't want you to know. Because if you know, it might be the end. He wanted Nellyfish to shut up before she ruined it for him. He's terrified of losing you all over again, Lex. And now there is Summer. He loves her like she's his own. Until you give him an answer, he's going to keep holding on to that hope. Unfortunately..." her voice dropped, heavy, "...Nelly just found out how far he'll go to protect it."

Her words sank like a stone in my stomach. I rocked Summer gently, pressing her closer, searching her tiny face for comfort I couldn't seem to find anywhere else.

"Okay," I whispered, finally forcing the words out. My throat scraped raw. "I'll talk to him... tonight."

Maddie's expression softened for half a heartbeat before she straightened, brushing her hair from her shoulders, already pulling herself back together.

"Well, I've got to go," she said lightly, though her eyes still carried the weight of everything she'd just told me. "Ray and I have an appointment. Tell Lucas I said goodbye."

I nodded, my voice too tight to trust. "I'll tell him."

She gave me one last look, half warning, half encouragement, before she turned and left, her heels clicking softly against the linoleum until the door swung shut behind her.

The silence afterward was suffocating. Too big. Too loud.

I looked down at Summer, her tiny chest rising and falling against me, her soft whimper pulling me back just enough to breathe. I brushed my lips over the crown of her head, whispering into her hair.

I really am going to have to talk to him. I can't let him carry this weight, can't let him take it out on other people. I don't want him angry or hurting because of me.

One way or another, this had to end.

I sighed, rocking her a little harder, the steady rhythm a weak attempt to calm the storm inside me.

*God, why can't anything ever be simple?*

# Chapter 35
## Lucas

The door clicked softly behind me as I stepped back into the cafe. My chest felt tight, my steps heavier than they should've been.

The moment my eyes found Lexi, with Summer curled against her chest, the ache hit again, fear, guilt, want, all of it tangled into one.

"Are you okay?" I asked, my voice quieter than I intended. I hated how uncertain it sounded, like I was walking on glass.

She coughed softly before answering, and the pause nearly gutted me. "Yes…" Her voice was thin, strained. Then her eyes lifted, sharp in their softness. "Is Nelly okay?"

Shit. My stomach dropped. I rubbed the back of my neck, heat crawling up the side of my face. "I couldn't find her," I admitted, wincing at how pathetic it sounded.

"She's a fast one. I looked everywhere, but she just disappeared. She's so damn short... she's hard to find."

The joke fell flat, crashing into the silence between us. She didn't laugh. Didn't even smile. Just hugged Summer tighter, rocking her gently, her anger simmering so clear it made me restless.

I shifted my weight, scratching at the back of my neck again, my eyes darting everywhere but hers. "Don't worry. I'll track her down and apologize for being an ass."

Her reply was sharp, tired, and it cut straight through me. "You really were."

I swallowed hard and nodded, shame crawling in deeper. "I know."

The silence after that was brutal, the kind that presses in until it's choking you. I stared at the floor, then back at Summer in her arms, the little rise and fall of her chest so peaceful it almost hurt. She had no idea the chaos circling around her.

"Can you take us home?" Lexi's voice broke through, steady but worn. My head snapped up, a flicker of relief rushing through me. She wasn't shutting me out completely. She still wanted me near.

But then came the second blow.

"And when we get there," she added, quiet but firm, "we need to talk."

The second her words landed, *we need to talk*, my whole body locked up. Shoulders stiff. Breath stuck in my chest. I knew what that meant. This was it. The beginning of the end.

I followed her through the cafe, my stomach in knots, every step dragging heavier than the last. She held Summer close to her chest, like I wasn't even a thought in the picture anymore. And I couldn't blame her. Not after today. Not after the shit that just came out of my mouth.

I caught her profile when she glanced ahead, and I swear she could see straight through me. Haunted. Guilty. Desperate. That's what I felt. That's what I was. My own thoughts taunted me like a neon sign.

*Shit. I really did fuck up today. She's going to tell you to leave her alone. And what then? What the hell are you going to do if she tells you to stop coming around?*

I'd been enjoying it too much, being there, helping, pretending, for a second, like we were a family. Like maybe I could belong. And if she took that away from me… I didn't know how I'd survive it.

I dragged in a breath, ragged and uneven, but it didn't shake the sadness weighing down my chest. It clung to me, pressing heavier with every step, all the way out to the car park.

The cold afternoon air hit sharp against my skin, but it didn't cut through the tension. Didn't lighten the heaviness between us. We walked in silence, across the car park, past the glowing lamps and empty spaces, until we reached my car.

I opened the passenger door for her, careful, quiet, the way I always tried to be with her now. My fingers brushed the frame like it could anchor me, like touching something solid might keep me from falling apart.

She slid inside, Summer bundled tight in her baby seat, and I shut the door softly behind them.

By the time I circled around to the driver's side, my chest was aching with the truth. The talk waiting for us wasn't something I could charm my way out of. It wasn't something I could outrun.

And fuck, I was terrified of what she was going to say.

# Chapter 36

## Nelly

The room was dim, blinds half-drawn, thin streaks of gray daylight slicing through like knives I hadn't asked for. Shadows stretched long across the wreckage, bottles, pills, the usual entourage. The air reeked of stale whiskey, sharp and sour, coating my throat with every breath.

I hunched on the couch edge, elbows to knees, staring at the floorboards until they blurred into nothing. My chest pulled tighter, every second dragging like chains.

Then the phone lit up, buzzing against the cushion, the shriek ring shattering the silence like glass.

One look at the name and my stomach twisted, bile rising. My throat locked. I dropped it like it burned.

"Not now," I muttered into the empty room, my voice raw, brittle.

But the ringing came again, louder, longer, like it knew I'd cave. My hands dug into my hair, pulling, shaking, tears smearing my vision.

"He made his feelings clear," I snapped to no one, broken, the words splintering as the tears spilled.

When the ringing finally died, the silence that followed pressed harder, heavier, like the room itself wanted to suffocate me.

"He was right though," I breathed, hollow. "And not just about the girls."

The ache spread through my chest until it felt like rot. Parents who hadn't wanted me in years. Every time I reached out, I got the same cold sermon: an afterthought, a burden. My sister, months between calls, and when she did bother, her voice already halfway out the door.

The phone lay silent beside me now, its blank screen louder than the ring. The stale air settled, thick, suffocating. And I sat in it, swallowed whole by the emptiness.

"I'm too busy," she always said. "I'll call you back when I have more time." She never did. Time always ran out when it came to me.

The memory rattled around my skull as I hugged myself tight, rocking on the couch edge like some broken clock. My breath came shallow, uneven, like even oxygen didn't want to stick around.

"Everyone at work hates me," I muttered into the heavy dark. My voice sounded foreign, thin, cracked, barely human. "They don't get me. My boss shoved me out like trash."

The phone lit up again, not a call, just the group chat. Notifications bubbling over with laughter, jokes, plans I wasn't invited to. They said they loved me once. They said they were just busy. But I wasn't stupid.

"I see what they're doing," I rasped, bitterness clawing at my throat. "They treat their other friends differently. Better. They don't love me the same, if they love me at all."

The words carved me hollow.

"They probably don't even notice I've pulled back; I have withdrawn." My fists pressed into my eyes, but the tears came anyway, hot, relentless. "And that's the worst part. I miss them so much… and I know they don't miss me. My absence is nothing to them. But to me? It's everything. A hole I cannot fill."

My hand fumbled for the whiskey bottle. It slipped, clattering back onto the table like it was mocking me. I stared at it, chest caving in around the void.

"All I ever wanted," I whispered to the shadows, raw, trembling, "was someone to love me the way I love them. To care like I care."

My voice cracked, more rasp than sound. My whole body shook, every nerve screaming empty. "Is that really too much to ask?"

The silence that answered was suffocating. Not peaceful. Never peaceful. The kind that crawls under your skin, presses hard on your chest, makes every breath taste like dirt.

I curled tighter on the couch, knees crushing into my ribs, arms wrapped around me like a shield full of holes. My head drooped heavy, stone-filled, like gravity was already trying to drag me under.

The shadows stretched long and cruel, curling in the corners like they were laughing at me. Even the hum of the fridge and the tick of the clock sounded like mockery, background noise to the suffocating weight pressing me down.

Everyone else seemed to have it… love, family, belonging. People who noticed when you went quiet. People who cared if you woke up the next day.

Me? Not so much.

"Apparently that's too much to ask," I whispered into the stale air. My voice came out hoarse, foreign, like it belonged to a ghost. "Even my parents can't stomach me. And their love's supposed to come with a no-return policy."

The truth split me open, raw and rotting. Shame twisted in my gut, folding me in half until my forehead pressed to my knees like I could crush the ache out.

"In the end, it's always the same," I muttered against my skin. "I'm unlovable. Always have been." The confession slithered out like poison.

"People try, sure. But eventually they get it, there's nothing here worth loving. Not really."

The last word snapped in my throat, jagged as glass. A sob tore free anyway, my chest heaving as I rocked in the dark, wishing, pathetically, that someone, anyone, might prove me wrong.

I swallowed hard, but the lump in my throat refused to budge. My whole body shook like it was crumbling from the inside out.

"I'm broken. I'm worthless." The words carved themselves out of me, sharp and cracked. My voice fell to a whisper, shaking into the emptiness. "Pointless."

The word echoed. *Pointless. Pointless.* Each repetition heavier, louder, until it pressed so hard on my chest I could barely breathe.

I hugged my knees tighter, trying to keep myself from spilling apart completely. Tears blurred the floorboards into streaks of gray.

And the silence? It didn't soothe. It suffocated, thick, endless, swallowing everything until all that was left was the weight of my own despair.

And in that silence, I knew what had to come next.

And Lucifer, it scared me how easy it was. How simple to decide this was the cleaner way out. The better way. For them. For me.

I sat up straight, steadied my trembling hands, popped the pill bottle and poured them all into my palm. Whiskey in the other hand, my holy communion.

"So long, cruel world."

I slapped the pills into my mouth, tipped my head back, and drowned them in liquor. Classy exit.

An hour later, the world was darker. Blurred. Fuzzy around the edges. The floorboards were cold against my cheek, damp from tears that had already dried into nothing. My body sprawled face-down, limp, heavy. The air was thick with whiskey and finality.

Empty pill bottles lay scattered like evidence at a crime scene, proof of surrender, proof of failure, proof of just how pathetic I'd become.

Then came the knock. Loud. Violent. Like a gunshot.

"It's been over a week, Nelly!" A bellowed, muffled voice through the door, rough, merciless. My landlord. "You need to be out."

Another knock. Harder. Rattling the thin door, rattling my bones. "I've got another low-life waiting to move in. I was nice enough to give you the week. But you're out. Now. I don't care if you've got nowhere to go."

Each word landed like a lash, dripping with venom. The pounding came again, the whole room vibrating with it.

"Open this door," he snarled, "or I'll let myself in."

I stared at the cracks in the floorboards, frozen. My body was coffin-ready, no movement, no care left to summon.

I could see it, it was like I was out side my body, looking down at myself and the pathetic excuse I had become. Watching my eyes stare vacantly, unblinking into space as my breathing barely scraped through. Hearing the banging like it was down a series of tunnels. And all I could think was how I didn't care. How peaceful not caring was.

His growl came again, low and dangerous, followed by the slow count.

"One."

The walls shuddered with it. My chest tightened, breaths scraping raw.

"Two."

Tears burned at the corners of my eyes, but I didn't move. Couldn't. My heartbeat was a slow deliberate war drum in my skull, loud enough to drown the world.

"Three!"

His voice thundered, final, unforgiving. Still, I lay there, limp, broken, the walls caving in like a tomb.

"Oh, fuck this shit," he growled. Then… BANG.

The door splintered, the crack echoing like a cannon. The floor vibrated, hinges screamed, then silence… before the heavy stomp of boots invaded my final resting place. Each thud shook my skull, dragging me out of the fragile nothingness I'd been clinging to.

"No point playing dead, Nelly," he sneered, voice slicing sharp through the fog, though it sounded distant, like I was underwater. "That ain't gonna get you out of moving out."

*Dead.* Lucifer, that sounded perfect right now.

I wanted to laugh, or cry, or both, but nothing came.

The couch screeched across the floor, his boot slamming it aside. The jolt rattled the boards, nudging my arm, but my body stayed limp, a marionette with cut strings.

"Nelly?" His voice cracked this time. Different. Thin. Boots scuffed closer. A shadow fell across my blurred vision, darker than all the rest.

"Nelly??"

He dropped to his knees, the empty pill bottles clattering across the floor as he shifted closer. His heat pressed the air around me. Panic seeped into his tone, leaking through the cracks.

"Oh, Nelly… what have you done?"

My chest barely moved, breaths shallow, ragged. The world tilted, the edges blackening. I tried to respond but I couldn't muster the energy to speak. To move. I was on my way out, and I couldn't be happier. Peace was on its way. I felt the side of my lip lift slightly.

Plastic clicked. Metal scraped. His voice shook. A phone.

"Yes, I need an ambulance," he stammered, words tripping over themselves, frantic. "A young girl… overdosed, looks bad. Hurry."

No. No. No. Just let me go.

But the plea stayed trapped inside my body, echoing softly, like a ghost that never got to leave.

The words scraped wrong. I was too old, too broken, to be called *young* anymore. Nothing young about rotting.

His voice warped, distant, like it was drowning in black water. My body sank heavier, pinned by invisible hands that didn't care if I ever got back up.

And in that emptiness, one truth circled like a vulture: maybe this was all I'd ever be.

A burden. A cleanup job. A mess someone else had to call an ambulance for. A corpse-in-progress, waiting for someone to file the paperwork.

# Chapter 37
## Maddie

Every second stretched long, the ticking clock drilling into my nerves until I thought I might scream. My fingers wouldn't behave, I kept twisting them together, then forcing them apart, then twisting again, like if I stopped moving, I'd shatter.

Ray sat beside me, solid as ever, though the weight of his tension pressed against my skin. His leg bounced once before he stilled it, rubbing at his chin, trying to look calm for me. He always tried.

Across from us, the fertility specialist adjusted her glasses, her smile practiced, warm, but professional. "Good to see you two again," she said evenly. "So, you're here to get the results from your blood test this morning."

"Yes," I managed, though the word came out too light, too tight. My chest felt locked up, like I'd been holding my breath all day and didn't know how to let it go. "It feels like today has dragged on forever."

She gave a sympathetic nod. "Yes, waiting to see if FET has worked or not is always hard."

Always hard. Always waiting. Always hoping.

She picked up the sheet of paper, scanning it with the kind of calm that made me want to reach across the desk and shake it out of her. Ray leaned back in his chair, stiff, holding himself together the way I couldn't.

The doctor finally looked up, her eyes catching mine. "So, I won't make you wait any longer."

My heart hammered so loudly I was sure they could both hear it. My knuckles ached where I gripped the armrest, every muscle braced for impact.

"Your progesterone levels look good and strong," she said, pausing. Then her lips curved, just slightly. "And I am happy to say you have traces of HCG, the pregnancy hormone."

The words hung in the air, suspended between us, as though the whole room was holding its breath with me. My lungs locked, my chest tightening until I thought I'd burst.

Pregnancy. Hormone. Positive.

My breath caught in my throat, and suddenly I couldn't tell if I was about to laugh or sob.

"Now, they're low, as it's only the first two weeks," the doctor continued, her tone careful, almost like she knew how fragile hope could be.

"But they are typical for this stage of a normal pregnancy. So, everything looks good. Congratulations, Mom and Dad."

Ray's face broke instantly into a grin, the tension that had been wound so tight in him finally loosening. His shoulders sagged, his whole body softening as if the words had physically lifted a weight off him.

Me? I didn't move. I couldn't. My body froze, my eyes wide, the word echoing through me like it couldn't possibly belong to me.

Pregnant.

After all this time. After the needles and the waiting rooms, the heartbreaks that nearly swallowed me whole. After watching everyone else get their happy endings while I plastered on a smile.

Pregnant.

"Thank you so much, Doc," Ray said, his voice bright, shaking his head like he couldn't believe it either.

The doctor tilted her head. "Do you have any questions?"

Questions. I had a thousand. But my throat was tight, locked, like the air itself refused to move.

I opened my mouth, but nothing came.

Ray chuckled, his warm hand slipping over mine, steadying me. "Seems as though the news has left my normally very chatty wife speechless."

The doctor's lips curled in amusement, but my heart was still hammering, my body buzzing like I'd been plugged into a socket.

Ray leaned forward, practical as always. "What happens now? Do we just do this like a normal pregnancy? Or…?"

"We will monitor you for the first six to eight weeks," the specialist explained. "Maddison will need regular blood tests to make sure the HCG levels are tracking well. But if all goes well, then we'll discharge you to your normal OB-GYN."

Ray's brow furrowed, his voice dipping low, quiet but steady. "And if something goes wrong?"

The words lodged in my chest, sharp. I stopped breathing, bracing myself for an answer I wasn't sure I could survive.

The doctor set the paper aside, his eyes steady and firm. "We will deal with that if it arises. But for now, there is no reason I can see that this won't be a normal pregnancy."

Ray let out a long breath, nodding, his relief tangible. "Okay. Thank you, Doc."

The specialist gave us both a warm smile. "I have to go, I have my next patient. But take a few moments, let the news settle in, then you can go."

And just like that, she was gone, the door clicking softly behind her.

The silence that followed wasn't really silent at all. My heart was thundering, my breath shaky, my body trembling in the chair.

Pregnant.

The word circled me, wrapped me up, terrified me, thrilled me, and weighed me down all at once.

Pregnant.

For the first time in so long, hope didn't feel like a cruel joke waiting to break me. It felt real. Fragile. Terrifying. But real.

Ray turned to me, and the look on his face nearly shattered me. His whole being seemed to light up, joy sparking in his eyes in a way I hadn't seen in years. "Oh my God, baby… we did it." His voice cracked with laughter, disbelief, and relief all tangled together. "We're going to be a Mom and Dad… finally."

I blinked, my throat tightening, my breath catching somewhere between a sob and a laugh. "So… I didn't hear wrong?" I whispered, almost afraid to speak it into existence. "I'm… pregnant?"

"You sure are, baby." His smile was unshakable, full of wonder.

And that was it, the dam inside me burst. Tears flooded hot and fast, spilling down my cheeks before I could even wipe them away.

My hands shook, my body folding as the years of pain and disappointment came crashing back, every injection, every failed attempt, every month of waiting for a call that only ever broke me.

It all collapsed into this one moment.

Ray froze for a heartbeat, startled, then he was beside me, pulling me into his arms without hesitation. His embrace was steady, warm, the safest place I'd ever been.

He kissed the top of my head, his hand stroking my back as my sobs shook us both. "It's okay, baby. Let it all out. We finally did it. We can finally get excited."

I clung to him like I was drowning, burying my face into his chest, the fabric of his shirt soaking up years of heartache.

"I can't believe it's finally happening," I whispered, the words trembling out of me like a confession. "That all the hard work… all the heartbreak… it's finally worth it. It feels like a dream."

Ray held me tighter, his lips brushing the crown of my head. "It's not a dream. "It's our reality now. We're going to be parents."

He leaned back just enough to grin down at me, his eyes glinting with that cheeky spark I knew too well. "You want me to pinch you, baby? I know the perfect place to pinch."

I gasped, shoving at his chest with no real force, my tears colliding with a reluctant laugh. "No! Stay away from my ass. We're at the doctor's, Ray."

He wiggled his brows, utterly unashamed. "Yes, but we're in a room. No one will see. And you need to be sure this isn't a dream..."

I rolled my eyes, though the smile tugging at my lips gave me away. For the first time in years, it wasn't forced, it was real. It was mine. "No, I think I'll be fine."

And just like that, tears still wet on my cheeks, joy and fear twisting inside me like two sides of the same coin. I let myself believe it.

We were finally on the other side of hope.

The room softened around us, full of laughter and quiet relief, until the penetrating ring of my phone cut straight through it.

Ray groaned, leaning back. "Ignore it, Babe."

But it rang again, insistent.

I shook my head. "No, it might be important."

Reaching for it, I glanced down at the screen. My stomach tightened. "Oh, it's Nelly. I've got to get this. Something happened today at lunch; I have to make sure she's okay."

I pressed the phone to my ear, relief flickering through me when the line connected. "Hello? Nelly? Are you okay?"

But instead of her voice, a calm, unfamiliar one came through the receiver. "May I ask whom I'm speaking to?"

Confusion rippled through me, and I frowned, gripping the phone tighter. "My name is Maddison… Who are you? Why do you have Nelly's phone?"

"I've been going through her most recent calls," the voice explained, calm, almost too calm. "You were the first to answer. I'm an ER doctor, and I'm looking to speak with Nelly's next of kin. She has nothing listed on her records."

The room tilted. I gripped the edge of the desk to stop myself from swaying. Panic clawed at my throat. "What happened to her? I'm… I'm one of her closest friends. I've known her forever. Is she okay?"

The pause on the other end stretched too long, each second heavier than the last. My stomach twisted, the silence filling in answers I wasn't ready to hear.

"I'm sorry," the doctor said finally, his tone professional but clipped, almost cold. "Due to privacy laws, I'm unable to discuss her condition with you. I need to speak with family, a husband, or a legal next of kin."

My throat closed. Nelly didn't have any of that. She barely had us.

I clutched the phone tighter, my hand trembling. "She doesn't talk to her family. She isn't married. I don't even know if she has anyone listed as next of kin. She doesn't have many people in her life. Please, I need to know if she's going to be okay."

There was a low hum in the background, the faint, steady beeping of hospital machines I knew too well. The same sounds from the night of Joshie.

The doctor's voice came again, steady, clinical, offering no comfort. "I suggest you come down. We can try and sort this all out."

I swallowed hard, though my throat felt like it was closing in. "Okay," I whispered, forcing the word out. "We're just around the corner at the clinic. We'll be there soon."

When the line went dead, I lowered the phone, my pulse racing so hard it made me feel dizzy.

The room blurred, and for a moment all I could think was, please, God, let her be alive when we get there.

Ray's eyes locked onto mine instantly, his face pale, like he already knew he wouldn't like what I was about to say.

"What's happened?" he asked, his voice raw, bracing for the worst.

I swallowed hard, my throat thick and dry. "Nelly's in hospital. Something's happened. They won't tell me anything else." My voice cracked, panic clawing its way up my chest. "We have to get there."

Ray didn't hesitate. He just nodded, his jaw tightening, like he was trying to carry both my fear and his in that one movement.

We didn't speak as we moved. We just ran, out of the doctor's office, down the long corridor, past the blinding white walls of the clinic.

My footsteps stumbled, uneven, but Ray was steady behind me, his hand brushing my back every few strides as if to keep me upright.

All I could hear was the frantic thrum of my pulse and the echo of Nelly's name slamming around inside my skull.

Please be okay. Please still be here.

The world blurred, faces, voices, the city outside, it all melted into background noise as we pushed forward, straight toward the unknown.

The hospital hit me like a wall. The smell of antiseptic clung to everything, sharp and merciless, but beneath it lingered something heavier, like grief absorbed into the paint, into the very walls.

We were hurried along and directed to the room Nelly was in. Machines hummed faintly, the steady beep of a monitor slicing through the silence.

My chest tightened as my eyes found her.

She looked so small. So breakable. Lying there in the hospital bed, swallowed whole by stiff white sheets. Her skin was pale, almost translucent, her lips dry. Her chest rose and fell faintly, but her eyes stayed shut, as though she was somewhere else entirely.

The sight made my stomach twist so violently I thought I'd be sick. "Oh, Nelly…" I whispered, my hand flying to my mouth as the weight of it hit me all at once.

"How is she, Doctor? What happened?" The desperation in me was too sharp, too loud. I was terrified of the answer but needed it anyway.

The doctor lowered his eyes to the clipboard in his hand, his face grave, his tone careful. "This is an unusual case," he said slowly. "We managed to get in contact with her mother. And…"

He paused, the silence weighted, like he was trying to soften a blow that could never be softened.

"She told us she has disowned Nelly. She said she's happy for us to speak to whoever is willing to claim her."

I stopped dead, the words slamming into me so hard it was like my chest caved in. My ribs ached under the weight of it. "That's… terrible," I whispered, barely able to breathe.

Beside me, Ray stayed silent, but I could feel the fury rolling off him. His jaw was tight; his hands curled into fists at his sides.

The doctor let out a tired sigh and pushed on. "We really don't have a precedent for this sort of thing. I spoke to the head of emergency, and he's cleared me to speak to you about her condition, given her mother's consent."

A cold shiver climbed my spine. My throat ached as I forced the words out. "Why would she say that? Why would any mother…?" My voice broke, the crack sharp as glass. "Is she going to be okay? What happened to her?"

The doctor's eyes dropped again, his pen tapping lightly against the clipboard like he needed the rhythm to stay steady. "Her landlord was in the process of evicting her," he said quietly.

My stomach dropped. "What?"

"But when he busted through her door," the doctor continued, "he found her unconscious on the floor."

I gasped, shaking my head hard, as if that might make his words untrue. "I don't understand… she didn't say anything at lunch today about having to move out. Unconscious? Is she ill? She seemed okay at lunch today?" My voice trembled, disbelief cutting through every syllable.

The doctor's tone shifted, heavier now. "The landlord handed in an empty bottle of strong painkillers. The script was only filled a couple of days ago, but the bottle was empty."

My heart seized. "She… ?" The single word fractured in my throat.

"Yes," he said quietly, grim but gentle, like he'd spoken this truth too many times before. "We pumped her stomach, but we don't know how long the pills were in her system."

The floor tilted beneath me. My knees gave out, and I sank into the chair by her bedside, my palms pressed flat against my thighs to keep myself from shaking apart. My eyes burned, but no tears came. Not yet.

"Her vitals have improved," the doctor went on. "Now we're just waiting for her to wake up."

I forced the words out, my throat raw. "Has there been any damage?"

"At this stage," he said carefully, "the initial tests suggest we caught her just in time. But we'll know more once she wakes and we can run further tests."

My chest tightened until I could barely breathe. "Do you know when she'll wake up?"

He shook his head gently. "We can see no real reason for her to still be unconscious. Just… when her body is ready. When it's recovered."

I reached for Nelly's hand, limp and cold against mine, and squeezed it desperately, like I could pull her back with nothing more than will. "Come back to us, Nelly," I whispered, my voice cracking. "Please… just come back."

I turned toward Ray, my words sharper than I meant, grief twisting them into blades. "But why this, Ray? Why try and take her own life?"

He let out a long breath, his face drawn with something I couldn't fix. "Sometimes, when you're lost… this feels like the only way out," he said gently. "The easiest way. They convince themselves that the world would be better off without them. That they're sparing the people they love."

I shook my head violently, clutching Nelly's hand as though I could anchor her here with me.

"But she's wrong. I would miss her. I *do* miss her. I love her, Ray." My voice broke, tears slipping. "And I can't believe she was hurting this badly and I had no idea. At lunch today, I knew Lucas upset her, but before that she laughed. She acted like everything was fine. She fooled me."

Ray's expression softened, his tone low and careful. "Sweetheart… when someone doesn't want to talk about their pain, they learn how to hide it. They become experts at pretending. She's probably been doing it for years."

He reached for my arm, grounding me. "You couldn't have known unless she wanted you to. And from the looks of it, Nelly thought she had to fight her demons alone."

I squeezed her hand harder, the monitor beeping steadily beside us, cruel in its rhythm. "Well, look where that's gotten her," I muttered, brittle, though underneath it, all I felt was fear.

Ray stepped closer, looping his arm around me, his voice soft. "When she wakes, we'll be here. We'll tell her she doesn't have to do this alone anymore. But, baby…" His voice lowered, pleading. "If you show her anger, she'll only retreat further. What she'll need most is love."

His words sank deep, but all I could do was press my forehead to Nelly's hand, whispering inside my heart the truth I couldn't let her go without knowing.

"It's not fair," I choked out. "That I had good parents. That I was taught love and kindness. And Nelly… she never got that. She never had what we have."

The ache inside me turned jagged. "What chance did she ever really have? How do you survive in a world that's never shown you what love is? How do you believe in it if you've never received it?"

Ray didn't answer this time. He just held me tighter, like he knew there wasn't one.

My tears spilled harder as I looked down at her pale face. "I don't want her to leave this world without knowing. Without knowing she *is* loved. That someone actually wants her here."

I pressed her limp hand to my cheek. "I'll tell her every day if I have to. I don't care if she rolls her eyes or shuts me down. I'll make sure she knows."

Ray met my eyes, his own heaviness mixed with something that looked a lot like pride. "That's exactly why she needs you. Why she's lucky to have you."

Resolve sparked inside me, fragile but fierce. I brushed a strand of hair from Nelly's forehead. "She's not going to go through this alone. Not while I'm still here."

I turned toward Ray, my voice trembling. "How do you do it? How do you always know the right things to say?"

He gave a small shrug, a sad smile tugging at his mouth. "I don't know… just good parents, I guess. And an amazing wife."

A shaky laugh escaped me. "Shush, you."

Then, like lightning, it hit me. My stomach twisted. "I have to tell Lexi and Lucas. Lucas is going to blame himself. He lost his temper and said something… something mean before she left lunch. Oh god, he's going to take this hard."

Ray's voice was firm. "Well, he needs to know."

"I know," I whispered, dread already sinking in.

My fingers trembled as I pulled out my phone. The glowing numbers blurred through tears as I dialed. It rang repeatedly before Lexi finally answered.

The moment I hung up, I sagged back in the chair. The weight of the hospital, the machines, the silence, it felt unbearable.

Ray's hand rested steady on my knee. "You did the right thing," he said softly.

I nodded, though my voice cracked. "It doesn't feel like it. It feels like I just set off a bomb."

The silence pressed in again. I turned toward Nelly, her chest rising faintly, tethered only by fragile breaths.

"She has no idea what she means to us," I whispered, brushing her hair back. "She thinks she's a burden, but she's wrong." My tears burned hot. "God, she's so wrong."

Ray squeezed my shoulder, letting me pour it out.

And so, I waited, waited for Lexi and Lucas to arrive, waited for Nelly to wake, waited for the chance to tell her the words I'd say a thousand times if I had to:

"You're not a burden. You never were."

# Chapter 38

## Lucas

The living room was too still, the kind of silence that crawled under your skin and made you itch.

I lingered near the door, trying not to look as restless as I felt, though my chest was tight enough to crack. Lexi stood a few feet away, her bag clutched like a shield, her eyes darting anywhere but at me.

"Thank you for dropping us off," she said, her voice steady but… not steady. Too practiced. Too forced.

I nodded, shoving my hands deeper into my pockets, because if I didn't, I'd wring them raw.

She'd been so damn quiet in the car. Barely said a word. Just stared out the window, picking at the hem of her shirt. And I knew. I knew this was it, *the talk*. My stomach twisted, guilt gnawing at me like teeth.

*Why did I say that to Nellyfish?*

The words echoed, burning in my skull. Why did I lose my temper like that? I saw her face again, the way it crumpled before she bolted. What if she never wants to see me again. Fuck!

I tried to breathe past the panic, but the silence between us was suffocating. Finally, I turned toward her, the words rough in my throat. "Look, Lexi…"

"Look, Lucas…" she blurted at the same time, and for half a second, the tension cracked.

We both laughed, soft and nervous, the sound fragile as glass.

But it didn't last. The quiet snapped back in, heavier than before. I cleared my throat, shifting my weight, forcing myself to say it. "I'm sorry I went off at Nellyfish like that. I lost my cool. I shouldn't have. It won't happen again."

My voice dropped lower, weighted with the truth I couldn't shake. "I'll track her down and apologize. Make it up to her."

I met Lexi's eyes, just for a second, and the regret must've been written all over me. Because it wasn't just Nelly I'd let down. It was her too, and my little princess.

I exhaled hard, my shoulders slumping like the weight of it all had finally crushed me. "I really don't want you to tell me to stay away."

The words were out before I could stop them. Too raw. Too desperate. But it was the truth. The thought of her looking me in the eye and saying *don't come back*... it would end me.

Her head snapped toward me, her mouth parting in shock. "Why would you think I'm going to tell you to stay away?"

Because I knew how these things went. Because women didn't stick around once they figured out what I wanted. They walked. They always walked.

My voice dropped, quiet, heavy. "Because you said you wanted to talk. And that always means something bad."

She shook her head, fumbling for words, her gaze darting to Summer, sleeping peacefully in her pram. I could see the nerves twisting in her chest the way mine were twisting in my gut.

"No... I just need to talk to you about..." She faltered, her voice catching, breath trembling. "I have recently become aware of..."

But nothing else came.

The silence between us felt like it might choke me. My heart hammered as I stepped forward, closing the space, because I couldn't stand watching her struggle anymore. If she couldn't find the words, maybe I could hold her steady until she did.

I reached for her hand before I could second-guess myself. Her skin was soft, trembling, but I laced my fingers through hers like it was the most natural thing in the world. Like I'd done it a thousand times before … because I had in my head.

Her pulse beat frantic under my touch. Mine wasn't much better. My thumbs brushed over the backs of her hands, slow, soothing strokes that I hoped would keep her from pulling away.

God, I didn't even know if she realized how much I needed this. How much I needed her. I needed Summer.

"You can talk to me about anything," I said softly, holding her gaze, refusing to let her look away. My voice cracked with everything I couldn't say. "I'm always here for you."

Even if she broke me. Even if this ended with her walking away.

She drew in a shaky breath, her palms slick, but she forced the words out anyway. "I wanted to clear the air and talk about what is happening between us. I wanted to tell you how I feel."

My whole body locked. The air slammed out of my lungs like I'd been hit. My hand twitched in hers, useless, because what the hell do you do when the woman you've loved for forever finally opens that door?

Oh my God. This is it. She's going to tell me. I'm about to find out if she actually wants me, if she's ever wanted me. If I've been building castles in the sand all these years, or if there's finally ground to stand on.

And then, like the universe couldn't resist screwing me over, her phone rang. Loud. Demanding. Over and over as we stared at each other, waiting for it to stop.

Maddie's name blazed across the screen like fire.

Her sigh cut through me, guilt lacing her voice. "It's Madz. She doesn't seem to want to give up. I'm gonna have to get it."

I nodded, stepped back, releasing her hand, even though every muscle in me screamed *no.* I could feel the moment slipping like sand through my fingers, and I didn't know how to grab it back.

She pressed the phone to her ear. "Hey Madz. You're persistent. What's up?"

I watched her face as it changed, watched the color drain, the way her body froze, eyes wide, mouth trembling. My stomach dropped like I'd swallowed a stone.

Her voice cracked, breaking apart in real time. "She did what?" Then softer, desperate: "No… is she going to be okay?"

My chest caved in. My skin went cold.

She covered her mouth, shaking, and the dread in my gut turned to steel. Maddie's voice on the other end must have shattered her, because I could see it all over her face.

"I'm with Lucas now. We will be right over." Her words wobbled as she ended the call, her hand trembling so badly I wanted to grab it again to steady it, but I was too afraid of what she was about to say.

"What is it?" My voice was low, urgent, but I already knew it wasn't something I wanted to hear.

Her eyes met mine, wet and burning, and the words came out jagged, like they were cutting her throat on the way out. "Nelly tried to kill herself. We need to get over to the hospital now."

The world stopped.

My body went rigid, every drop of blood draining from my face. My chest burned, a fire of horror and disbelief, and my knees almost buckled under me.

"Oh my God..." The words tore out of me, raw and broken. My hands pressed hard into my face, useless against the truth slamming into me. "Oh my God... what have I done?"

Because I knew. I knew I was the last one to push her. I'd said the words, sharp and cruel, and now they echoed in my skull like gunshots.

And if she didn't make it, if she was gone, I'd never forgive myself.

I sucked in a sharp breath, the air catching hard in my lungs. The words hit me like a punch I couldn't block.

*She tried to kill herself.*

They dropped into me like stone, heavy and cold, and before I could even process it, the world around me started to blur. The walls, the floor, even Lexi's voice, all of it faded to the edges, distant and useless.

All that remained was the pounding in my chest. Urgency. Fear. Guilt. A storm I couldn't control.

Nelly.

The image of her face, defiant, sarcastic, alive, clashed with the thought of her lying still somewhere, silent, because of words I'd thrown at her like weapons.

My throat burned, my head spun, but there was no space for collapse.

Only one thought anchored me, repeating louder than the rest:

*I can't lose her.*

# Chapter 39
## Lucas

The hospital room was too quiet. Too still. The only sounds were the steady beep of machines and the low hum of the fluorescent lights buzzing overhead. The smell of antiseptic hit me the second I stepped inside, sharp, chemical, suffocating. It clung to my skin, to my clothes, sinking in until my stomach twisted.

And then I saw her.

Nelly lay pale against the thin white sheets, her chest rising and falling in weak, fragile movements. She looked smaller than I'd ever seen her, shrunken, hollow, like someone had pulled the life right out of her and left only what was barely enough to keep her here.

I froze in the doorway, Summer clutched in my arms, my throat closing around the words I didn't want to say. "Oh my god," I whispered, my voice breaking before I could stop it. "What did she do?"

Maddie turned, her face streaked with tears, shoulders hunched like she was carrying the whole damn weight of the world. "The doc said she took a bunch of painkillers," she rasped, brittle and breaking.

My head shook before I even realized it. No, that couldn't be right. That wasn't Nelly. My chest tightened as my eyes dragged back to her, to the tubes and wires anchoring her to the bed. "Why would she do such a thing?"

"I don't know." Maddie's words cracked. She scrubbed at her cheeks like she could erase the truth. "I had no idea she was this sad."

Her words trembled, but I barely heard them. All I could see was Nelly. All I could feel was the guilt burning holes through my chest.

Because I knew.

I knew my words at lunch had cut deeper than I'd meant. And now she was lying here, pale, still, because I'd been too much of a dick to keep my mouth shut.

My voice came out hoarse, barely a whisper. "Is she going to be okay?"

"The doctors said they think she will," Maddie answered, her voice fraying at the edges. "But they can't say for sure until more tests are run when she wakes up."

Her words should have been a relief, but they weren't. They landed heavy, like a weight I couldn't shake. I clutched Summer closer, holding her as if she were the only thing keeping me upright.

My voice cracked before I realized I was speaking. "Why would she do this?" "After Joshie? She knows how hard this is. Why would she do this to herself?"

"I don't know," Maddie whispered, shaking her head, eyes wet.

Ray's hand tightened on her shoulder, grounding her, before his gaze shifted to me. "Are you alright, man?"

I jerked my head up, startled, caught in the guilt I couldn't claw free from. "Argh, me… yeah. Just a bit of a shock."

My voice was rough, hollow, a pathetic attempt at pretending I wasn't drowning in it. My eyes dropped back to the floor.

Ray nodded firmly, steady in that way he always was. "It will be alright."

I rubbed the back of my neck, restless, skin hot with shame. "I hope so," I muttered, though it felt more like a prayer than belief.

The silence that followed was suffocating, broken only by the steady rhythm of the monitors. Each beep seemed to mock me, reminding me she was here, but not really here. Alive, but slipping further away.

I bit down on my lip until I tasted blood. "When do they think she'll wake up?" My voice was soft, frayed with fear.

Maddie exhaled shakily, barely meeting my eyes. "They aren't sure."

I turned back to Nelly, my chest tight, throat raw. I willed her to open her eyes, to glare at me, to spit out something sharp and sarcastic that would sting. Anything would've been better than this endless, terrifying quiet.

Maddie's face was pale, streaked with exhaustion. Her voice trembled. "We just have to wait."

Wait.

That was all there was left to do. And it was torture.

Minutes bled into hours. No one spoke. The silence said enough, fear, helplessness, guilt, all of it hanging heavy, pressing down until it was hard to breathe.

Sometimes Maddie broke, burying her face into Ray's chest, her sobs shaking her whole body. Other times she collapsed into me, her pain raw and heavy. I held her tight, whispering empty words meant to comfort her, though I was really just trying to keep myself from shattering.

But even then, even with her in my arms, I felt empty. Hollow. Like part of me wasn't even there. I could hear the machines. I could feel Summer's small weight against me. I could see Nelly lying pale and broken. And still, it felt like I was standing a step outside of myself, watching from some cold, distant place.

Once, I caught Maddie watching me, worry etched deep. "Are you alright?" she whispered.

I forced the tightest smile I could muster. "I'm fine."

But I wasn't. I was anything but fine.

Because the truth was eating me alive. Nelly was here, barely breathing, and I couldn't shake the thought pounding in my skull:

*I put her here. I pushed too far. I lost my temper, and I broke her.*

And now all I could do was wait, wait and pray she'd wake up, pray she'd give me the chance to say the words I should've said years ago.

But no one is fine after something like this.

I could feel Maddie's eyes on me, full of unspoken questions I wasn't ready to answer. My chest was tight, my throat raw. Silence was safer. If I opened my mouth, everything inside, guilt, shame, fear, would come spilling out. And I wasn't sure I could survive that.

So, I popped Summer into her pram, and I slipped out.

The hallway was harsh with light. The buzz of fluorescent bulbs filled the air, and the smell of disinfectant stung my nose. My hands dug deep into my pockets; shoulders hunched like maybe I could fold myself small enough to disappear.

I stood frozen, staring at the sterile tiles, trying not to fall apart. Nelly in that bed kept flashing in my head, the machines, the tubes, the pale stillness of her face. And every time, the thought hit harder.

*I did this. My words pushed her further into the dark.*

Then her voice broke through the silence behind me, soft, cracked.

"Lucas…"

My jaw clenched. I didn't turn. Couldn't. If I looked at her, Lexi, I'd lose it completely.

"Yeah," I muttered, my voice low, flat. That single word felt like gravel in my throat.

Her footsteps shuffled closer. "What is going on with you?" she asked, gentle but trembling.

I balled my fists inside my pockets, nails biting into my palms. What was going on with me? Everything. Too much. And none of it was something I could say out loud.

"I'm fine"

Truth was, this was tearing me apart. I couldn't stand being in that room pretending I wasn't breaking. I couldn't look at Nelly without seeing my own words carved into her skin.

"Lucas…"

"I told you, I'm fine." The words came out flat, brittle, hollow. My eyes stayed locked on the far end of the hall. If I looked at Lexi, I'd crumble.

"You aren't," she fired back, sharp and certain.

That made my head tilt, just a fraction, a weak attempt to stall, to hide. "I'm not?"

"No, you're not," she snapped, her voice trembling with something deeper than anger. "You're out here wandering the hallways while Nellyfish is in there fighting for her life. We need you in there. *She* needs you in there."

Her words sliced straight through me. She was right. God, she was right. But the guilt was louder, dragging me under.

So, I did what I always do. I deflected. I shoved the pain down and grabbed the nearest distraction.

"I was just checking the notice board," I muttered, forcing casualness I didn't feel. My eyes flicked to the posters I hadn't even read. "There are a lot of people looking for work. Did you know they do a kids' book club here? Maybe we should take Summer. Sounds good."

Even I heard how insane it sounded. But pretending normal was easier than admitting I was unraveling.

Lexi voice cracked like a whip. "Are you serious?"

I turned to her then, shrugging weakly, my chest burning. "What?"

Her eyes blazed. "Surely you're not this heartless? I thought I knew you."

The words hit harder than any punch. For a moment I couldn't breathe. Because she didn't understand, I wasn't heartless. I was drowning. And the only way I knew how to survive was to pretend. Wear a mask.

Her voice cut again, sharp and shaking. "Really, Lucas?"

The sight of her standing there, Summer tight in her arms, eyes blazing with fire and hurt, knocked the air from my lungs. My mask slipped. My chest heaved with everything I couldn't say.

"I…" My throat closed, words tangling. God, what had I done? My silence. My detachment. The way I'd lashed out at Nelly, all of it was crashing down.

I dragged a hand through my hair, pacing a step, desperate, my voice rough when it finally broke free.

"You think I don't care?" I snapped, harsher than I meant, fear boiling under my skin.

"You really think I could hold *her*..." I gestured toward Summer, "...like that, be here day after day, and not care?"

Her eyes widened, but I couldn't stop. The words kept spilling out, jagged and raw.

"I care too much, Lexi. That's the problem. I care about you. About Summer. About Nellyfish. And it's eating me alive because I'm not good at this. I don't know how to show it without screwing everything up."

My chest rose and fell hard, my hands trembling as I shoved them into my pockets, like maybe that would hold me together.

I looked at her then, my voice cracking low. "What I said to Nelly today... I can't take it back. And if she doesn't wake up..." My voice broke, sharp and unsteady. "That's on me. I'll never forgive myself. And I was the one that gave the drugs to Joshie. I killed both our friends."

*And then there was Sammy.*

The hallway went silent, except for the faint hum of the hospital lights above us. My jaw clenched, but when I finally spoke again, it was barely a whisper.

"So, if you want me gone after this, just say it. I'll walk. But don't ever think it's because I don't care."

Her arm slid around me, her warmth pulling me in when I least deserved it. I stood there stiff, useless, my arms hanging at my sides like I didn't even deserve to hold her.

Her voice, fierce and trembling, pressed against the wall of shame crushing me. "This is not your fault," she whispered into me. "And Joshie was never your fault."

God, I wanted to believe her. I wanted her words to sink into the cracks in me and make them whole again. But I couldn't. The guilt was too sharp, lodged in me like glass that no amount of kindness could pull out.

I let out a rough, broken laugh, bitter in my own ears. "You're just being nice," I muttered, hollow. "Trying to fix me when we both know I'm already broken."

My throat burned. I couldn't look at her, couldn't bear to see her eyes when I said the next words. "But I know the truth, Lex. I've always known."

My jaw clenched hard, my voice breaking. "Joshie's dead because of me. Nelly's lying in that bed because of me. And if I keep standing here, sooner or later, you and Summer will end up broken because of me too."

The confession scraped out of me, raw and ugly. My chest heaved, hands still trembling inside my pockets.

I wanted to pull away, to stop infecting her with the mess that was me, but some selfish part of me stayed. Her arm around me was the only thing keeping me from falling apart completely.

Then she said it. That nickname that always broke me, *Lukey*. She always got me when she called me that. No matter how much I wanted to stay buried in the dark, that one word dragged me up just enough to breathe.

Her hand came up, cupping my face, her touch so soft it made me flinch inside. I didn't deserve it. Didn't deserve her. But her thumb brushed across my cheek, slow and steady, like she was wiping away the shame that had sunk too deep to ever be cleaned.

*How?*

How does she do this to me? When I feel like nothing but filth, when all I can see in the mirror is failure, how does her touch make me feel like I might be worth something?

My chest burned as her eyes stayed locked on mine, steady, unyielding, like she could see through every wall I'd built.

And for a moment, God help me, I believed her. Believed I might not be the man who ruined everything he touched. Believed I could be the man who stands by her. The man who doesn't walk away. The man who proves her parents wrong.

Why does she have this hold over me? Why does she make me want to stay when everything in me says I should let her go?

Because letting go of her feels like letting go of the only piece of light I've got left.

Her voice cut through the noise in my head, firm but breaking at the edges. "Lukey, it's not your fault. We all say things in the heat of the moment. This is not what caused her to do what she did. Look at me and know, this is not your fault."

I swallowed hard, my chest tightening like it wanted to cave in. The words scraped out of me anyway. "But..."

She didn't let me finish. "But nothing, Lukey."

And that was it. No room for argument. No excuses. Just her, staring at me with those emerald eyes that saw through every shield I'd ever built. The sadness in her gaze gutted me. *Fuck, she looked at me like I was worth saving. Like she needed me to believe her.*

I couldn't. I didn't know how.

And then, before I even understood what was happening, she leaned up on her toes, pressed her lips against mine, and kissed me.

The world stopped. The sterile stink of disinfectant, the buzz of the fluorescent lights, the echo of voices down the hall, all of it disappeared. My body went rigid, frozen in disbelief. Her lips pressed against mine, soft, and trembling, and every alarm in my brain went off at once.

She's kissing me.

*Lexi is kissing me.*

For a split second, I couldn't move. Couldn't think. Panic and heat tangled in me, panic that this wasn't real, that I'd wake up and she'd be gone, and heat because *shit,* I'd imagined this a thousand times and now it was happening.

My stomach dropped, guilt and hunger twisting together in a violent knot. It blindsided me, her lips on mine.

For years I'd dreamed of this moment. Late nights, drunken thoughts, moments when I hated myself for wanting her this badly. I'd pictured it a hundred different ways. But nothing prepared me for the reality.

At first, shock rooted me to the spot. *Lexi is kissing me. She's actually kissing me.* My mind scrambled to catch up, but instinct took over before doubt could ruin it.

I kissed her back.

Fuck… *yes,* I kissed her back like I'd been drowning, and she was the only air left in the world. My hands found her waist, sliding down the curve of her back, pulling her closer like I'd always wanted.

The world outside us dissolved. Hospital walls, machines, grief, guilt, all of it blurred until there was nothing left but her. Just her.

And for one perfect moment, I felt whole.

Her lips tasted like fire and salt, fear and tears and something dangerously close to hope. My chest burned, butterflies tearing through me like I was seventeen again. Reckless. Helpless. Completely hers.

I didn't want to stop. Not ever.

But then the PA system cracked to life, static tearing the moment in two. "Paging Doctor Jones. Doctor Jones, you are needed in Resus."

The sound jolted us back into reality. The kiss broke, leaving us gasping, breath mingling like we'd just surfaced from underwater. My heart hammered in my chest, my hands still on her waist, reluctant to let go.

And then, I smelled it.

Popcorn.

Warm, buttery, sweet, faint but unmistakable. The scent curled through the sterile air, and something in me just… stilled. It hit me low in the chest, spreading warmth from the inside out. *Joshie*. I knew it.

It felt like he was right there beside me, clapping a hand to my shoulder, laughing that stupid laugh of his. *Finally… you did it, dude.*

A shaky breath escaped me, half a laugh, half a sob. For a second, I let that warmth sit in my chest, let it chase away the guilt and the cold edges that had been living there for too long. Joshie was here. Watching. Approving.

But the moment shifted as fast as it came. The warmth turned sharp, a reminder, not comfort. *Nelly*. She was still in the other room, fighting for her life.

I straightened, my heart sinking under the weight of it all. This wasn't the time. Not for this. Not for us.

I looked at her, really looked at her, and the truth slammed into me like a punch. I was in deeper than I'd ever admitted. And there was no way back.

The announcement crackled again, dragging me back to where we were.

My chest tightened, shame crawling up my throat like barbed wire. This… whatever just happened between us… it wasn't right. Not here. Not now.

Lexi's eyes searched mine, wide and uncertain. "Are you okay?" she asked softly, her voice breaking just a little.

I forced a smile, weak and half-formed. My hand went to the back of my neck, rubbing the tension that never seemed to leave me.

"If this had happened anywhere but here," I admitted, my voice rough with the truth, "I'd be doing cartwheels. I'd be screaming from the top of my lungs. And right now…" I laughed bitterly under my breath. "I'm probably acting like no man should after kissing such a beautiful woman."

Her soft giggle broke through the heaviness, nervous and fleeting, but it still managed to light something in me. *Fuck,* I'd missed that sound.

I sighed, my shoulders sagging under the weight pressing down on me.

"But we're here. Nelly's in that bed fighting for her life. And poor Summer's getting squished between us."

That pulled another laugh out of both of us, hers light and warm, mine shaky, barely holding together. But the silence that followed swallowed us whole again.

I swallowed hard, my throat dry, my chest aching. "And I just…" My voice trailed, the words caught between everything I wanted to tell her and everything I was terrified to admit.

Because I wanted to tell her I loved her. That she was the only thing holding me together right now. That I wanted to kiss her again, God, how I wanted to kiss her again.

But instead, I stood there choking on the silence, not knowing if I was brave enough to say any of it.

Her hand on my arm stopped me dead. Just that small touch, and I couldn't breathe.

"Shh," she whispered, her voice soft, breaking through the chaos in my head. "I completely understand. I'm sorry it happened this way. I just…"

I wanted to soak in every word she said, let it bury the guilt eating me alive. But all I could think about was the feel of her lips still burning against mine, the ghost of her hands, the way she'd looked at me like I wasn't the screw-up I'd always believed I was.

And then she said she was sorry.

*Sorry.*

God, it ripped through me. Why would she apologize for something that had just saved me from drowning? That kiss wasn't wrong; it couldn't have been wrong. Because for the first time in years, I didn't feel empty. I felt *alive*.

But I bit my tongue. This wasn't the place. Wasn't the time. Nelly was still fighting for her life just a hallway away, and here I was, falling apart because the woman I've loved for half my damn life finally kissed me.

I forced myself to speak, steady but strained. "Please don't apologize," I said, my voice lower than I meant, almost pleading. I searched her face, desperate for her to understand. "Never apologize for kissing me. I'm happy it happened, but…" My chest tightened, words catching. "I can't… I can't process it. Not now. Not while Nelly's lying in that bed."

Her eyes softened, and she nodded. She got it. Of course she did. But it didn't stop the ache.

We walked side by side down the corridor, every step heavy. The fluorescent lights hummed above us, sterile and unforgiving. My mind wouldn't stop replaying it, her lips, her warmth, the way she made me feel like maybe I wasn't broken beyond repair.

If only she knew how close I'd come to shattering before she kissed me. If only she knew how much I needed it. Needed *her*.

When she touched my arm again before we walked back into Nelly's room and whispered, "You're not alone… this is not your fault, Lucas," something inside me cracked.

I wanted to believe her. God, I wanted to. But all I could do was nod, tight and weak, because if I opened my mouth, the truth might slip out:

That I was terrified. That I didn't deserve her. That I had loved her for so long it felt like it would destroy me.

And that one kiss wasn't enough. Not by a long shot.

# Chapter 40
## Nelly

The first thing I noticed when I started to wake was the smell. Sharp. Sterile. Antiseptic, clinging to the back of my throat.

Then came the beeping. Slow. Steady. Mechanical. Each sound hammered at my skull, a cruel reminder that I was still here.

My body felt heavy, pinned down by the weight of the sheets, the wires, the fog in my head. I felt like I'd run a marathon, or at least what I imagined it would feel like if I'd ever run one.

My chest rose and fell, shallow and weak, but it rose. I was breathing. Still breathing.

*Damn it, I can't even do death right.*

Voices blurred at the edge of my hearing, low and muffled. I forced my eyelids open, and the world swam into view, too Bright, too vivid.

Maddie stood stiff at my bedside, her eyes swollen and red, like she'd been crying for hours. Ray hovered behind her, steady and silent, his hand uncertain near her back, as if touching her might either hold her up or break her.

Lucas lingered further back, shadows carved beneath his eyes, his whole-body carrying guilt like a second skin. And Lexi… Lexi was clutching her small, milk-spewing machine against her chest like she'd shatter without that tiny weight grounding her.

The sight of them all hit me like the first shovel of dirt on a coffin, loud, final, and exactly the kind of welcome I should've expected. I longed to retreat into the dark where the shadows could swallow me whole. It was easier there. Isolating. No one staring at me like I was already halfway gone.

Their stares were so loud.

But the silence in the room was worse, thick and suffocating, pressing down until it felt like I might choke on it. So, I forced my throat to work, my voice hoarse and broken but sharp enough to cut through the stillness.

"Well," I rasped, lips twitching into the ghost of a smirk, "don't you all look a sight. Why are you standing around like someone dug your grave and forgot to put you in it?"

The look on their faces, shock, relief, disbelief, was almost worth the pain of speaking.

*Almost.*

My throat burned, every word dragging out like rusted nails tearing free from rotted wood. But sarcasm was easier than silence. Easier than letting them see how close I'd really been to never waking up.

Ray's laugh rumbled low, warm, belonging to another world, one far away from hospital beds and suicide attempts. Maddie rolled her eyes, arms crossed, glare sharp enough to slice right through me. Some things never changed.

"Don't look at me like that, Madz," I croaked, my voice barely more than a rasp. "If I'm still alive, you don't get to kill me with your eyes."

She gasped, caught between exasperation and heartbreak, hands flying to her hips. "Do you think this is funny, Nelly? Do you have any idea what you've put us through?"

Her words hit harder than I wanted to admit. The sting behind my eyes sharpened, but I forced a smirk back in place, brittle and weak. "If I told you I didn't plan for an audience, would that help?"

Silence followed, heavy, raw, until Lucas finally shifted. He'd been standing off to the side, pale and hollowed out, like my almost-death had drained the life out of him too. His jaw clenched, eyes cutting into me, and when he finally spoke, his voice splintered like a cracked stone.

"Don't ever do that again, Nellyfish."

The nickname almost got me. Almost. My lips trembled without permission, but I held the smirk in place like it was the only armor I had left.

"Relax, *Lukey*," I muttered, though my chest ached with the lie. "I'm too stubborn to die anyway."

Even as the words left me, I knew none of us believed them.

The door swung shut behind Maddie as she stormed out, her anger trailing like smoke. I let out a breath that scraped against my ribs and forced a weak grin, even though my chest ached from the effort.

"Well, there goes Mother Hen. Storming out like she's gonna teach me a lesson."

Ray gave me that steady look of his, the one that always made me feel like he could see through the bullshit. "She's scared, Nelly. That's all it is."

I swallowed hard, shifting against the stiff sheets. The wires tugged at my arm; the monitor beeped steady and mocking. All I could think about was how fragile I must look to them. Broken. Pathetic. Exactly what I swore I'd never be.

I tried to laugh it off, but the sound came out hollow. "Well, she should be scared. I'm obviously a menace. Pills, landlords, near-death experiences... what's next? Maybe I'll set the world record for fuck-ups."

Lucas flinched, jaw tightening like he wanted to argue but didn't know how. Lexi shifted Summer closer to her chest, rocking the tiny human softly, her eyes still shining with worry.

"You scared us, Nellyfish. Don't joke about it."

Her voice cracked, trailed off on the last word, and for a split second the sarcasm slipped right off me.

I looked at the three of them, Lexi with her little clone clutched close, Lucas pale as a ghost, he almost looks hot as a goth, shame I go for girls, and Ray standing strong and solid. Seeing them there, sad and moping, just made me hate myself a little more. Like that list needed to get any longer.

I wanted to say I was sorry. I wanted to say I didn't mean to hurt them. But the words got stuck, too sharp, too heavy. So, I just smirked again, brittle.

"Relax, guys. I'm still here, aren't I?"

But deep down, the truth burned: I didn't know how much longer I wanted to be.

The door clicked shut behind Ray, and the silence that followed felt heavier than before. Just me, Lexi , the small human, and Lucas standing awkwardly by the wall like he'd rather be anywhere else but couldn't bring himself to leave.

I let out a low breath, throat scratchy. "You know, for a girl who's been unconscious for days, I'm suddenly very popular." My lips tugged into my trademark smirk.

Lexi looked at me like I'd just slapped her. Her grip on her little clone tightened, jaw set. But instead of snapping back, her voice was soft, almost pleading.

"You scared us, Nellyfish. You scared me. And I don't want to lose you."

I shifted on the bed, the sheets rustling, my eyes flicking to Lucas just to avoid hers. He was staring at the floor, hands shoved deep into his pockets, guilt practically dripping off him.

Great. One more person I'd broken without even trying.

I sighed, pressing my palms to my face, wishing I could disappear into the thin hospital mattress. "You don't get it. None of you do. I didn't want to be saved. I didn't want anyone worrying."

My voice cracked before I could stop it. "I just wanted the noise in my head to shut the fuck up for once."

The monitor beeped steadily, mocking me with its reminder that I'd failed at even this.

Lexi's eyes glossed with tears. "You don't have to go through that alone. We're here."

I dropped my hands, dragging my gaze back to her and the sleeping bundle on her chest. Something twisted inside me, sharp and deep.

"Yeah, well… maybe I didn't want anyone to be."

The room went quiet again, my words hanging like smoke. For the first time in a long time, I didn't hide behind a joke.

The silence pressed down, thicker than I could handle. Lexi's eyes burned into me like she was trying to peel back the bullshit. I wasn't going to let her. Couldn't.

So, I turned to Lucas, slouched in the corner like a shadow that didn't belong. He looked wrecked, shoulders tight, hand dragging over the back of his neck in that nervous tick he's always had. He hadn't said a word since telling me I scared him.

I smirked weakly, sarcasm my default weapon. "I think this is the quietest I've ever heard you, Lucas. Cat got your tongue?"

His head snapped up, eyes wide like I'd just caught him out. For a second I swore I saw something raw flash across his face, guilt? shame? ...before he looked away, like he couldn't bear me to see it.

Figures. He's always running from what's real.

"If you've got something to say, just say it. Don't stand there brooding like the tragic hero in someone else's story."

Lexi shot me a look; lips tight like she wanted me to shut up. To be softer. But I wasn't soft. Never was.

Lucas looked up at me then, wide-eyed, guilty, cornered. His shoulders hunched like he was trying to fold himself up and disappear into the floor tiles. His voice broke as he finally got the words out.

"I'm sorry for what I said, Nellyfish."

I scoffed, though my throat burned. "What? You think this is on you? You're more of an idiot than I give you credit for." My voice was raspy, weaker than I wanted, but sharp enough.

His eyes flicked up, raw guilt bleeding through. It made me sick.

"Why the hell would you think that, that had anything to do with this?" I demanded, my voice breaking through the dryness.

"What? You think one smart-ass comment at lunch made me do this? Newsflash, Lucas, the world doesn't revolve around you. Not everything is your fault."

He flinched, just barely, but I caught it. I always catch it. For all the years we've been throwing digs at each other, I know his tells.

And this? This wasn't about me. Not really. This was about Joshie. About the ghosts he still drags behind him.

I leaned my head back against the pillow, closing my eyes for a second. "Lucifer," I muttered hoarsely. "You really are carrying around every corpse, aren't you?"

The silence that followed was thick, almost unbearable.

I opened my eyes again, staring at him, softer now, but still cutting. "You're not that powerful, Lucas. You don't get to take credit for ruining every life in this room."

He coughed, awkward and broken, his weight shifting like he wanted the floor to swallow him whole. "Well… when we last talked… I said…" His voice trailed off, shaky. "I was wrong. I didn't mean… I'm sorry." His voice cracked on the last word, and for a moment, he didn't even sound like Lucas anymore.

I let out a hoarse laugh, shaking my head against the pillow. "Don't worry about it, Lucas. That wasn't why I did this. And you weren't wrong."

The way Lexi stiffened caught my eye. Her grip on the spewing machine tightened, her voice sharp with panic. "Nelly, no…"

I cut her off, dry, tired, but edged like a blade. "But I don't want to talk about it right now. I just woke up, and the last thing I want to do is sit here and rehash why I swallowed a handful of pills with a whiskey bottle chaser. Can we, for once, talk about something other than me being the fuck-up of the group?"

The words dropped heavy, sour, filling the room like smoke after a fire.

Lucas folded back into himself, jaw clenched, guilt pouring off him in waves. He didn't say a word.

Lexi just stared at me, eyes wet, searching my face for something, maybe for answers I didn't have. Maybe for some piece of me I hadn't already burned to the ground.

But what could I say? What could anyone say?

The truth was, I wasn't built for pity. I wasn't built for soft words or people looking at me like I might shatter if they breathed wrong. I'd rather be hated than pitied.

Still, as the silence stretched, I felt it clawing at me, that emptiness that had put me here in the first place.

I wasn't anyone's best friend. I wasn't anyone's first choice. And maybe that was my fault. Maybe I'd pushed too hard, kept everyone at arm's length with sarcasm and venom until they stopped trying.

My lips twitched into a bitter smile. "You don't need to know why I did it," I muttered. "Just know I didn't do it because of you." My eyes flicked to Lucas, then away again. "Not because of either of you."

Lexi clutched the pooping machine like a shield, and Lucas scratched at the back of his neck, trying to fold himself into the corner like a guilty little boy.

I cracked my eyes wide open, flicking between the two of them. Lucifer, they looked so damn uncomfortable, like they were at a funeral and didn't know what to say to the widow. A grin tugged at my lips, crooked and wrong, but it was all I had.

"Oh my Lucifer, look at you two," I rasped, my voice rough from the tubes. "Anyone would think I just tried to kill myself and this is awkward."

Their faces didn't even twitch: dead serious, both of them. I huffed out a laugh, dry as dust. "Come on, that was funny. Geez, tough crowd."

The silence stretched. I hated it. So, I did what I always do, went straight for the jugular.

"So," I blurted, tilting my head with a wicked grin, "have you two done it yet?"

Lexi's face drained of color, and Lucas's ears went scarlet. Jackpot.

I grinned wider, mischief sparking in my chest. "Yesss!!! Finally."

Lexi spun toward me, cheeks blazing. "No," she snapped, hugging her mistake tighter like I'd just accused her of murder. "It's not like that."

I leaned back into the pillow, the smirk deepening, my voice dripping with mock seriousness. "So, he just got a bit of booby action then?"

Lucas nearly choked on his own breath. Lexi looked ready to combust. Before either of them could stumble out a reply, the door creaked open.

Ray strolled in like nothing could rattle him, Maddie trailing right behind with that sharp-eyed look of hers.

Ray smirked, voice dripping with mischief. "Do you really want to know what sort of action these two are getting, Nelly?"

I snorted, the sound rough in my throat. "No, but I love how awkward it makes them."

Lucas coughed into his fist, eyes darting anywhere but me. Lexi joined in, awkward coughs and rocking Lexi junior so hard I hope the little human wouldn't get motion sickness. And me? I lived for this. Watching them squirm was the only entertainment I had left.

Maddie crossed her arms, that half-Mom, half-best-friend glare plastered across her face. "We've heard enough about their romance that's going nowhere," she shot, sharp but edged with softness.

"We bumped into your doctor in the hall. He'll be in soon to do some checks, and if all looks good, you can be released."

I groaned, loud and dramatic, making sure it filled the room. "Oh, wonderful. Can't wait."

Maddie narrowed her eyes. "I know that tone." Her voice gentled, but there was weight in it. "The doctor told us everything. That your landlord found you."

Her words hung in the air like smoke, heavy, suffocating.

Lexi shifted uncomfortably, rocking absently. "Lucas and I might give you some space," she whispered. We'll check on you tomorrow, sweetie."

That word, *sweetie,* stabbed right through me. I barked out a laugh, sharper than I intended. "I ain't ever been sweet."

The silence that followed said it all. Maddie's eyes softened, Lexi's face crumpled like she wanted to argue, and Lucas gave me one of those faint, awkward smiles, like he didn't know whether to pat me on the back or apologize again.

My throat tightened, but I shoved the feeling down, deeper, behind the smirk.

"Glad to see that you're still the old Nelly," Lucas said quietly, his voice catching in that careful way he used when he was trying to sound light but didn't quite pull it off. "Talk to you tomorrow, Nellyfish."

I forced a nod, lips stretched into something that looked like a smile. "Yeah. Talk tomorrow."

He and Lexi slipped out. Maddie and Ray lingered behind, their eyes heavy with pity, worry, disappointment, all of it itching at my skin.

"So… is this when the lecture starts?" I muttered crossing my arms.

Maddie sighed. "No lecture. But the landlord told the doctor everything. That you were due to be kicked out. That he extended your leave date. That he… found you. And what he found in your apartment. It looks like you'd been planning this for a while."

I shifted against the pillows, a bitter laugh scraping my throat. "Not like anyone was going to miss me."

The silence that followed was thick enough to choke on. Maddie's breath hitched, but she steadied herself. "Well, I know for a fact that I would have. And Ray has a soft spot for you too."

Ray chuckled, rumbling. "Who, me? Never." He winked.

"Oh, shush, you," Maddie shot back, elbowing him, though her lips twitched with affection.

Then her gaze cut back on me. "Ray and I have talked. We'd like you to come home with us. And to be honest, Nelly, if you don't, the doctors will put you on a seventy-two-hour suicide hold."

My mind froze. *Home.* The word felt jagged, undeserved. I forced a smirk before the ache could show.

"Home, huh? Looking to spice up your marriage? Better lock your liquor and medicine cabinets."

But my throat burned, because part of me wanted it. Wanted them.

Ray grinned, Maddie rolled her eyes.

"I am perfectly happy with my baby girl. She excites me enough," Ray said, smacking Maddie's ass.

I groaned. "Oh my Lucifer… STOOOPPPP! Or I'll ask the doctor to pump the rest of my stomach. You're making me sick."

They laughed. I didn't. Sarcasm was the only shield I had left.

Maddie folded her arms, her voice softer but edged with steel. "And if you stay with us, no more jokes about this."

I arched a brow. "What, the threesome?"

She sighed hard. "You know what I mean, Nelly."

The sarcasm drained out of me like blood. And then…

The faint smell of popcorn drifted through the air.

Warm. Buttery. Familiar. It hit me so fast my breath caught. For a moment, I thought I was losing it. Hospital meds were powerful things, combined with lack of sleep, hallucinations weren't out of the question.

But then that warmth spread through my chest, slow and steady, melting something frozen inside me.

Joshie.

It was him. It had to be. His quiet way of saying, *Do it, Nellyfish. Go home. Stop fighting what's trying to save you.*

My throat tighten. "Fine. No more jokes about the pills. Or any of this." My throat was dry, like sandpaper. "I sadly have nowhere else to go." The words slipped out raw, heavier than anything I'd said.

Maddie's expression softened. "Okay. Then it's decided. Tomorrow, if the checks are good, you're coming home with Ray and me."

I blinked, thrown. My lips parted, but nothing came out at first. When my voice finally did, it cracked. "Okay… and… thank you."

Her smile was small but real. "You're welcome, Nellyfish. Now rest. We'll see you tomorrow."

All I could do was nod. "Okay."

She leaned in, her smile warm despite the bags under her eyes. "I'm so glad you're okay. Love you, Nellyfish."

I swallowed hard. "Love you too."

Maddie turned for the door, footsteps steady. Ray lingered, gave me that damn wink. "See ya later, Nelly." Then he followed her out, leaving the room too quiet.

I rubbed at my eyes, fingers trembling against skin that still felt foreign. The sarcasm felt thin. Truth was, I was bone-tired. Fragile. And the demons hadn't gone anywhere. They were just quieter, crouching in the corners, waiting.

When my eyes finally drifted shut, it wasn't rest that came. Just uneasy sleep, haunted by thoughts I couldn't outrun.

And then, the next day, everything shifted.

The car ride was quiet. Maddie didn't push, and I didn't talk. I just stared out the window, the world rolling by in muted colors.

When we finally pulled up outside their place, the air felt… different. Like the start of something I wasn't sure I deserved.

Maddie pushed open the front door, her voice warm, steady, too steady, like she was carrying all of us on her back. "We have the spare room all set up for you," she said, leading me inside. "Spare towels. We got your stuff from your old landlord and brought it over. You even have your own ensuite."

I blinked, my eyes darting around their house. Too neat. Too bright. Too… safe. It didn't feel like a place I fit. My arms folded tight across my chest. "You guys didn't have to do all this," I muttered, sharper than I meant, because sharp was easier than honest.

But Maddie just smiled, that determined kind of smile that didn't leave any room for arguing. "Well, we're happy to have you."

I looked away, swallowing hard. My chest twisted. Part of me wanted to say *thank you*. Another part wanted to run. Because deep down, I couldn't shake the thought:

*What if they regret letting me in?*

I scratched at my arm, skin already raw, the familiar itch of nerves I couldn't shake. I wasn't used to this. People going out of their way for me. People making space where I didn't belong.

Ray's voice broke through, calm and steady as always. "Your room is down the hall on the left. Just make yourself at home. If you need us, just shout. We never go far."

For a moment, I just stood there. The words didn't make sense in my head. *Make myself at home.* When the hell had I last had a home? Not just a roof. Not just four walls where I existed, but somewhere safe. Somewhere people actually wanted me.

I swallowed hard, my voice coming out smaller than I wanted. "Okay… thanks."

I turned before I could fall apart under their eyes. The hallway felt too bright, too long. Each step echoed like I was walking into someone else's life, a life I had no right to. My boots scuffed against the polished floor, and I hated how loud I sounded in a house so calm, so clean.

The door to "my" room creaked when I pushed it open. The bed was neatly made, with black sheets and doona, just for me. Black folded towels on the chair. My old clothes in a bag by the dresser.

I stood there, frozen, staring at it all. It was too much. Too kind. Too foreign.

I dropped onto the bed, the mattress dipping under my weight, and pressed my hands to my face. Relief crept in, sharp and terrifying. Because if I let myself feel it, if I let myself *want* this, what happened when it got ripped away like everything else?

From down the hall, muffled voices drifted to me. Maddie's, soft but cracking; Ray's, low and steady. I couldn't make out the words, but I didn't need to. I knew what they were talking about.

*What if she tries it again?*

The thought twisted my gut. They were right to worry. I didn't even trust myself.

I curled onto my side, dragging the blanket up like armor, my chest tight. For now, I was safe here. For now, I'd pretend I belonged.

But deep down, the question burned like fire in my veins.

*What if I don't know how to be saved?*

# Chapter 41
## Lucas

It had been two weeks since Maddie pulled Nelly back from the edge. Two weeks since we almost lost her. Two weeks of Ray hovering like a guard dog and Maddie fussing over her in the only way Maddie knew how, fierce, stubborn love. Two weeks of watching Nelly try to adjust, to accept care she clearly thought she didn't deserve.

I pushed the door open, its creak giving me away before I even stepped inside. Some habits die hard, I still walked in like I owned the place, shoulders loose, grin half-cocked, like the world owed me space.

But I knew better now. That swagger wasn't armor anymore, just muscle memory. The grin tugged at my lips, playful out of habit, but I could feel the weight clinging at the edges. Tired. Hollow in places I didn't let anyone see.

It had been a couple of weeks since the kiss. That reckless, knee-weakening, earth-tilting kiss that knocked the ground out from under me and left me drowning in her. And still, it haunted me. Every night when I closed my eyes, I replayed it, the way her lips felt against mine, the way she leaned in like she couldn't stop herself, the way it felt like every part of me had finally found home.

But here we were. Acting like it never happened. Pretending.

I still came over like I always had. Still filled the silences with bad jokes and dumb stories. Still stayed until dawn watching movies, sprawled out beside her on the couch like nothing had changed. I kept slipping into her world the same way I always had, easy, natural, like I belonged there.

But deep down, I knew better.

The kiss hung between us, sharp as glass. Because no matter how many signs she gave me, her hand brushing mine, her fingers lingering on my thigh, the way she leaned in like she wanted me closer, I forced myself to ignore it. I had to.

Not because I didn't feel it. Hell, I felt it more than anything in my life. But because if I reached back, if I let myself believe it meant what I wanted it to mean and she pulled away… it would destroy me.

So, I played dumb. I erased it. I made it look like that kiss was nothing more than a moment of weakness, a mistake, a dream she might've imagined.

Even though for me? It was everything.

And the worst part was, I could see it in her eyes, the confusion, the hurt, and I hated myself for putting it there. But it was the only way I knew how to protect her. Protect me. Protect whatever fragile thing we still had. Because losing her completely? That would kill me more than pretending it never happened ever would.

The smell hit me first. Warm. Familiar. Comfort I didn't think I deserved.

"Smells good," I said, leaning against the doorway like I had all the time in the world. My grin stretched a little wider, boyish, pretending just enough to pass. "What are you cooking?"

She glanced back at me over her shoulder, her voice lighter than it had been in days. "Your favorite. Steak and chips, with a runny egg."

And God help me; I lit up like a fool. "With mush…?" I asked, grinning like a kid, even though my chest was twisting itself into knots.

"Yes, fried mushrooms," she interrupted, rolling her eyes, but I could hear it, the affection in her voice, the softness she didn't even try to hide.

And just like that, I was gone again.

"Hmmm, ohh, yes," I laughed, rubbing my hands together like an idiot, because it was easier to play the fool than admit the truth. My grin softened as my eyes flicked around the kitchen. Her space. Her warmth. Her scent lingering in the air like something I couldn't shake, even if I wanted to.

"Where's my little princess?" I asked, my voice quieter now, the weight of everything pressing down again.

"She's down for the count," Lexi said, smiling faintly. "The day in the park wore her out."

And my heart sank. Because I'd missed it. Missed her. Missed them. And I wanted it all, more than I'd ever wanted anything. I frowned and stuck out my bottom lip.

Her hip bumped mine playfully, her laugh light, but I felt it "I will keep her up next time so you can get time with *your* princess"

I nodded and gave her my best lopsided grin. "Good, I miss my girls if I don't see them"

The bedroom felt too warm, too soft, like it was pulling me into something I wasn't ready for but had wanted for years. Fairy lights glowed across the dresser, the hum of the TV flickered shadows over the quilt, and there she was, patting the spot beside her like it was the most casual thing in the world.

"Come on. It's fine," she said, smiling like she wasn't twisting me into knots. "The TV out there isn't working. I really wanted to watch this movie. The one in here is working fine."

I stood in the threshold of her bedroom, frozen, my hands twitching at my sides. My chest was tight, every part of me screaming to move, to cross the room, to give in to the thing I'd been dreaming about since forever. But my legs wouldn't work.

She shifted back against the pillows, sinking into the mattress, looking so damn at ease. Then she patted the spot again. "What are you waiting for, Lucas? Come lay down."

My heart slammed against my ribs. *She wants me here. She actually wants me here. In her bed!*

And still, I hesitated. I repeated the words, *You can do this, Lucas,* like I was some pathetic teenager psyching himself up for his first kiss.

My voice came out low, uncertain, weak. "I'm not sure this is such a good idea."

She rolled her eyes, brushing it off with that easy confidence that always leveled me. "Come on, Lukey, stop being silly. I don't bite."

God. If only she knew how much I wanted her to.

I dragged in a shaky breath and forced myself forward, sitting stiffly on the very edge of the bed. My whole body was coiled tight, like if I let myself relax, I'd slide right into her arms and never come back out.

I kept my eyes fixed on the TV, pretending it mattered, pretending I wasn't acutely aware of her warmth beside me, her perfume in the air, the dip of the mattress between us that felt like the thinnest thread of restraint I'd ever held onto.

My chest ached, my palms itched, and one thought screamed louder than all the rest: *What if this is it? What if she finally wants me to?*

But the fear was just as sharp. *What if I ruin it? What if I'm reading everything wrong?*

So, I stayed frozen on the edge, terrified that moving even an inch closer would shatter everything.

The silence between us grew unbearable, every second dragging like an anchor in my chest. Then she shifted... closer. Inch by inch, until her shoulder brushed against mine and the heat of her body pressed into my side.

My whole body locked up.

Her hair brushed against me, the faint smell of her shampoo tangling with the clean bite of soap and aftershave clinging to my own skin. My heart thundered so hard I thought it might break through my ribs. *She's leaning into me. She's choosing me. Oh, God, what do I do?*

Panic clawed at the edges of my chest. For years I'd wanted this, dreamt of it, but now that it was here, real, I felt like a fraud. Like the moment I gave in, she'd see I wasn't good enough. That I'd ruin it the same way I ruined everything else.

My throat went dry. My hands twitched, desperate to hold her, to pull her closer, but my brain screamed at me to stop before I destroyed the one good thing I still had left with her.

And I shifted over, moved more to the edge of the bed, trying to get some space between us.

But before I realized what was happening, I'd lost my balance and toppled, without a shred of grace, off the side of her bed and onto the floor.

Smooth. Real smooth, Lucas.

"Oh my God, Lucas." Her voice cracked, sharp with shock.

I froze, rubbing my hand down my face as I lay on the floor.

*Idiot.*

*Coward.*

*What the hell is wrong with you?*

She scrambled upright, her arms folding across her chest like she needed to protect herself from me. The sight made my stomach drop.

"What the hell, Lucas?" she snapped, her voice brittle, hurt cutting through every word.

The silence that followed stretched too long, pressing against my chest until I thought I'd suffocate.

I slowly eased my way onto my knees, raising my head just enough so she could see my eyes, and nothing else. I stared at her for a long moment, hands shaking, the words tangled in my throat.

I let out a long, shaky sigh, my shoulders collapsing under the weight of it all. And I sat up straight. And for the first time, I let her see it, me. Not the jokes. Not the grin. Not the easygoing act. Just me. Broken. Defeated.

The silence was crushing. I could feel it wrapping around my throat, choking me as I sat there on the floor, rubbing the back of my neck like the nervous idiot I was. I couldn't even meet her eyes. If I did, everything I'd been holding back would come spilling out, and I wasn't sure I'd survive that.

Her voice cracked through the air, sharp and trembling. "You're so confusing. I have no idea what is going on with you. One minute you can't be close enough to me, hanging off my every word, and then we share what I thought was this amazing kiss..."

I snapped my head up at the mere mention of the kiss. God, I remembered it too: every second, every spark, the way it felt like my whole world finally made sense.

I'd replayed it every night since. But hearing her say it out loud made the shame burn hotter, because she had no idea why I was pulling away.

Her voice shook harder now, the anger giving way to hurt. "And now it's like I have some sort of contagious disease. You literally fell off the bed when I moved closer to you. What the hell, Lucas?"

I ran my hand through my hair, hunched in on myself like maybe if I made myself small enough, she wouldn't notice how much I was falling apart. "It's… I… you…" The words tangled in my throat, useless.

She laughed bitterly, rolling her eyes like I was the biggest joke in the world. "I… you… it's… spit it out, Lucas. Because this has gone on too long and I have had enough."

Something in me cracked at her words, and a laugh slipped out, not because it was funny, but because it was insane. Because the truth had been sitting on my chest for years, and I was about to choke on it.

"Oh, this is funny, is it?" she snapped, anger sparking hotter. "I'm glad you think so, Lucas"

My chest burned. I finally forced myself to look at her, really look. The fire in her eyes, the confusion, the hurt. I'd put it there. My voice came out quieter than I expected, but steady, because it was the truth.

"Too long?" I repeated, shaking my head. "It's only been a couple weeks for you…" I swallowed hard, my throat raw.

"For me…" I let out a breath that felt like it had been trapped for years. "It's been years." The words lifted a weight I didn't even realized I'd been carrying.

"And...? I've been giving you all the signals. Are you just blind or what?" she fired back, confused.

I wanted to tell her I wasn't blind. God, I'd noticed every single one. Every brush of her hand, every lean against me, every look she thought I missed. I used to be a player; I noticed them all.

But this wasn't about missing the signs. This was about the fact that I'd been starving for them for years and was too scared to take what I wanted.

A broken, aching smile tugged at my lips. "No. I've seen them all. Every single one. I know what you want."

The way her face fell nearly gutted me. Her arms loosened around herself, her voice dropping so soft it nearly undid me.

"Oh... So, you don't want me? It was just me, then? That kiss... it meant nothing to you."

My head snapped up before the poison of her words could sink in. "No... no, that's not it." That kiss was amazing."

I meant it. Every syllable. And still, I watched her tremble, fingertips brushing her lips like she couldn't decide whether to cry or scream.

"Oh my God, Lucas!" Her chest heaved, her arms folding tight again like she needed protection, from me, from the mess I was making. "You're making no sense. Do you want this or not?"

For a second, I almost laughed at how simple she made it sound. *Do I want this? Want her?* She was the only thing I'd ever wanted.

Have you ever woken on Christmas morning, rushed to the tree, and opened one present you'd begged for all year: the thing you secretly prayed for? And when it's finally there, right in front of you, you don't know whether to laugh or cry. The emotions are too big, too much. Happy because you finally got it. Sad because… what if it's the only time? What's next? What if it's not everything you imagined it to be?

I rubbed the back of my neck, my eyes glued to the floor. My body felt too big, too awkward, shifting like I was a teenager again. But I wasn't that boy anymore, I was a grown man.

Taking a deep breath, I forced myself to look at her. And just like that, the walls I'd built cracked wide open. I knew she could see it, all the truth I'd buried, raw and desperate, laid bare in my eyes.

"Yes," I whispered, my throat tight. "I want this. I want you. More than I've ever wanted anything. But wanting and deserving… that's not the same thing."

Her lips parted, her eyes wide and searching.

"I want this," I admitted, my voice barely above a whisper but heavy with everything I'd held back. "More than you'll ever know. But I don't want to just sleep with you. I don't want you to think you're like the other women I've been with. I don't want to rush into this and ruin it."

Dragging my hand down my face, I lean back against the wall, trying to steady the storm inside me.

"I've waited so damn long to taste your lips, to even get this chance. And now that it's here, I'm terrified I'll screw it up. That you'll think I'm just sleeping with you because that's all I want. And that's the last thing I want. Well… it's not the last thing. I do want to sleep with you… badly… but not just that. I want it all. Everything with you. I just don't want to be like all the other men in your life. I want to be the one that lasts."

Her eyes locked on mine, wide and unblinking. The way her lips curved, the way her chest rose and fell, it nearly wrecked me.

She shifted closer to the edge of the bed; one hand pressed to her chest like she was holding herself together. Her voice cracked, but her words wrapped around me, fragile and unshakable. "Aww, Lucas.

You should have talked to me. We could have worked this out together. It's been weeks."

I swallowed hard, my voice rough. "Actually… it's been years."

The air between us grew impossibly heavy. My heart slammed against my ribs.

"And now that I'm this close… to you, to us… it's scary as hell. But it's exciting too. And I just… I just want to make sure you don't get hurt. I couldn't stand it if I hurt you."

Her eyes softened. Her hand brushed my arm, her body leaning in, her scent wrapping around me like temptation itself.

"I'm not glass Lukey, I won't break. I am quite tough. Amongst other things." She smirked, eyes glinting, voice low and teasing.

"Le Le…" I rasped, her name breaking out of me like it burned. "You don't know what you're asking. It's taking everything in me to resist you. I'm just hanging in there."

But the way her smoldering eyes locked on mine told me she knew exactly what she was asking.

And worse… she wanted it just as badly.

Every nerve in me screamed to close the gap, to finally taste what I'd been starving for. My hands twitched at my sides, aching to grab her, pin her against the bed, lose myself in her.

But still I froze, torn clean in half.

"Then don't resist anymore. I'm a big girl. And like you said, it's been years."

Her finger curled, beckoning me closer, her smoldering eyes burning through me. And damn if it wasn't the sexiest thing I'd ever seen

*Holy fuck.*

I clenched my jaw, my voice low and rough. "If I start, Le Le… I don't know if I'll be able to stop."

"Who says you have to stop?"

Her words hit me like fire, searing through my chest, burning straight into places I'd kept locked down for years. Then she moved, slow and deliberate, and I swear my heart stuttered, like it couldn't keep up.

Her fingers brushed against me first, light as feathers, tracing their way up my chest one fingertip at a time. Each touch branded me, pulling me closer when all I wanted to do was grab her and never let go.

Then she looked up at me. Only inches from my face. Wide eyes, shimmering, dangerous with promise, hope, hunger, everything I'd ever wanted to see staring back at me… *from her.*

*Fuck. Fuck. Fuck.*

I couldn't move. My body was wired tight, strung like a bow ready to snap, but I stayed frozen, waiting. Always waiting. Always too goddamn scared of ruining it.

And then, she leaned in.

Her lips pressed against mine, soft at first, then sure. She was kissing me. *Again.* Just like last time, she was the one closing the gap, the one taking control.

And all I could think was… why? Why was I always leaving it to her? Why couldn't I be the man I was with everyone else, cocky, confident, always one step ahead?

Because with her, I didn't want games. Didn't want mistakes. I wanted it to be real. I wanted it to be perfect.

And that terrified me.

# Chapter 42
## Lexi

At first, the kiss was awkward, hesitant. I could taste his nerves in the way he moved, the way he hovered close but never fully consumed me. He was holding back, cautious, like one wrong move might shatter me… or worse, shatter whatever *this* was between us.

But I didn't want careful. Not from him. I wanted *him*. I wanted experienced version, not the hesitant teenager.

So, I pushed, deepening the kiss, slipping my tongue past his lips, telling him without words that it was okay. That *I* was okay. That *I* wanted this as much as he did.

And then it happened. I felt the shift, the spark, when awkward, cautious teenager Lucas turned into confident, fierce, *experienced* Lucas. It hit like lightning through my veins. His restraint broke, and suddenly he wasn't cautious anymore.

He was there, *really there*. That same kiss from the hospital, the one that left me shaking for days, the one that lived in my chest like a secret I couldn't stop replaying, only now it was stronger. Fiercer. Consuming. *Real.*

He finally let go, and I realized just how much he'd been holding back all along. And it wasn't just a kiss. It was pleasure. It was passion. It was a promise.

A promise that I wasn't just another woman to him. That I wasn't just another night to forget. This was deeper. Heavier. This was Lucas showing me he wanted more.

My hands trembled as they found the hem of his shirt, slipping beneath the fabric to brush against his skin. The heat of him made me gasp against his mouth, my fingers curling as I began to lift it higher. I needed to feel him, *really* feel him, skin to skin, heart to heart.

But then… he stopped me.

His hand caught mine, gentle but firm, hesitation etched into every line of his face. I felt the weight of his concern before he even spoke, the storm of fear and restraint swirling behind his eyes.

So, I silenced it.

I kissed him deeper, tugging softly at his lower lip, sucking just enough to tell him without words that I was okay with this. That I *wanted* him. That I wasn't afraid. And in that kiss, I prayed he finally understood.

His hands trembled when he let mine go, like he was afraid that if he didn't hold on tight, I might vanish. My breath caught as I pulled his shirt over his head, tossing it aside. The air between us thickened, humming with something electric and undeniable.

The room didn't just feel quiet, it paused, as if the world had stopped, letting us have this moment.

This wasn't just a beginning. It was a shift. A before and an after.

Lucas lifted me gently from his lap and moved me to the bed. He hovered over me, balancing his weight on one arm as he stared into my eyes. With the other, he brushed my hair from my face.

He didn't rush. He didn't devour or demand like I'd braced myself for. Instead, he savored. He moved with a kind of patience that cracked me wide open, every touch deliberate, every kiss weighted with meaning.

His lips traced me like I was something sacred, mapping me slowly, carefully, as if I were a story he'd been aching to read his whole life.

And I let him.

Because for the first time in my life, it felt safe to surrender. He made me feel *seen*, truly seen, in a way I hadn't even realized I'd been craving. Every sigh, every shiver, every tentative gasp he met with tenderness, with care, with adoration that left me unraveling piece by piece.

This wasn't just desire. It was connection.

And God, he showed me, without words, only through the way his hands and mouth moved over me, that I wasn't just some fleeting moment to him. He touched me like I was precious. Like I was his world.

And it didn't stop at just one moment between us. When we both climaxed, he wasn't like every other man I'd been with, rolling off and falling asleep. It was like now that he had me; he wasn't going to let me go.

His hands stayed on me, his lips never strayed far, always keeping some part of him connected to me. He wasn't going to leave me at one undoing; he made sure to unravel me over and over again.

He hadn't been wrong when he said he wouldn't be able to stop.

The only thing that stopped him was the only girl I think he thinks about more than me.

Summer.

When she cried for her three-a.m. feed, before I could even lift my head, he was already leaping out of bed like a damn Energizer Bunny. "You aren't going anywhere; I've got this one." He threw on his pants, and in a few quick strides, he was gone.

I couldn't help but smile, watching his silhouette disappear through the doorway, his muscley frame, those low-cut jeans showing just enough of his cute ass. A giggle escaped as I caught sight of his usually groomed hair now tousled, post-sex messy.

One benefit of him being a player: he knew all the right areas to focus on and all the right buttons to push. And now I know why he was so popular. Lucas was all about making sure I was taken care of. I guess he hadn't changed too much from the kid I knew in high school, always putting other people's needs first. I never thought that would extend to the bedroom.

I yawned, eyelids heavy, tugging the blanket up to my chin. After keeping that boy, hmm, no, that very well-endowed man, up until three in the morning, I figured I'd earned my rest.

Rolling onto my side, I let sleep pull at me like a tide.

But then the bed dipped. A warm, firm hand slid over my hip, curling across my stomach. A hard, very hard, chest pressed against my back.

"Le Le," his voice was low, teasing, laced with satisfaction. "Did I wear you out?"

A soft laugh slipped from me. "I wasn't expecting you to be so… enthusiastic." I tilted my head toward him, eyes still closed, lips twitching. "So very dedicated."

He shifted impossibly closer, pressing a kiss to my cheek before nudging my head forward to bury his face against my neck.

"I don't want to sound creepy," he murmured, his lips brushing my skin, "but you have no idea how many times I've done this to you in my head over the years."

I giggled, cheeks warming. "That *is* a little creepy."

I paused, then tipped my voice into a playful tease. "So, tell me, which version of me is better?"

He groaned softly, pulling me tighter against him, his words rumbling against my neck. "Oh, definitely you. People say fantasies are better than reality… but you, Le Le, you're better than anything my horny teenage brain, or my asshole player days, could have dreamed up."

I could hear the smirk in his voice when he added, "Although… fantasy Le Le did come up with a few things I'd be more than happy to try with you. She was quite the little vixen."

I twisted slightly and gave his shoulder a playful punch. "Yeah, I regret asking. I do *not* want to know where your mind goes when you're left alone, unsupervised with your thoughts."

"Only ever to you.," he whispered, pressing another gentle kiss to my neck. His breath deepened, sleep tugging him under, but not before he murmured, "Goodnight, Le Le."

Heat bloomed in my chest and crept up my face, but I smiled into the darkness. "Goodnight, Lukey."

His breathing slowed into steady, heavy pulls, and I lay there wrapped in him, grinning like a fool.

Lucas wasn't the man I thought I knew, not the reckless playboy who stumbled from one night to the next, chasing highs that never lasted. Not the troublemaker who wore his smirk like armor and hid his pain behind too many girls and too many lies.

He was more. So much more.

He was the man I'd been blind to all these years, the one who had stood right in front of me, patient, steady, carrying a quiet devotion I had been too broken, too afraid to see.

And now, here, with his lips pressed to my skin and his hands holding me like I was something fragile but worth protecting, I finally saw him. *Really* saw him.

And I loved every moment of it.

The way he touched me like I was precious. The way he looked at me like I was the only thing that mattered. The way every barrier I'd built around myself, every defense I thought was unshakable, melted the second he whispered my name like I belonged to him.

For once, I didn't feel like I was being used. Or tested. Or tolerated.

For once, I felt wanted. Needed. Cherished.

And maybe it was reckless to admit it, not out loud, not even to him yet, but in the quiet of my heart, I knew.

I was falling for Lucas.

And this time, I wasn't afraid.

# Chapter 43
## Maddie

It had been three months since everything changed. Three months since Ray and I brought Nelly home from the hospital. Three months since she tried to leave this world at the exact moment we discovered we were bringing new life into it.

The first month had been… rough. She was darker than usual, sharper than usual, and coaxing her out of her room was near impossible. But living under our roof meant hiding wasn't an option.

If I wasn't vacuuming obnoxiously right outside her door until she got irritated enough to move, I was marching in to strip her bed and forced her into the sunlight. And if it wasn't me, it was Ray, roping her into gaming marathons.

Ray was sneaky. He told her the network point in her room was "broken" and that she had to set up in the office. He even bought a desk and sat her right next to him. Half the time, they sat there, headphones on, talking through microphones like strangers online, even though they were literally side by side. I still didn't get it.

Today, though, I had something different in mind.

"Nellyfish, come sit on the lounge."

She rolled her eyes dramatically as she finished making a sandwich. "What have I done now? If this is about your fancy glass, that was Ray's fault. He jumped out of nowhere and scared me."

"I was merely crossing the hallway, Nels," Ray chuckled.

"Without announcing yourself! I thought you were at work!" she shot back, glaring at him.

"I just came home for my wallet. Didn't realize I needed to announce my presence in my own house… Duchess of Darkness."

I narrowed my eyes at him immediately. I *hated* that nickname.

Ray shrugged innocently. "It's her online screen name, baby cakes."

"Well, I don't like it."

Nelly tilted her head, chewing her sandwich. "Thanks, Maddie. Glad you hate my name."

I whipped my head toward her, finger raised like I was about to give a lecture. "That is not your name, Nellyfish."

She gave a long, exaggerated sigh. "And neither is that. Come on, get it over with. What have I broken, ruined, or made unbearably depressing this time?" She bit into her sandwich again, smirking.

I shook my head, unable to hide a smile. "You're not in trouble. Ray and I just… have some news."

Her chewing slowed. She looked between us warily, eyes darting like we were about to drop a bomb. She swallowed, deep, heavy. "What news?"

"Don't look at me like that," I said quickly.

"News…" She scratched her head, narrowing her eyes. "Well, it's not a proposal, Ray already has you shackled. You already own this house… unless you're selling and moving?"

I shook my head.

She froze, her eyes widening as realization hit. "Holy Grim Reaper. No. Fucking. Way."

I nodded, and Ray's grin lit up the whole room. "You're harboring a parasite."

"NELLY!" I snapped, but Ray burst out laughing.

"She's not wrong," he grinned, pointing to my stomach.

I glared at him, arms crossed. "Do not encourage her."

"Well," Nelly muttered, waving her sandwich at me dismissively, "it's feeding off you. That's parasite behavior."

Ray chuckled. "Technically, for it to be a parasite the host has to be a different species…"

"RAY!" I cut him off, glaring harder.

He threw his hands up, still grinning. "Just being factually correct."

I pointed between them both. "Neither of you are calling my baby a parasite ever again."

Ray slid behind me, wrapping his arms around my waist and pressing a kiss to my cheek. "Fine. Our *beautiful* baby."

I rolled my eyes, but I couldn't stop smiling.

Nelly slumped on the couch, eyes falling to the floor. Her voice came out low, defeated. "I'll start looking for a job… be out of your hair soon."

Ray and I froze.

"Nelly, no," I said quickly. "We never said anything about you moving out."

She didn't look at us. "You don't want me here when the womb invader comes along. You'll want your space. You'll want to be a family."

Ray leaned forward, his voice steady. "And who do you think you are, Nels?"

She looked up, confused.

"You're family," he said proudly.

I nodded. "We're keeping the baby in our room for six months, then turning the office into the nursery. You're not going anywhere."

Her fingers twisted together, her mouth tight. "Why would you want me around with a mini human?"

Ray smiled gently. "Because you're the godmother, Nels."

Her head snapped up, eyes wide. "Wait… what? You want me… as godmother?"

We nodded.

"You and Lucas, godparents" I said softly. "So, you'll have to play nice."

She blinked at us, mouth open. "You want me to have *responsibility* over another human being? Over your little clone?"

I giggled. "Yes. If anything ever happened to us, we'd want you there for the baby as they grow."

"But you'll have to stop calling it parasite, clone, loaf of flesh, or, ugh, the one I hate most, womb invader."

Ray chuckled, his whole body shaking against mine.

Nelly rolled her eyes. "Fine. What am I supposed to call the little bag of bones then?"

"Baby!" I scolded, trying not to laugh.

"So boring."

Ray grinned. "If boring means he's safe and healthy, I'll take it."

I nudged him. "Stop calling the baby 'he.' You'll give her a complex if it's a girl."

Ray tilted my chin, eyes twinkling. "It's a boy. Strong Y chromosome. Runs in the male seed, sweetness."

"Na na na na!" Nelly shoved her fingers in her ears, eyes squeezed shut. "Tell me when you stop polluting my air with your gross splof talk!"

I threw a cushion at her. "Oooofff! Rude!"

She flopped back dramatically. "Guess I'll just have to teach the Y chromosome how to dodge."

Ray laughed so hard he nearly fell over and dropped to the floor.

I groaned. "Great. Now she'll call the baby Y Chromosome for the next five months."

Nelly smirked. "So... you're three months pregnant?"

I nodded.Then it hit: warm, buttery, familiar. Popcorn.

The smell drifted through the room like sunlight cutting through dust, faint but real enough to make me and Nelly freeze. We exchanged a look, wide-eyed, knowing, and I knew she felt it too.

Nelly's voice came out small, trembling. "You smell that?"

I nodded slowly, my eyes glassy. "Popcorn."

Ray frowned, glancing between us. "What popcorn?"

Neither of us answered. We didn't need to. The air had shifted, soft, charged, full of something that wasn't grief but peace.

Nelly's lips quirked into a shaky half-smile, her gaze flicking upward. "Guess that's your way of saying you approve, huh, Joshie?"

The smell lingered, curling gently around us before fading into nothing, but the warmth stayed, sinking deep into my bones.

It wasn't just an answer. It was approval. A quiet, unseen *I'm here. I'm happy with what I'm seeing.*

And Nelly didn't argue anymore. She didn't need to.

"Nothing changes, Nelly," I said, smiling so wide my cheeks ached. "We want you here. Always. You're part of our family."

For once, Nelly didn't have a comeback, just the tiniest, softest smile tugging at her lips before she stood and drifted toward her room.

I turned to Ray. "She's actually happy here. Not that she'll admit it."

He wrapped an arm around me, chuckling. "Oh, she's happy. Trust me."

# Chapter 44
## Lucas

Bang. Bang. Bang.

I groaned, dragging a hand over my face. Whoever it was could take the hint and leave.

Bang. Bang. Bang.

Cracking one eye toward the alarm clock on my nightstand, Nine-a.m., I groaned louder and shut it again.

Bang. Bang. Bang.

If this was a Jehovah's Witness telling me God could save me from my sins, or worse, a salesman pushing vacuums or insurance, I'd lose it.

Swinging my legs out of bed, my feet hit the cold timber floor and I shuddered. Adjusting my morning glory with a wince, I yawned my way down the hall.

Bang. Bang. Bang.

"All right, all right, hold your horses!"

I cracked the door open, leaning against the door, eyes half-closed.

"What took you so goddamn long?"

Lexi shoved the door wide open before I could reply, storming straight into my living room. Summer's capsule thudded onto the floor as she set it down.

I closed the door behind her, raking a hand through my hair. "And good morning to you too, beautiful."

Her cheeks pinked, sheepish. "Sorry. I've had a bad morning."

Now awake enough to actually look at her, I noticed the details: hair a little wild, blouse wrinkled, faint milky stain down her shoulder. Summer's calling card. Probably smelled by now. And yet… I grinned. God, I loved it. Loved what it meant. Lexi as a Mom. Summer marking her like territory.

"Didn't you have that…" I started.

"Yes." She cut me off with a sigh. "My interview. It was a disaster."

I crossed the room and pulled her into me, arms locking tight around her. Yep, she definitely smelled faintly of sour milk. Didn't matter. Weirdly, I loved it. It was them. My girls. My family. My home.

Her voice was small against my chest. "I'm sure it wasn't as bad as you think."

She rolled her eyes, exhaling hard. "The babysitter canceled, so I had to take Summer. She puked on me before I even got inside. The interviewer looked at me like I was a hopeless case. Like that's who I'll be if she hired me."

I cupped her cheek, brushing away the tear that slid free. "You should've called me. I'd have watched Sumz."

She shook her head quickly. "No. You worked late last night. I didn't want to wake you."

Then her eyes widened, scanning me, messy bed hair, sleep in my eyes, standing there in nothing but jocks. "Oh my god, Lucas. I'm sorry. You worked late. I should've remembered, that's why I didn't ask."

I chuckled, my voice still thick with sleep. "How about I grab a coffee, wake up properly, and then we'll talk?"

She nodded, still buzzing with nervous energy.

"Want one?" I asked over my shoulder.

"No. Too wired already."

I poured myself the world's largest black coffee, threw on gray track pants and a white tee, then joined her on the couch. Her knee bounced like it might take flight. I set my hand over it, steadying her.

"So… tell me what's really going on."

She bit her lip, glanced up at me with those wide, pleading eyes. My chest squeezed. God, she was killing me, independent, fierce Lexi, looking at me like I was the safe place she could finally fall. I shouldn't swoon over her worry. But I did.

"I can't pay my rent," she whispered. "I need a job, fast. I might have to go back to my old one."

I gave her my best unimpressed glare. She rolled her eyes.

"I'm running out of options, Lucas. Summer needs stability. Food. Heat. A home. And I'm failing. You've been amazing and helped me so much, but these are my responsibilities. I'm failing, just like my parents said I would."

"Stop." I caught her hands in mine, lacing our fingers tight. "You are so far from failing, Le Le, that word shouldn't even exist in your head."

She dropped her gaze, but I held steady.

"You're an incredible mom. Summer is healthy, happy, loved. That's more than most kids ever get… including you."

Her lips curved into the faintest smile.

I grinned, pointing at Summer drooling happily on her foot. "Look at her. No one with a foot in their mouth, is that joyful and suffering."

Lexi laughed softly, brushing at her eyes.

"Some things are worth more than money, Lex. You can't buy what you're giving her."

I cleared my throat, heart hammering as I reached into my pocket and pulled out the small box I'd hidden there when I got dressed. Dropping onto one knee.

Her eyes went wide, frozen.

"Would you do me the honor of…" I paused, grinning, as I opened the box, "…moving in with me?"

Her hand smacked my shoulder. "You asshole! I thought you were proposing! You scared the shit out of me."

I smirked. "Good to know how you feel."

"We've only been together three months, Lucas!"

"Best three months of my life."

Her lips parted, stunned. "I didn't come here for this. You don't have to instantly fix my problems…"

"Lex." I gestured at the box, the key inside. "You think I just pulled this out of nowhere? I've been holding onto it, waiting. Planning."

She squeaked, speechless.

I stood, tugging her hand, leading her down the hall. "There's something else. I know you don't come here much. But that's good lately. It's given me a chance to do what I wanted."

She frowned. "What have you been up to?"

I stopped at the spare-room door and took a deep breath. Then I opened the door. Her gasp filled the air.

The walls were painted pink and white. A cot stood in the center, dressed in unicorn sheets with a matching mobile dangling above. Fairy lights twinkled across the wall. A pile of plush toys waited in the corner beside a white rocking chair.

Her hand slid over the cot rail. "What did you do, Lukey?"

I wrapped my arms around her waist from behind. "This is Summer's room. I've been working on it whenever I wasn't with you."

She turned in my arms, eyes shining.

"I love her, Lex. I love *you*. I've loved you since high school. I'm not wasting another damn minute. Move in with me. Make this your home."

She stared, hesitation flickering. My stomach dropped. Then her arms looped around my neck, pulling me down. "I love you too, Lukey."

My mouth fell open, not what I expected. She smirked, nudging my chin shut with her fingertip, then kissed me.

I didn't hesitate. My hands tangled in her hair as I kissed her back, deep and hungry. Body to body. Soul to soul. Between gasps, I whispered, "I'll take that as a yes."

She nodded, and I laughed, lifting her off her feet, spinning her in my arms, not breaking the kiss for a second.

This girl. My girls. My family.

# Chapter 45
## Epilogue – Nelly

*5 years later*

I threw my hands up in surrender as the tip of the sword pressed against my throat. His gruff little voice growled like a pint-sized executioner.

"Was it you?"

I shook my head quickly, keeping my face serious. "Nope." Total lie.

"Is that your final answer?"

I stood perfectly still, praying my eyes wouldn't betray me. Only a squeak escaped my lips.

"Aunty Nelly, I can see the chocolate all over your mouth." He rolled his eyes and lowered his sword. This kid was already too much like his father.

That did it. I doubled over, clutching my stomach, cackling like a villain in a bad horror movie.

Joshua sighed, like the weary old man he clearly thought he was, and stormed down the hall. "Dad! Nelly ate the last of my choc-chip cookies!"

"Wow, way to throw me under the guillotine, pirate Joshua." I chased after him, catching his shoulder. "I thought we had an alliance. You don't rat to the parentals."

He crossed his arms, glaring at me with all the fury a four-year-old could muster. "That was before you ate my last cookie."

I snorted. "Good to know what I'm worth around here. One damn cookie."

Before he could reply, I leaned down. "If you bothered to look, you'd see I put a whole new packet in the pantry this morning. But shhh, don't tell your Mom. If she catches you eating them before breakfast, she'll kill me."

And right on cue, like she had supernatural Mom-radar, Maddie appeared.

"Kill you for what this time, Nellyfish?"

I pressed a finger to my lips and whispered to Josh, "Stick with me, kid. If we don't crack, she can't win."

We both turned in unison to stare her down. Maddie narrowed one eye, arms crossed, the picture of maternal judgment.

"Tell me now, Joshua, or no sleepover with Summer tomorrow."

Traitor-boy cracked instantly. "She was gonna let me eat cookies!" he yelled, then bolted into his room, door slamming like a courtroom verdict.

I crossed my arms, glaring at the closed door. "Why that little…"

"Language, Nellyfish."

"I thought I trained him better. Stick together. Loyalty. Best friends for life."

Maddie just laughed. "Looks like Summer trumps you."

I rolled my eyes, throwing my hands up as I headed for my room. "Whatever. She won't buy him cookies, she's broke."

I stopped, spinning back dramatically to point at Maddie. "And she's never written a book and dedicated it to him!"

Maddie just shook her head, smiling like she knew me too well. "Josh loves his Aunty Nelly to the moon and back."

"Ugh. Who says I want the moon and back? More like the fire pits of hell and back."

"Nelly!"

"Fine, fine. Since I'm not appreciated, I'll just go back to my crypt, sorry, *room* and finish writing."

I stomped off with all the theatrics of a scorned goth aunt, Maddie giggling under her breath behind me.

Back in my room, I settled at my workstation. I've been living here for over five years now. Never left after *the incident*, the one Maddie refuses to let me call by name. Just the *incident*. The thing that broke me but also built me into something new.

Maddie and Ray showed me what family actually meant. What being loved felt like. Not that I'd ever admit that out loud. I'm still me, grumpy, sarcastic, cold as a grave, but they see through it. Somehow.

I hate the word *happy*. Makes me think of rainbows, unicorns and sparkles. All things I'd happily set on fire. But if I had to admit it? Yeah. I'm closer to happy here than I've ever been.

They supported me while I figured out what the hell I was supposed to do with my life. It took a while, but being asked to be Josh's godmother flipped a switch in me. That kid made me want to *create*.

So, I started writing and illustrating children's books. Don't look at me like that. They're not sunshine-and-daisies crap. They're about a bat. *Bailey the Bat*. He's dark, broody, misunderstood, sound familiar? But his stories teach kids about listening to that inner voice, and how to feed it with the good stuff. Not toxic garbage. Real lessons no one else is brave enough to write about.

And you know what? People love them.

First book was for Josh. Second was for Summer. The third I'm writing now… is for Edward.

Maddie and Ray only had Josh. After years of fertility treatment, Ray swore he wouldn't put Maddie through it again. Which made Josh even more special. Spoiled rotten too, mostly by me. And I don't regret it. Not one bit.

I don't know if it's because I owe Maddie and Ray everything, or because they named him after Joshie, or because he's just… cool. But that kid owns me.

My work schedule is mine to control, which means when Maddie and Ray head off to work, I get him. My little shadow. My best friend.

I haven't got him into wearing black yet, or appreciating death metal, but give me time. He's only four.

And yeah, I'll miss him on my book tour next month. But I won't stay gone long. I made a promise to myself never to stay away from *home*.

Because that's what this is now. Home.

A place where I'm loved. Where I'm wanted. Where no one calls me hopeless.

And when Josh looks at me with those big eyes, full of love and mischief and adoration, there's no better feeling in the world.

Even if he is a damn traitor over cookies.

# Chapter 46
## Epilogue – Lexi

*5 years later*

I buried my face in my hands and sobbed. "I can't do it."

A warm arm wrapped around my waist, pulling me back against a chest I knew too well.

"Yes, you can."

I shook my head fiercely. "No… no, I really can't."

Lucas chuckled softly, tugging me tighter until I was pressed hard to his chest. "She'll do fine."

I turned in his arms, pressing my face into him. "How did this happen? I swear it was only yesterday I was pushing her out of my…"

His laugh rumbled in his chest as he rubbed my back. "Yeah, I was there. Remember?"

I pulled back and frowned up at him. "Not funny, Lucas. How can you laugh at a time like this?"

He reached up, cupping my face in his hands. His thumbs brushed away my tears. "Because she's ready.

She's growing up, Lex. This is a big day, but it's a good one."

He wrapped an arm around my waist and gently turned me as he rested his chin on my shoulder. "Look."

I followed his gaze.

There she was, my Summer. Laughing, waving her hands around as she spun some elaborate story to a group of wide-eyed kids, the same way she always did with us at home. She spotted me, then grabbed a little boy's hand and dragged him over.

"Mom, this is Brody. He's in my class. He's my new friend." She turned to him, smiling proudly. "This is my Mom, my Dad, and my baby brother, Eddie."

I glanced at Lucas. His whole face lit up, that wide grin I adored. He still beamed every single time she called him Dad.

Summer knew the truth, that he wasn't her biological father. We'd given her other dad chance after chance, and Lucas had stood by us both through every disappointment. But Summer had made the choice herself one day. She wanted Lucas to be her Dad. And he'd been glowing ever since.

"Nice to meet you, son. Be nice to my princess," Lucas said warmly. Then he crouched, eyes soft on

Summer. "Now, behave yourself, princess. We'll be back this afternoon to pick you up. Enjoy your first day of school."

He placed a gentle kiss to her forehead.

Summer nodded seriously, then threw her arms around us both, hugging tight before kissing Eddie's head where he slept peacefully in his pram. She scrunched her nose with excitement, then darted off as the bell rang.

My throat tightened all over again, tears stinging my eyes

Lucas pressed a kiss to my temple. "Now, now. Don't cry. Let's get Eddie home for his nap. Maybe we can make use of all this… free time." His eyebrows wiggled playfully.

I narrowed my eyes. "Don't you have work to do?"

He smirked, running a hand through his hair. "Best part about being the boss, I can take the day off."

He slapped my ass, grabbed the pram handles, and started walking us back toward the car.

I couldn't stop smiling. I still couldn't believe how my life had turned out.

Lucas and I had been married two years now. He'd proposed on the beach at sunset, and I hadn't even let him finish asking before I said yes. He'd been perfect ever since. Said it took this long to get me, he'd make sure I never regretted choosing him.

He bought a bar with an apartment over it so he could be close to home, close to us. He never let me feel like I had to choose between being a mom and being loved.

And then, a year later, came Edward. Named for Joshie, Edward was his last name. As soon as we found out it was a boy, Lucas insisted. Eddie was our way of keeping him with us.

Now, here we were. A family of four.

Sometimes I wondered what life would've been like if Lucas had spoken up earlier, or if I would have been ready earlier. Would we have made it? Or would we have been too young, too reckless?

I knew one thing for sure: I wouldn't have had Summer. And as much as her conception had been a mistake… she wasn't. She never could be. She was my everything.

Lucas had been there the day I almost gave her up. He'd talked me out of it. Given me the courage to keep her. And for that, I can never thank him enough.

And Maddie and Nelly, they'd all been there too. Pushing us, pulling us, forcing us to keep showing up when we didn't want to.

I sometimes think Joshie had been wiser than any of us. Maybe that's why he'd made us promise that night to always keep meeting, no matter what.

He knew that each of us needed to survive.

We didn't need the forced weekly café meetups anymore. We were family now, woven into one another's lives.

Josh and Summer were inseparable. Nelly still called Summer things like "host for germs" or "human vomit vessel," but the way she loved her was undeniable. She loved all the kids like her own.

The four of us, tied together by one boy's dying wish.

And somehow, against all odds, that promise had turned us into exactly what we all needed most.

Family.

# Chapter 47
# Epilogue – Joshua

*5 Years Later*

I can finally say goodbye.

I can finally let go.

They're all on the paths they were always meant to walk, finding pieces of happiness I always hoped they'd reach.

Maddie... she has Nellyfish now. She's learning that plastering fake smiles over every crack isn't strength, it's poison. She's not at Nelly's level of brutal honesty, let's be real, nobody ever will be, but she's braver now. More honest with her friends, more honest with herself. And being a mom has only made her stronger, steadier, more assertive.

Nellyfish... she tried to join me too early. She was disappointed when she found me waiting, convinced she was destined for fire and brimstone. But I sent her back. She wasn't done. She had a family waiting for her, a home she didn't even realize she had.

Now she's found it, opened herself up to love, to being loved. She's learned to accept what she can't change about her blood family and to pour herself into the ones that truly matter. The ones that keep her grounded, alive, and whole.

Lucas… he finally became the man I always knew he could be. He stopped hiding behind guilt and bravado, stopped numbing himself with meaningless nights, and finally told Lexi how he felt. Now he's a husband, a father, a provider. His pride isn't in conquests anymore, it's in keeping his kids smiling, in loving his wife the way she deserves.

And Lexi… my Lex. She always knew what she wanted, but she searched in all the wrong places to find it. Until one day she finally looked up and saw what had been in front of her all along.

She has the man she deserves now, the love she's been craving her whole life, the kind her parents never gave her. She's blossomed into a confident, loving mother, every step steadied by Lucas's devotion. They had no idea how much they needed each other. But I did. I always did.

I knew all of them needed each other, that without one another, their lives would stay fractured, empty.

Now? Now they're a family. A real one. And because of that, I can finally be at peace.

I take one last look as they gather around a Sunday dinner at Madz's house. Kids laughing. Food being passed. Smiles lighting every face. It's everything I wanted for them. Everything they deserved.

As the sound of their laughter fades, I feel myself pulled upward, toward the soft, glowing horizon. Warmth wraps around me, flooding me with comfort, with love.

My task is complete.

I am free.

# About the Author

Hope is an Australian romance writer who crafts raw, emotional stories about survival, second chances, and the complicated path to love.

She began writing in 2017 on an animated story app, using it as an escape from the realities of chronic illness. In those early chapters, she discovered her voice in creating characters who fight to overcome the odds, no matter how heavy the burden.

After a breast cancer diagnosis in 2024, Hope returned to writing with a renewed passion, and a promise to tell stories that make readers feel deeply. Her words are a tribute to strength, healing, and the kind of love that refuses to give up.

*Dying Wish* is her first standalone novel, born from her own journey of chronic pain, depression and hard times.

When she's not writing, Hope can be found daydreaming new plot twists, sipping Coke Zero, or enjoying fun activities with her family, the people who inspire her to keep creating.

My social Media:

Instagram: @hope_epi

TikTok: @hope_everly_

Facebook Hope Everly

Website:

https://hopeeverly.company.site

Other books by Hope Everly are *Wicked Games and Deadly Games* Books in the *Rise of the Broken Heart* series:

www.ingramcontent.com/pod-product-compliance
Lightning Source LLC
Chambersburg PA
CBHW011548190726
48287CB00010B/2791
*9781764227292*